For the Love of Spumoni!

by

Mary Lou Piland

with

Jenna Barrett Bernstein

MaryLou Piland

This is a work of fiction. Names, places, characters, and incidents are either the product of the author's imagination or are used fictitiously. Any resemblance to actual persons, living or dead, actual events or locations or other public venues is entirely coincidental.

Cover Design: Peacock Design

Editing: Christina Miller

Proofing: Anthony Piland & Nancy Esposito

Formatted by: Brenda Wright at Formatting Done Wright

fortheloveofspumoni.com

Dedication

This book was written from a series of life lessons, some out of fear but always out of love. I dedicate this book to my husband Anthony who made me chase him, my dad who made me choose love and my mother who is the boulder of our family. To my Nonna Maria: the patience and love you have taught me has redirected my whole life. To my sons Anthony, Michael and Marcanthony; you are my world, my moon and my stars. To my sister Nancy, thank you for putting up with me, even when I divided the room we shared with duct tape and charged to enter and exit. To my brother Anthony; I will always have your back. To my little sister, Teresa, my world is different with you in it. To my Zio Mimi, Zia Teresa, Zia Evelina and Zio Luigi, thank you for always treating me like a daughter. Rosie, I love you and thank you for all your support, always. To Mrs. Joe the best English teacher on the planet, please don't look for any typos! To Cynthia Riggs, who gave my name to Meg Bowles, I would not have had a ticket on this rollercoaster without either of you believing in me. To my ghost writer Jenna Bernstein, thank you for bringing your infectious peace and knowledge into my life. Love Knows No color, the message heard around the world.

Table of Contents

The Nightstand

Tuscany, 1984

You could say I'm a girl who knows how to get what she wants. I've always gotten what I wanted, one way or another.

It's how I ended up with the nightstand, and it's how I ended up with my Anthony.

"What's that, Zia?" I asked, pointing at the little piece of furniture nestled in the far corner of my Nonna's abandoned childhood home. It seemed more like a garden shed than a house.

"It's staying," Zia Pina said, arms crossed. "And that's final."

The little wooden nightstand was the only piece of furniture left in the house. I felt magnetically drawn to it, as if it was calling me closer for a better look. Made of dark, ancient wood, the nightstand had a pattern of leaves carved along the edges. An elegant "Q" decorated the cabinet door. It had some kind of inscription, too.

Bending down, I squinted in the dark room to make it out.

Maria Terni.

My grandmother's name.

"Zia, look at this—Nonna's name!" I said.

"I know. It's been here as long as I can remember."

Marveling at the old piece of woodwork, I could feel the history stored in the grains of its wood. "I've got to bring this home."

"No. *Questo sta qua,*" my aunt said firmly. *This stays here.*

Not a chance. I brought my nose to the nightstand's surface and inhaled the smell - wood, dust, dirt and time.

I tried to open the cabinet door to see if anything was inside, but it seemed glued shut or stuck. I couldn't get it open.

"Hey, Mar." My cousin Rosie poked her blonde head around the door and looked from me to our aunt. "We better go. We don't want to miss our flight."

She was right—time was short. But I had to have that nightstand. Something about it … "Rosie, come and help me move this."

Rosemary tottered over on her platform heels, looking as if she'd just stepped out of the business casual pages of Vogue. "Help you move what?"

I pointed to the nightstand.

"That thing?" She folded her arms in her maddening older-cousin way.

"We've gotta move—now. We can't miss our flight or I'll miss my first day of high school." I pushed past her and hurried to one side of the nightstand. "Grab the other end."

We hefted the nightstand a couple inches off the ground, then set it back down. "Whoa, that's heavy," I said. "What kind of wood is this?"

"Walnut. It's been here for sixty years, and it'll be here another sixty. Now leave it, " Zia said, hands on her hips.

Rosie and I carried the nightstand past her. We paused at the door, and I leaned on the windowsill to rest. By chance I looked out the window, taking in its beautiful uphill view. A giant walnut tree stood on the hill, silhouetted in the rich afternoon Tuscan light. Nonna was right, it was beautiful. Absolutely mesmerizing.

"Your Nonna and her parents used to come up here every fall to harvest the walnuts to sell in Colle and the neighboring towns," Zia said, clearly noticing my lost gaze and hoping to distract me, perhaps.

I could imagine my young Nonna bending over to pick up walnuts from below the tree. Then I blinked and snapped back to the nightstand. We had to go.

"So amazing to see you, Zia. Thank you for the nightstand. It means so much to me." I shot Rosie a look that should have kept her from asking any more questions. We bent to pick it up again.

"Nonna doesn't want you to take it." Zia's voice rose an octave. "It should stay here, in her home."

"Her home is in the United States now, Zia Pina," I said. "This thing is coming with us. *Grazie, ciao!*"

She stood scowling, wordless, in the doorway of the cold little shack.

Rosie and I struggled with the heavy nightstand, lugging it down the steep, grassy hill toward the street below.

"Mar, you have got to be kidding me. How are you going to bring this from Colle to Connecticut?" Rosie whispered-yelled. Taking baby steps in her heels, she stumbled and almost lost her grip on the surprisingly heavy piece of furniture.

"You're family, so you should know the answer. I'll find a way—always do."

Nunzio, our cabbie, scrambled out of the Fiat. With his wrinkled white shirt, rumpled black tie, and little driver's cap, he looked as if he'd slept in the taxi. He took one look at the nightstand and waved his hands. "No, no. *Troppo grande* ... too much, too big. No, no, can't fit that."

Rosie and I set the nightstand down behind the Fiat, the Italian version of the yellow cab. I reached around Nunzio to pop the trunk and started rearranging our bags.

One block over, a parade crossed our street, a crowd watching. The smashing of cymbals and the melody of flutes and horns carried to our ears. Between Zia Pina yelling, Rosie whisper-yelling, and now the cabbie yelling, we seemed to be attracting more attention than the parade. The crowd had turned around to stare at us, wide-eyed and curious. A few of the clarinet and trombone players even lost time, glancing over in our direction instead of keeping with the music.

"Rosie, here—move this and hold that." I shoved a suitcase in her hand. "Can we fit this in the front with us?"

"It's not going to fit," Nunzio kept saying in Italian.

Yeah, it wasn't going to fit in the trunk. I piled all our bags back in and thought a minute.

Rosie shot me a "What gives?" look.

My mind raced with bad ideas, until …

"Rope. Anyone have any rope?" I desperately eyed Nunzio's tie.

Five minutes later, we drove down the winding cobblestone street, the nightstand strapped securely to the roof of the cab by Nunzio's tie, suspenders, and white shirt. We came to a complete stop when we got to the intersection, where the parade blocked our road.

"We're definitely missing our flight now," Rosie sighed.

Nunzio, wearing his white undershirt and black cap, blared on the horn and shook his head. The parade had come to a complete stop in front of us. The music went on, but it sounded a little off-key, probably because all the musicians were turning to look at the honking car.

Seizing the opportunity, I opened my door and jumped out.

"What are you doing?" Rosie grabbed at my shirt as if to pull me back into the car.

"Come on, let's take a picture. Look at all of these cute guys … Hey! Can you look over here?" I called to the trombone players, who were marching in place. I held out my disposable camera until Rosie got out of the car and took it from me.

"Fine. Pose."

I whipped myself around and posed with the band behind me, who had stopped marching in place and now posed with me for the photo.

"Got it."

Nunzio honked the horn in staccato and called out the window, still shaking his head. When we'd gotten back in, he gunned the car through the gap in the parade. "I don't believe it. This parade, Festa della Madonna—one hundred and fifty years old. Never stop-a the band or parade. She crazy, that one!" Nunzio said, jerking a thumb back in my direction.

"Tell me something I don't know," Rosie said. "Mar, do you always have to get what you want?"

I paused in thought. "Well, sometimes it might take a little more time and effort, but yup, I eventually get what I want."

I turned around to catch one last glimpse of Colle, the ancient castle walls, the surrounding houses, and the rolling green hills dotted with groves of walnut trees, all backdropped by mountains. It was magical here. I sighed and sank back into the leather seat, leaning my head into the headrest.

How many times had my Nonna walked this road?

~~~~~

Two days later, when I got back to the States, the first thing I wanted to do was show my Nonna the nightstand.

"Nonna, you have to come downstairs and see what I brought you from Italy." I could hardly contain my excitement.

"Okay, Mary Lou," she said with a genial smile, pronouncing my English name with her Italian accent. I took her hand and led her down the painted blue wooden steps to our apartment on the first floor.

"Wait, close your eyes." I opened the door and led her inside and around my sister, Nancy, who sat on the couch, reading as always. Then I guided Nonna close to the nightstand, where it stood dark and old in the middle of our living room. I could clearly see the "Q" in the light. When she was positioned just right, I told her to open her eyes.

I watched Nonna's face closely as she stood there, gazing at it. At first, her expression registered nothing. Did she recognize it? "Do you know what this is, Nonna?"

Nonna touches it and said "Yes."

"Well, do you like it? I saw that it had your name on it, and I thought it belonged here, in the United States, with you." My voice trailed off as I wondered if I'd made a mistake in bringing it here.

I'd never seen Nonna blinking hard and wringing her hands like this. What had happened to her always-cheery mood, especially around me?

She blinked a few more times and then looked away. Her hand cradling the side of her face, she seemed lost in thought, her gaze far away, her expression sad.

"Nonna?" I asked quietly, approaching her. She moved to sit on the couch. I sat next to her and laid my hand on her knee. "What is it? Don't you like it? Do you want me and Nancy to carry it upstairs for you?"

"I wish you'd left it where it was."

A sinking feeling spread in my stomach. I'd wanted to make Nonna happy, but it looked as if I'd made her sad instead. Why didn't she like it? I'd only wanted to surprise her with something from her past. I thought it would be like a sweet childhood memory for her. But suddenly I got the feeling she'd left it in Colle because she'd never wanted to see it again.

After a moment, she got up, gingerly approached it, and placed her hand on it. She closed her eyes. "You like this. I want you to have it."

Me? "Thank you, Nonna. I love it, I really do. I'll move it into my room right now."

"Good," was all she said.

Her fingertips lingered on the surface of the nightstand for a few seconds, then she walked out of the house almost as if she was in a trance, something I had never seen her do. I looked back at the nightstand in the middle of the room, her name inscribed in block letters on the drawer.

I kneeled to inspect the small wooden door and noticed an indentation, as if one of the leaves on the border had fallen out. Had it been like that before? Had it gotten damaged in transit? I couldn't remember.

Nancy was busy reading, so my brother, Vinny, helped me carry it to my room. There we tried to pry open the door, but the long flight hadn't loosened it at all. We placed it right next to my bed. It fit perfectly.

Waterbury, September 1984

On an ordinary Tuesday, a few weeks into my freshman year, my life changed forever.

It started out like any other day. That morning, Nancy, and I fought over who got to control the radio while we got ready to leave for our two different rival Catholic high schools. I won, of course, so we got dressed in our uniforms and brushed our teeth to the sounds of my Whitney Houston instead of her Doors.

By the time Nancy and I were dressed, my mom had eggs, homemade sausage, and toast with butter and jam on the table.

My dad drove me, Nancy, and Vinny to our three respective schools in the family's red Chevy blazer on his way to work.

When we got to Sacred Heart, my dad put the car in park and bid me goodbye with an old adage: "Don't forget, it pays to be good," and then the blessing, "This is the day that the Lord has made. Let us rejoice, and be glad in it."

"Uh, thanks, Dad," I said, confused, closing the car door.

Walking toward the school, I spent a few seconds thinking about his comment before brushing it off. I never understood my dad's vague religious riddles.

As soon as I walked through the double doors of the foyer, I saw Mrs. Joe, my English teacher.

I needed to talk to her about my recent homework assignment, so I hurried to catch up to her. In my family, Cs flew, but Ds didn't. "Mrs. Joe, is there any way I could do a little extra credit?"

She was about to open her mouth to say, "No," in one form or another—I was sure of it.

Just then, a sudden rush of wind hit my bare legs. Goosebumps travelled up both legs, the full length of my spine, and down along my arms too.

I turned toward the doors, the wind blowing back my hair. Time slowed like I was in a dream.

Brown leather jacket, black oiled hair, mocha skin, a look so calm and cool I thought he must have walked right out of a Michael Jackson music video.

The angels and saints—the ones my crazy Italian parents were always talking about— started singing hallelujahs, and bright heavenly light spotlighted his gorgeous face. Maybe my parents weren't the crazy ones, after all. Without meaning to, I committed his features to memory. He moved with such ease, it seemed almost as if the wind were escorting him in.

He was, without a doubt, the most beautiful boy I had ever seen.

"Yoo-hoo, Mary Lou?" Mrs. Joe said.

I was frozen.

I stared at him, urging him to *look at me, look at me, look at me*. But he just breezed past, without even a glance in my direction. He hiked his backpack up onto his broad shoulder as he headed out of the foyer and down the school's main hall.

Time resumed its normal pace. I watched his backpack bump down the hall as long as I could.

"Mary Lou, what are you staring at?"

At Mrs. Joe's words, I suddenly remembered she was there. She asked so genuinely, too—as if no one else had noticed the utter perfection I had just witnessed.

I couldn't have been the only one, right?

I looked around in a daze. Did anyone else around me feel faint or weak in the knees?

Mrs. Joe looked down at me curiously through her red-rimmed glasses, her perfectly coiffed hair swooping away from her face on either side.

I prefer to call it admiring, I almost said, but I held it in. "Him, the boy with the curly hair and dark skin," I said, as if there weren't thirty-five other people in the hallway. "Didn't you see him?"

"Yes, but do you know it's not polite to stare? Or to drift off in the middle of a conversation?"

I wasn't sure if she was asking me or telling me. It didn't matter. I had to know his name. She would know, right? After all, she taught English. Everyone has to take English.

"I know, but I can't help myself." I figured there was no point in lying. It felt out of my control. Could this be love at first sight? I melted a little more inside just at the idea of it. I'd always wanted to be in love.

I'd never seen him before, I was sure of that. It was a small town, and everyone looked at least a little familiar.

Except him. He looked brand new, fresh, incredible, hypnotizing.

I had certainly never experienced any time-stopping moments or exhibited any previous staring problems that I could recall. If this was a regular occurrence, I'm pretty sure I would have already sent myself to therapy.

Replaying his walk-by in my mind, still not caring about Mrs. Joe's befuddled amusement, I fell into another trance while recalling his face. He wasn't just attractive. He was drop-dead gorgeous, exotic. He had a commanding presence about him, too, in his posture, his stance. Between his features, the bronze skin, his thick, curly black hair, and those full lips, he'd cast a spell on me.

"Is he a senior?" I asked.

"He's a junior. He was a student in my English class last year. Bright young man, polite."

"What's his name?"

"Anthony Knight."

"Well, Mrs. Joe," I announced in a determined daze, "I'm going to marry him someday."

"Marry him?" Her chuckle made her sound unconvinced. "Let me get this straight. Five minutes ago, you didn't even know his name, and now you're walking down the aisle to get married?"

I didn't concern myself with her skepticism. I could already see our monogrammed towels and stationary: MLK.

"Knight, Knight ..." I'd heard that name before, even if I hadn't seen his face. I started scanning my memory like going through a filing cabinet.

On the way to my locker I thought of it. My dad owned a garage, and his sister might've brought her car there to get it fixed one time. That was an angle I could work. Fiddling with my locker combination, I noted to myself: extra make-up tomorrow ... better hairdo ... and my bandana had to match my sneakers.

The day passed in a blur. I couldn't wait to go home and start planning my outfit and strategy for tomorrow. I walked the twenty-minute route home with my friends Daniella Mancini, Tanya Capparelli and Izzy Spinoza, who also lived in the neighborhood. Daniella always had her big, curly hair piled up on top of her head in a colorful scrunchie. She chewed bubble gum as if it was part of her wardrobe.

I couldn't help myself. I was nearly exploding with love and excitement, so I shared it with my friends, the first ones to know about my crush. As coolly as I possibly could, I told them about this new Anthony Knight guy I'd seen.

"Who introduced you?" Daniella smacked her gum.

"Did you talk to him?" Izzy chirped.

"Did you get his house phone?" Tanya asked, hoop earrings swinging.

"Mrs. Joe did, kind of ... no ... and, no. Look, girls, it's a work in progress. It's only day one. But I have a good feeling." When you know, you just know.

"Same as your good feeling about Sam?" Daniella laughed with a teasing smile, popping a pink bubble between her teeth.

I rolled my eyes. "Just wait until you meet Anthony. You'll see what I mean. He's perfect husband material."

As crazy as it was, I fell that fast. All it took was one sighting to confirm that yes, he was the one, and no, there would be no other one.

I saw him, and without even consciously deciding, my heart and mind chose.

Despite my friends' skepticism, I felt confident. I'd been given a whole new purpose, a new reason to show up to school every day. Besides being well-liked and already being friends with more than half the school, now I had a future to pursue, a goal. I had four years of high school ahead of me. I wasn't thinking about college or careers. I just wanted a boyfriend. No, a husband. A family of my own. Don't get me wrong—this was no game. My heart was dead serious, and my mind was determined to figure out a way to make it happen.

Halfway home, Tanya said, "The American girls at school are so skinny. Do you see their lunches?"

"Yeah, peanut butter sandwiches with the crust cut off," Danielle said.

"I wish my mom would pack that instead of giant leftover mortadella sandwiches or lasagna," I said. Maybe then I would look more like the "American girls" at school. "Although I've got to say, I do love mortadella."

"I think our moms must be in a competition for who has the best-fed kids." Tiny blonde Izzy laughed, but it wasn't that funny. I thought of my mom's routine at dinner, coming over to spoon a second helping of mashed potatoes onto my plate. I think I might be winning.

"Anyone want to start going to the gym?" Tanya said, drawing laughs.

In my month of high school so far with these "American" students, I'd been experiencing something like culture shock. Sure, I still had tons of friends from my Italian neighborhood and my majority-Italian middle school, but now I was making all these new friends who knew absolutely nothing about being Italian.

"What's that?" A new friend, Sadie McLane, asked at lunch the next day. Fair-haired and freckled, she was definitely not Italian. She stared skeptically at my messy muffaletta sandwich. I looked from her thin ham and cheese on Wonder Bread with the crust cut off, her bag of Lay's chips and pre-packaged chocolate chip cookies to my dense muffaletta sandwich, with its layers of ham, mortadella, salami, provolone, mozzarella, and olive spread, dripping oil and sauce down its brown paper wrapping.

"Muffaletta sandwich," I said. "Want to try it?"

Tanya flipped her brown hair. "You've never heard of muffaletta? It's like the best Italian sandwich."

I held it out, and Sadie grabbed it. When she took a bite, her eyes popped out of her head. "Wow, that is so good!"

I nodded and gave her a second bite, then she offered me some of hers. I tried it, only to be nice. Nothing beats muffaletta.

Wait, she hadn't even heard of muffaletta, so what else didn't she know about? Or was I the one missing out on something? What didn't I know about? I eyed my friends' neat sandwiches with the crusts cut off, ignoring my greasy brown sandwich-wrap paper.

I always thought my neighborhood and family lifestyle was the way everybody lived, but apparently, Americans did things differently.

Didn't everyone have huge extended families, a mom who makes home-cooked meals every night, and a giant backyard garden? Didn't everyone have two frugal, loving parents, two kitchens, and plastic-covered couches? When I say frugal, I mean really frugal. So frugal, my mom kept scores of plastic bags hung up on clothespins from our hanging fruit baskets in the kitchen.

I'd been imagining all my life that everyone went home to the same routine.

Now that I was out of my largely Italian Catholic elementary school, I guessed I was starting to learn what it meant to be American, and how different my life was from some of my friends'.

Coming up to my house, number 7 Walnut Lane, that evening, I waved bye to my friends. Tanya was my cousin. In Italian neighborhoods, everyone's related somehow.

We lived in the north end of Waterbury, a mostly "fresh off the boat" Italian neighborhood. That meant everyone spoke Italian, and everyone's parents or grandparents had been born and raised in Italy. The houses all looked the same, and nobody had a house of their own. Everyone lived in units of three family houses, as we did.

My family lived on the bottom floor of a tall, narrow three-family house.

In our front yard stood a homemade shrine to the Virgin Mary. An old bathtub stood upright, buried a quarter of the way underground, forming a perfect shelter for Mary. The edge of the tub—I mean, shrine—was decorated with rose garlands, flowers, and votive candles. Even in a cookie-cutter neighborhood, my parents found ways to make our house our home---mostly through their deep devotion to Catholicism.

Instead of going in the front door, I walked around the side of the house to the backyard, and in a heartbeat stepped out of the city and into the rural Italy of my parents' childhoods. We had a big multi-box above-ground garden, surrounded by a high chicken-wire fence to keep out the birds, rabbits, and squirrels—and Pasqualina, our nosy Italian neighbor.

Our backyard garden provided us with enough food to end world hunger. Beans, potatoes, corn, lettuce, tomatoes, squash, peppers, onions—we grew it all. We even had a pergola for our grapes to grow on, which my dad would later turn into homemade wine. That same garden would supply all the tomatoes for the two hundred jars we canned every year so we could, of course, have homemade sauce every Sunday. Some days my work wasn't done at the sound of the last class bell. There was always more to be done in the garden.

My mom and Nancy were already out there.

"Good day at school, Mar?" Mom said it like *mare,* short for Mary. "Did you eat your lunch?"

Even though it wasn't a neat little ham and cheese on Wonder Bread, it tasted too good to pass up. I had devoured it. Now I didn't even crack a smile. "Yes, Mom."

"Good."

I helped them for a little while, weeding the dirt between the plants while they picked lettuce and tomatoes.

Mom and Nancy chatted, Mom eventually encouraging her to "take a break from her studies" to hang out with other kids outside of school. Focused intently on cutting lettuce, Nancy said, "I'll think about it."

Mom watched Nancy, diligently do her duties. Then, as if a lightbulb went on over her head, she said, "Maybe you could tag along with Mary Lou if she has plans this weekend, hmm?"

She looked at me expectantly. I gave a non committal shrug in response. This weekend was still a mystery. It was only Monday. There was a dance on Friday, but I wasn't sure I'd want Nancy hanging around while I flirted with Anthony.

I didn't let on about the momentous events of my day. Not to my parents or to Nancy, with whom I had the great fortune of sharing a tiny room.

Brushing my teeth that night, I kept meeting eyes with another small statue of Virgin Mary, which Nancy had placed on the shelf.

My parents and Nancy were obsessed with religion and had

placed statues of Catholic saints and prominent figures all over our house, "for protection." We had a huge wooden plaque of Padre Pio hanging in the living room and various statues and paintings of the essential saints in every room of the house. There was St. Francis, the saint of animals, despite the fact we didn't have any pets. We had St. Rita, my middle namesake as well as Nancy's, whom my mom had nicknamed "the saint of the impossible." St. Anthony—every house has to have one, because he's the saint you pray to if you lose something. And then, of course, the classics: Mother Teresa, Virgin Mary, and Jesus.

We had a Jesus on the cross hanging dutifully on a wall in the living room, visible from the dining room table. Among photos of family on side tables, my parents included a framed portrait of Mother Teresa, strewn with fake flowers forever in bloom. My mom kept portraits of Jesus, Mother Mary and some of our ancestors, surrounded by candles and rose petals, in a corner of the kitchen counter, right under the hanging fruit basket that doubled as the recycled plastic bag dispenser. There was at least one Bible and at least one set of rosary beads that usually smelled like roses, hidden in a drawer or hung on a picture frame or statue of a saint in every room. I didn't share my share my family's enthusiasm for religion. My mind was occupied with other things like – being American and finding a husband.

Mouth full of minty Crest, I rinsed, then examined my smooth skin in the mirror, my silky brown hair. Not bad.

Tomorrow would be the day.

I was sure I'd be able to win him over. By the end of the school day, I'd be one step closer to getting to know him, dating him, kissing him, walking down the aisle with him … you get the picture.

I noticed the statue of Mary behind me in the mirror, her smooth porcelain skin, her white hands together in prayer. Under her gold-trimmed hood, she wore her typical expression, benevolent, peaceful, slightly disapproving. As if she knew my plan.

I turned off the light and left her in the dark. I needed my beauty sleep.

~~~~~

The next morning I woke up early and spent a solid two hours on my outfit, hair, and makeup. Eyebrows done, eyelids shadowed, lips glossed.

I ignored Nancy, who whined and pounded on the bathroom door, until my dad's booming voice came from the other side and demanded I unlock it. Begrudgingly I did, and had to share the mirror with Nancy as I put the finishing touches on my hair: a pretty pink bow that matched the laces on my white canvas sneakers.

"Have a blessed day!" my dad called out the car window as I ran toward the double doors of school.

Once inside, I strategically stationed myself in an inconspicuous corner, a perfect place to watch for Anthony's approach, but it also happened to be right outside the nurse's office.

"Not feeling one hundred percent today?" Ms. Sheffler, the nurse, asked, and then so did all my friends who passed by while I waited.

Let me tell you, I got asked a lot. I'd befriended every Italian Catholic this side of town at my middle school, so that meant I was already friends with about a third of my new high school. The other two thirds were new territory for me, but given how easily I'd made friends at my old school, I was pretty sure Sacred Heart would be a breeze.

"Are you sick, Mar?" Anna Pesce asked in passing. She was my friend and all, but did I really look sick to these people? I'd spent two hours getting ready this morning. Seriously.

Finally he appeared, and he was hard to miss.

Anthony came down the hall dressed in a preppy bright yellow cardigan, his curly black hair gelled and neat. He was headed straight toward me.

For a second, I thought we were making eye contact, but then I realized he was just looking straight ahead. I watched him coming, counting down the moments, summoning my courage. When he was close enough, I started walking the same direction and fell in step with him for a beat or two.

Walking side by side in a nearly empty hallway, our strides in perfect pace, the clicks of our shoes matching, he still didn't seem to notice me until I cleared my throat.

Those eyes. He slid them over in my direction without turning his head. A wave of nervousness covered my face. We were close enough that I could smell him, a rich, spiced, musky scent that made my head swim. Sweat beaded at my hairline. I ignored it.

"Hey, you're Anthony Knight, right?" I said, just as I'd rehearsed in my head a million times that morning.

He raised his eyebrows at me and nodded, like *Yes, of course I'm Anthony Knight.*

I decided to stick with my rehearsed script, pretended to think for a second. "I'm pretty sure my uncle fixes your sister's car. She has a Fiat, right?" I blurted, pointing enthusiastically.

He eyed my finger as if it was a dirty rag.

I'm Italian—I use my hands. It's what I do. Was I saying "right" too much?

"That's nice." We walked a few more paces before he added, "And it isn't polite to point."

Like a mean kid with a tack and a balloon.

He looked straight ahead again, as though he'd already forgotten about my existence, and power-walked away.

"And it isn't polite to walk away while someone's talking to you," I muttered, slowing down.

He kept walking.

"I think she takes her car to my father's garage," I called, rising up on my tip-toes, hoping he could still hear me. He was already a good way down the hall, disappearing behind other students.

"Cool" he called back, barely turning, his voice echoing off the walls. Then he rounded the corner, out of sight.

I stopped walking and just stood there, feeling like a deflated *sformato.*

That was it? Wasn't he going to ask my name? Or what year I was in? If I was going to the dance Friday night, or better yet, if I would take his hand in marriage? I hadn't anticipated him being this difficult.

Among my premature wedding plans, one thought did cross my mind. What would Dad say? What would Mom say? Could they ever accept us?

~~~~~~

Green wallpaper with a pink hydrangea pattern lined the walls of our room. I never liked it, but Nancy did.

Sitting on my bed, painting my toenails fluorescent pink, my mind full of my new crush, I tried to ignore Nancy on her side of the room. She was reading barely out loud to herself, her lips mouthing the words, whispering quietly.

"What are you doing?" I groaned. "Are you reading the dictionary?"

"The Encyclopedia Britannica," she said without looking up.

"That's weird." I hunched over to dab paint onto my pinky toenail. "What letter are you on?"

"D. I hate that smell." Nancy blurted.

"Well, I hate sharing a room."

Flexing my toes, I thought I'd done a pretty good job. I could be a professional pedicurist if I wanted to.

I stood up, careful not to smudge the polish, and clicked on the cassette player. Michael Jackson bopped out of the speakers. Soon enough he was singing, "Beat It." I wished that was what Nancy would do.

It took her about ten seconds to object.

"Do you not see that I'm reading? Turn that off."

"Can't you just ignore it or something?"

"Shouldn't you be doing your homework or something?"

"Shut up, Nancy."

"Dad!" Nancy screamed.

"Fine. I'll turn it off."

I smacked the cassette player and froze as the sound of my dad's footsteps came stomping through the house.

I flashed her a threatening look. If he came in here and yelled at me because of her …

After a few seconds, the footsteps faded away. He must've sat back down, thank goodness.

I glared at Nancy, but she was already back to the page, lips moving. Only one thing could stop us from fighting while we attempted to live as roommates, and that was the footsteps, coughs, and sighs of my father. The threat of his wrath was enough to force you to suck up whatever was bothering you and "play nice." My sister could never be at fault. It didn't matter, there would be no fighting. We just had to get along.

It was futile to bring a fight with Nancy to my father, anyway. Nancy had always been the perfect, obedient child. Literally, since before she was born. My father swears that when Nancy was in utero, he'd often bend down and say, "move" to my mom's belly, and Nancy would do it. She'd jump or kick. I've been hearing this story since I was just a little kid. I remember the first time I heard it. I said, "You mean to tell me she even listened from the womb? How unfair is that?"

This is what I was up against.

Part of me wanted to smack her as she sat there, head pressed back against her pillow, knees up under the blanket to prop up the encyclopedia. But it wouldn't help, and I'd feel bad if I did. I wiggled my toes while I waited for them to dry.

~~~~~

By the end of October, I had gotten to know Anthony better.

Well, actually, I had gotten to know his schedule better.

Mrs. Joe helped me get a non-existent filing job in the guidance office as a way to get some extra-credit points for her class. My parents had this clever incentive plan to keep our grades up, in which every A we got on a report card earned us ten dollars. Every B made five, but Cs earned *niente*. While Nancy consistently came away with fifty bucks per report card, I usually walked away with fifteen.

I had a C in English. As far as I was concerned, C's get degrees and I thought they were cool, but my parents didn't think the same. I thought if I could raise it to a B, they'd get off my back.

Still, I liked my new office job. Ms. Kent, the head of Guidance, would come to me at my little desk and ask for so-and-so's file, and I'd run my fingers through the folders and give her the right one.

Technically, I wasn't supposed to be opening files— something about students' confidentiality. I thought about changing some of my Cs to As, but I figured that would undermine Mrs. Joe's idea about giving me the job in the first place.

After trying to watch Anthony in the halls for a while, I knew

I needed more information, but he didn't seem as if he'd divulge it willingly. Whenever I tried to talk to him, our interactions went pretty much the same as the first time. He'd brush off whatever I said and walk away as if I was nothing more than dust floating in his air.

But I couldn't get his face, that heavenly musky scent, or visions of us kissing out of my head.

So I breached some confidentiality agreements. So what?

So I bribed two freshmen boys to fake a fight to make Mrs. Kent leave the room. So what?

So I "accidentally" dropped his file on the ground and got a pretty good look at his schedule. So what?

If only I could study my schoolwork as well as I studied that boy's file. Within the hour, I had his schedule, locker, and locker combination memorized.

And so, as it happened, we began to see each other in the halls more frequently.

Falling into step with him on his way out of the cafeteria, I said, "Hey! Going to the dance on Friday?"

He looked over at me with those eyes, those incredible hazel eyes, and my insides squirmed. The skepticism in his expression only slightly detracted from his beauty.

"Yeah, but I'm going with somebody already."

My heart sank. What? Who? We both slowed our paces.

"But I'll still see you there," he said as if he was trying to soothe hurt feelings. As if he cared.

"Yeah, totally." I pointed at him the way I knew he liked.

Anthony rolled his eyes at my finger. "Learn some manners?" Then he smiled. "Gotta get to class. See ya."

So studious. And just like every other time, he walked away, leaving me lovestruck and alone.

Going to the dance with somebody? Who goes to school

dances together unless they're girlfriend and boyfriend? The more I thought, the further my heart sank.

I left him alone for the rest of that week until we passed each other by accident on Friday. When I saw him, my heart jumped to my throat. He waved, for once, finally starting to warm up to me. It had sure taken him a while, but he still didn't stop walking.

"Want to get ready for the dance together?" Tanya asked on our walk home from school that Friday.

"I'm gonna skip this one," I said.

"What? You were so excited about it last week. Is that Anthony guy not going or something?"

The opposite.

I should never have told them about my fiancé-to-be. At this point, my odds weren't looking too good. "Just not in a social mood tonight. Kinda tired."

"'Not in the social mood?' You are *Miss* Social!" Tanya looked at me, all dolled up with her blue-powdered lids, her hoop earrings, like, *Come on, what's really going on?* "Are you okay?"

"Of course." I waved my hands and tried to look normal. "Everything's fine. I'll come to the next one. Promise."

I breezed through the house without seeing anyone and went straight to my room. I was glad it was empty. Dropping my backpack on the floor and sitting down on the bed, I stared at the floral wallpaper, and then over at my posters of Michael Jackson and Whitney Houston hanging on the wall above the head of my bed.

I trudged over to the stereo, turned on my favorite tape, and stood in front of the speakers as Whitney Houston started to sing, "Saving All My Love for You." Flopping onto the bed facedown into the pillow, I thought about Anthony, afraid to imagine what he was doing right now or what would happen at the dance that night. I rolled over and sighed, floating in my melancholy, wishing for Anthony's love. *"A few stolen moments is all that we share. You've got your family and they need you there. Though I've tried to resist being last on your list, but no other man's gonna do, so I'm saving all my love for you,"* Whitney sang. She got me.

Somehow, no one bothered me for those hours that afternoon and evening. After I'd cried and listened to the whole cassette twice, which involved standing in front of the player for what felt like forever to rewind the tape, I finally turned off the music and listened for sounds of activity in the house. I ventured to the living room to see what the rest of my family was doing. Huddled around the coffee table in chairs and on couches, in the dark wood, deep red, religiously anointed walls of the living room, a small group of guests had gathered.

The first thing I noticed was Sister Victoria's habit and veil, the customary wear of a Catholic nun. Yes, my mother's best friends were nuns. And yes, they were frequently invited over for dinner at our house. There was also an older man I'd never seen before, sitting on the other end of the couch from Sister Victoria. The nun, the old man, and my parents sat around the coffee table, chatting happily in Italian in our warmly lit living room.

Nancy sat at the kitchen table, now reading the Bible instead of the encyclopedia. I went in to fill up a glass of water. From the kitchen we could hear my younger brother talking in his room with a friend, doing who-knew-what. Trading baseball cards? It didn't matter. He could've been in there looking at dirty magazines, and my parents would've excused it. If Nancy was the princess of the family, Vinny was the prince. He could do no wrong, not by my family or anyone else.

"Mary Lou, come over here," Dad said during a pause in their conversation.

Water in hand, I returned to the living room and stood by my dad.

He laid his hand on my shoulder. "Massimo, this is my second daughter, Mary Lou. Mary Lou, this is Massimo Costada. He didn't have dinner plans tonight, so I invited him to break bread and pray with us." Dad raised his chin authoritatively, like the godfather.

The old man, Massimo, nodded a hello in my direction. "Buona sera."

"Buona sera," I returned, and then, to the nun, "Ciao, Sister Victoria."

The beautiful young sister smiled warmly at me as she always did, her face smooth as a statue's, a living saint. Of my mother's nun friends, Sister Victoria was always the kindest to me. We'd spoken before, about Jesus and God, about kindness and helping others, and patience. Honestly, I always thought my mom put her up to some of those talks, but either way, I liked Sister Victoria. Once I even asked her what it was like to become a nun. This pleased my parents and got them temporarily excited at the possibility of their daughter having a future as a woman of the Lord.

Even though being a nun sounded peaceful, and it would make my parents proud, I knew I'd never be able to have a family that way. So yeah, my one and only "career" my parents wished for me, quickly went out the window.

Perfect Nancy always had direction and purpose. She studied hard and gave herself stomachaches if she thought she'd scored less than a ninety-nine on a test.

I guess I was more of a free spirit, the black sheep, if you will, of the family. For me, school was a social event. I got to see all my friends. Hello, I was there building my future social network. Mary Lou Knight, remember? Building a future for Nancy had a different meaning. For me, getting a seventy was passing. Seventy-five was cause to celebrate and take a week off from studying.

I looked at my dad—did he want something else from me? But he took his hand off my shoulder, and the adults resumed talking about how Irish immigrants were still getting more jobs than Italians.

"But the garage is a great success, no? You're helping young Italians get good, clean jobs as mechanics, and that is admirable. And you extend such wonderful Christian kindness to everybody." Sister Victoria glanced over at our increasingly emotional guest, Massimo.

"Grazie, grazie." Massimo's voice quavered, his eyes moist. "Truly, Antonio, your generosity is boundless. I've been so lonely since my wife passed away last year." Sister Victoria laid a gentle hand on his shoulder. "You're among friends tonight."

"It means so much to spend time in a Italian household like this one." He wiped his eyes and gazed around the table. "It makes me miss my Catarina less, and more."

Oh man, I was about to start crying again. Watching Massimo's gentle old eyes sparkle, I could tell how much he loved and missed his wife. I wanted, more than anything in my life, to feel that kind of love too. It's the only thing I'd ever wanted since I'd started wanting things. Just love, and to start a family of my own with the right person. I'd never thought about what it would be like to lose that person, though.

"We are happy to have you," my mom said, her voice strained as if she was nearly moved to tears herself. "I'm glad my husband brought you home from the shop. We love company, and you are welcome any time."

"Good thing I brought my car to Antonio's garage." Massimo laughed.

"Happy to have more Italian business," my dad said.

As the conversation continued, I excused myself and started toward the kitchen. But before I got there, I slipped out the front door of our three-family house and ran up the steps, past the second floor, where a nice newlywed couple lived, and up to the third floor.

My knuckles met the door, and in moments my Nonna opened it. Her sharp, long face appeared in the crack of the door, her wild nest of old-woman hair reaching straight out from her head like Einstein's. Already in her slippers and nightshirt at five o'clock, she brushed crumbs from the soft off-white fabric spotted with little bouquets of flowers like my wallpaper. She smiled, her whole face crinkling.

"Granddaughter, my namesake—come in, come in," she said in Italian. Nonna stepped aside, let me through the door, and swung it shut behind me. We hadn't spoken of the nightstand since I brought it home, but for my grandmother, it seemed to have disappeared into the past like a bad dream.

Neither of my grandparents spoke any English. My parents came to the United States young enough to learn the language and become fluent, although Dad never lost his accent. When my grandparents moved from Italy in their fifties, they hadn't bothered to learn English.

Nonna's apartment felt the way I imagined her house in Italy must have felt—sparse but cozy, with old, dark wood furniture and grandmotherly curtains hanging on the windows. The couches and chairs were all covered in blankets that either Nonna or my mom had crocheted or knitted.

On a little table by the couch, a lamp emitted gentle light. Beside the lamp stood a framed black and white photograph of my Nonna as a little girl, standing between her parents on a hill with huge mountains and wide-branched trees in the background. In the photo, they all had the grim looks of hungry people.

Other framed photographs stared at me from the walls and nightstands. Nonna and Nonno on their wedding day, stoic as soldiers, Nonna holding my mom when she was a baby. Sketches and hand-written letters lay strewn on the coffee table. Small plants grew inside too—herbs and flowers blooming in their pots on the windowsills and tables.

Nonno sat sleeping in the comfy chair, his head leaned back, snoring. His bony hands rested on the upholstery.

I went to the couch as usual and fell into its springy cushions. Nonna banged around in the kitchen for a minute while I sat there, sinking deeper into the couch, trying not to think about my friends getting ready for the dance. Was Anthony getting ready now too? I could just see him, combing his hair in the mirror, checking himself out. He had to put effort into looking that good. There was no way it was natural. Who looks like a male model from a Michael Jackson video without trying?

Nonna shuffled over to the coffee table and set a silver tray down with a kettle, two tea cups, and a box of Social Tea Crackers— our favorite. I sipped the rose tea and felt the warmth in my belly. The gentle, floral aroma filled my nose. I sighed. Having my Nonna next to me made me feel even better.

We sat in silence for a minute, sipping, breathing in the steam. I reached across the cushion and grabbed her hand. She squeezed back.

We stayed up there, talking about Nonno and school for a while. Even though I was trying to keep Anthony off my mind, talking about school obviously made me think of him. I was about to bring him up to Nonna when another knock came at the door.

Nancy's voice carried through the wood. "Mar, Mom wants help setting the table." Without waiting for a response, she went back downstairs.

Nonna and I exchanged a look and both knew we'd be back up here once the dishes were done.

A lot of families probably value their dinner traditions, but at my house, family dinner was like the main event, day after day, seven days a week, without fail. Kinda like church, but every sigle day.

Some of my American friends talked about how they got to eat TV dinners on the couch, or went out to dinner with friends. That would be so cool.

Not me. Family dinner at the house was absolutely mandatory every night until I was at least fifty. No excuses. So far I'd never tried to get out of it, except for middle school parties or dances, but typically these took place after dinner, so there'd been no conflict. Yet.

My father was usually the first to sit down. He twiddled his thumbs or prayed. My mother, my grandmother, my sister, and I shuffled between the kitchen and the dining room. We ferried massive plates of delicious, home-made Italian food from the counters, stoves, and ovens to the dining room table. On the odd nights that my father had to work late and was the last to sit down, we waited for him before we even touched a crumb of food.

That night the table was set for nine. My family, my grandparents, Sister Victoria, and Massimo all crowded around our wooden table, laid with a soft plaid tablecloth and nine placemats.

Once we were all seated, my dad cleared his throat, folded his hands in prayer, and bowed his head. We all followed suit.

"Hail Mary, full of grace," he began in his thick Italian accent.

He proceeded to repeat the prayer two more times for good measure. He was superstitious and did everything in threes because of the Holy Trinity. For my dad it was the Father, the Son, and the Holy Spirit. My mom had a holy trinity of her own, the holy trinity of Italian cooking: olive oil, salt and pepper.

"Amen," the table chorused.

Just when we thought it was finally time to eat, my dad dove into one more set. "Bless us, O Lord, and these Thy gifts, which we are about to receive from Thy bounty, through Christ our Lord, amen."

"Amen," I said, my voice lost in everyone else's. Trying hard not to roll my eyes, like three Hail Mary's weren't enough!

I glanced up around the table, where Mom and Nancy gazed lovingly at Dad, sitting serenely in the afterglow of prayer. My brother played with the Garbage Pail Kids cards in his hand, and Nonna Maria caught my eye and winked at me across the table.

"And now," Dad finally said, "we eat."

Roasted potatoes and vegetables from the garden, homemade pizza, rice pilaf, and a tender, marinated chicken. As usual with my mom's cooking, there were no complaints, a solid round of seconds, and nine clean plates.

My mother insisted on home-cooked meals for breakfast, lunch, and dinner.

Every time we drove by a fast-food restaurant, my siblings and I begged my mom to stop. Without fail, she not only drove right past it, but then she lectured us on how home-cooked food is healthier and how much cheaper she could replicate the meal at home.

Dutifully, our mom made us homemade McDonald's cheeseburgers made of extra-lean ground meat from our freezer, complete with freezer burn. She delicately sandwiched the four-inch high clump of meat between two pieces of Home Pride whole wheat bread. We always tried to peel back the thin layer of bread, which was now colored pink from the ketchup, to see if she'd put cheese on it. Sometimes, when she ran out of American cheese, she used mozzarella, also from the freezer. Yup, just like McDonald's.

Growing up in an Italian neighborhood surrounded by other Italians made for a pretty limited worldview. We had Italian friends, Italian relatives, Italian parties, Italian food, Italian churches, Italian prayers, and Italian dreams. We all lived in our own little Italian bubble.

One thing was for sure, though. Even if it wasn't the same as American fast food, my mom could cook a homemade Italian meal better than any restaurant, or anyone else I knew, for that matter.

Back up in Nonna's apartment, I was full from another delicious homemade meal, I thought I might be permanently attaching to Nonna's couch.

I didn't had any wine, but I felt dizzy and drunk, maybe from the good food, or the good company. I ended up sharing my new found secret infatuation with Anthony.

"Am I crazy, Nonna?" I said to her in Italian. "From the second I saw him, I was in love with him. I barely know him, but I feel like we're meant to be."

Nonna watched me from her spot on the couch, one hand resting on her belly.

She took a minute to think. I listened to the faint sound of the second-floor tenant's classical Italian music floating up through the floorboards.

"Love is a funny thing. Sometimes it takes your entire life to find … some people never find it, but you think you've found it now, so young. Is it the real thing? A blessing? Or a curse, if it is lost." Her voice raspy, her gaze faraway, she seemed lost in time for a moment. Then she leaned toward me, her eyes suddenly intense. "Once you've found it, don't ever let it go." she whispered.

That night in bed, Nancy was reading as usual, I turned Nonna's words over in my mind. *It is the real thing?* I heard her ask, again and again. Was it the real thing?

How do you know when it's real love, and not just an obsession? Well, I'd never been obsessed with anything quite this way before, different from scrunchies, different from a favorite song, although kind of similar too. Like a new Michael Jackson release, Anthony was on repeat in my mind.

It was real for me, I felt a hundred percent sure. These squirming stomach feelings, constant thoughts, and mild "stalking" behavior suggested my feelings for him were very real.

But how did he feel about me? So far, it didn't seem as if he felt much.

On my wall I could see Michael's face, hovering over his trademark red leather zippered jacket. He looked down at me gently, tenderly, his eyes caring yet intense, sexy.

"You've got this, Mary Lou," I imagined Michael saying to me. "Anthony's gotta be crazy not to love you right back. But he will. Only a fool would pass you up, Mar." He winked at me, and then fell back into his typical silence.

"Thanks, Michael." I stood up in bed and kissed Michael's cheek on the wall.

Nancy sighed and rolled toward her own wall.

I snuggled back down in bed and turned away from her, towards the hydrangea wallpaper, and let out a heavy sigh. *Once you've found it,* Nonna's voice echoed in my head, *don't ever let it go.*

My Bathing Suit is Too Tight

Over Thanksgiving break, I had the bright idea of looking up Anthony's number in the phonebook. He consistently deflected my advances in person, although our friendship did seem to be growing. Maybe he'd be more responsive if I could get him on the phone at home. He hadn't given me his number yet, but here we were, three days into break, and I couldn't help wondering what he was doing. If he wasn't away, maybe we could hang out.

There was only one "Knight" listed, but the address was in a different town. I knew it wasn't him, but I picked up the phone and called anyway. I was hoping that maybe, by some miraculous chance, he would be there visiting. Better yet, maybe the person on the other line would say, "Oh, Anthony, he's my nephew," or "He's my cousin. He doesn't live here, but here's his phone number."

Yeah, well, that didn't happen. Nothing happened. It rang and rang and rang. I pressed the phone harder to my ear, waiting for someone, anyone to answer—for *something* to happen. But there was no indication that the phone was ringing in an inhabited house. Come on, who doesn't even have an answering machine? After the forty-eighth ring, I hung up.

Sitting down at the kitchen table, I guessed I would have to wait until after the break to see him at school. I could only imagine how he was filling his days.

Luckily, my imagination worked around the clock.

Listening to Whitney Houston's "I Wanna Dance With Somebody," I jumped around my room, singing, imagining what Anthony could be doing. If he was away, maybe he was skiing somewhere, barreling down a mountainside.

Or maybe he was somewhere warm and exotic, snorkeling with tropical fish, his rich skin dappled by the water in the sunlight. Could he be hiking in the rainforest, at the theatre in the city, dressed in a nice button-down and slacks for the performance? What was he doing in his down time, reading a book? Playing baseball? Watching a movie or listening to music? Playing Pong, or shopping at the mall? Was there any way, any possibility that he could be out there, where he is, dreaming about me the same way I dreamed about him? I imagined both of us gazing out windows at the same starry night sky at the same time, thinking the same thing: *I wish I was with you.* I had to wonder—did I even cross his mind?

Thanksgiving break was a boring time. Pretty much all of my friends were busy doing things with their families or traveling out of town. So I had to stay home and hang out in my house all day, which meant I had to stay home and hang out with Nancy all day.

At least we had an eventful Thanksgiving. Even though my family was culturally Italian, my siblings and I (well, more me and Vinny, not so much Nancy) begged to adopt American customs and traditions. Our Thanksgiving meals were "Italianized," of course, but we still had turkey.

Everyone came to our house: my godparents, ZiaTeresa and

Uncle Dominic, who we all called Zio Mimi and my cousins, the shared family German shepherd, Lupo, my dad's mom, Nonna Annunziata, plus anyone whom my dad invited home from the garage. It was usually a handful of older people, widows or widowers, and sometimes younger people who had just moved to town and didn't have family in America. Oh, and I can't forget the nuns.

My dad went around filling everyone's wine glass with his homemade Chianti. Our neighborhood revered him as one of the holiest, most generous and God-loving men around. To be invited to our house for dinner was a big deal, but Dad thought he was just doing his part to help the community. Italians helping Italians, he'd say, and then give a speech in broken English about how he loves America and "the humanity," and how it always "pays to be good." His favorite sayings. My dad loved giving advice and was always spouting words of wisdom cloaked in mystery at the breakfast table, on the drive to school, out shopping in the mall, to a roomful of Thanksgiving guests, wherever he could strike up a conversation.

We had so many people over for Thanksgiving that year, there was no point in setting a table. Nancy, Nonna, Zia Teresa, and I helped my mom serve massive, delicious plates of food. We set everything out buffet style. Some of our new guests had eyes as big as plates, in awe of my mom and aunt's incredible cooking. Before we dove in, though, of course we said grace.

"Amen," I said with everybody else, looking around the room at our village of friends and family—burly, dark-haired men, big-haired women, some thin, some curvy, all ages, little kids and grandparents. Then it was time to eat.

Steaming manicotti dripping in cheese, colorful arrays of garden vegetables, a huge bowl of seasoned mashed potatoes, a twenty-two pound golden-brown stuffed turkey, but also a rack of lamb and a roast ham too. We liked our meats, and we liked our options.

Between what we made to eat and what all our guests brought, we'd wind up with enough dessert leftovers to last until Christmas. Cannoli, tiramisu, pumpkin pie, rice pudding, crema, sfogliatella, rum cake, sponge cake, apple pie, and my favorite, Spumoni! Seriously, it was no wonder I was always trying to lose weight. I loved to eat, and thanks to my mom and relatives, we had an abundance of the best food on the planet.

Sitting down with my slice of spumoni, I marveled at the pretty layers of gelato cake. My Zia Teresa had made it, and it looked more like Easter dessert than Thanksgiving. The bottom layer was chocolatey and sprinkled with hazelnuts, the middle layer pink with strawberry chunks, and the top layer vanilla with crunchy little pistachios mixed in. The whole thing was topped with homemade vanilla whipped cream. I took a bite and tasted all the flavors and textures mixing in my mouth.

That's what I liked about spumoni—it has a little bit of everything, all at once.

Lupo the German Shepherd laid his chin on my knee, waiting patiently for Thanksgiving leftovers under the table. We spoke to him only in Italian, and he ate only Italian leftovers. He didn't whine once the whole evening. At the end of the night, when used plates sat stacked all over the kitchen, my mom cut the top off a gallon milk carton and filled it with scraps.

"Lupo, *siediti*," my mom said. He obediently sat on our yellow kitchen tiles. "*Bravo*," she said encouragingly and put the carton down for him, petting his head.

When the guests had gone and the dishes were done, I rolled myself into bed and finally thought about Anthony.

Did he have a big family Thanksgiving too? I pictured next year's Thanksgiving, another big, fun, loud, boisterous Italian gathering, and saw Anthony's face mixed in with the rest, happy, talking to Zio Mimi, glancing over at me as if he'd just been talking about me. I let out a heavy sigh in the dark.

At Anthony's Thanksgiving, they probably didn't serve spumoni for dessert. I bet he had a Thanksgiving as American as apple pie. They probably served apple pie for dessert or at least pumpkin, I hoped.

During the two weeks of Christmas break, I once more started wishing I had a "normal" American family. By this point in the year, I was pretty confident that we didn't all live the same lifestyles outside of school.

All my American friends were vacationing at ski resorts or Disney World. I'd asked Anthony about his plans, hoping against all odds that somehow he would be staying here in the freezing Connecticut winter too. He told me he was going to North Carolina to visit with his family.

"Oh, totally, have fun," I half-heartedly wished him, wanting more than anything to ditch my ultra-Italian family and go on vacation with an American friend. I could only imagine the people he would meet in North Carolina. Hopefully it would be strictly a family affair. All of the girls loved Anthony. I wasn't the only one following him around or trying to befriend him. Practically every day I watched him deflect cherry greetings and invitations from cute girls, with his cool skeptical face.

My Italian family spent that Christmas break eating, visiting relatives, *Compares* and *Comares*, eating more, and re-gifting. We had an entire liquor cabinet full of "re-gifts." I know this for sure because my sister and I drew a green star on the label of a bottle of Amaretto, and two Christmases later, that same green-starred bottle was back in our liquor cabinet.

A few days before Christmas, I went shopping with my mom.

As we walked up and down the crowded aisles, casually scanning the shelves, my eyes stopped when they came across a yellow phone in the shape of a banana.

Call me crazy, but I saw that phone and immediately saw myself on it. I would be the coolest, hippest girl with my yellow banana phone, and it matched Anthony's yellow cardigan. I begged and pleaded with my mom. I even promised her that, if she bought me that phone, I wouldn't ask for anything for the rest of my life. That's how bad I wanted it. I was desperate. I had to have it.

"We'll see," she said. "I have to talk to your father."

Why does she have to have a conference with my dad about a twelve-dollar present?

Because that's how an Italian household runs.

I was quick to answer myself with an Italian mindset that I was fully aware of, but yet I couldn't quite understand. Most Italian women make no independent decisions. Everything revolves around the "man of the house." If I wanted to do something or go somewhere, I had to ask my dad, and I got only one shot. If he said no, it was no. So I had to learn to approach with caution and try to catch him when he was in a good mood. I didn't have the same patience for this practice as my perfect older sister had. She probably didn't even need any well-thought-out strategy in getting a "yes" from Daddy.

Christmas was calm and beautiful, as usual. I loved Christmas. My birthday happened just a week before, so I always felt a little connected to Jesus' birthday, even if it wasn't actually on Christmas. Mostly, I loved the lights and the spirit and everyone's cheery mood. That year, I wanted so badly to give Anthony a gift. I brainstormed a whole list of possible presents.

"Do you think that would be creepy?" I asked Daniella over the phone.

"Um ... not creepy, but maybe a little much."

I knew she was right. It would be weird to give him something when we didn't know each other that well. But I couldn't help dreaming up future Christmases, in which we'd curl up in tacky Christmas sweaters by a fire, with two stockings hanging from the fireplace mantle. Anthony and Mary Lou would be written on them in my neat, fancy cursive handwriting. The tree behind us would glow with lights and glitter with ornaments. In my mind, we were so comfortable, so close with each other. He had his arm around me, and I snuggled up under his chin, leaning against his chest.

I closed my eyes and urged him to think about me, wherever he was in North Carolina.

That Christmas, all I wanted was him. I fantasized the appearance of a postcard in the mail: *Hey Mar! The weather's great here. Hope you're staying warm. Thinking of you! Anthony.*

Literally nothing would have made me happier. But every day, when I checked the mail, there was nothing for me. I was being delusional and I knew it. We had never talked about writing each other. But I couldn't help but dream. My mind and heart were really out of control.

That year, I ended up getting the banana phone I wanted. My mom nodded an approving patience-is-a-virtue smile as my gaze skittered toward the awesome new accessory.

"Here's another one for you, Mary Lou," Vinny said, grabbing a small present from under the tree.

"I didn't even notice this one." I shook it gently, then I carefully removed the star-print wrapping paper to reveal a small angel statue. Holding her in my cupped palms as if she were a living thing, I raised her closer to my face. Dark hair, eyes closed, hands pressed together in prayer, she wore a brown dress with green trim. My name and birth date were inscribed in looping cursive gold letters on the base.

My dad looked pleased with my response.

None of my other siblings had gotten a little statue like this. Usually my parents gave us the same thing. We each got a new hat, a new pair of socks, and a new book or cassette tape that we'd wanted. I got a skateboard, too, and Nancy got a new set of Hardy Boy mysteries and Vinny got a new Walkman, but no one else had gotten a little angel.

Immediately, I fell in love with her. I got up and went to my dad's side to hug him and kiss his cheek.

"Thank you, Papa." I hadn't called him Papa since I was eleven, when I found out that "American kids" call their parents "Mom" and "Dad."

"You are very welcome, Mary Lou. I saw it, and I thought-a of you." He patted my back. "Don't forget, you're my little angel."

Wow. I almost cried. Was he trying to apologize for something? All those years of Nancy-favoritism, maybe? Whatever the reason, it meant the world to me. I placed the little statue on the dark worn wood of my special nightstand from Italy.

~~~~~

The break came and went and so did the rest of freshman year—uneventful and unnoticed.

I spent the spring pining for Anthony, making unsuccessful attempts to spend time with him, and getting repeatedly blown off because he only had eyes for Candy Russell.

Yeah. Candy. Her name was really Candy.

After watching him long enough, I realized he had a pattern. Just like me, he seemed to strategically place himself around the school, in search of …

Her.

One day he stood against a wall, tapping his thumb and pointer finger together, watching Candy get books out of her locker.

No, please, don't go up to her. Don't go talk to her.

But he did. He went up to her and said, "Hey, Candy. How was your weekend?"

Hiding a cringe, she closed her locker. "Hey."

Slowly but surely, she edged away from him against the wall of tan lockers.

The bell rang, and she jumped on it. She gestured over her shoulder, mouthed, "Gotta go," with a fake-apologetic expression. He waved after her with the look of an over-eager fan who just got blown off by their pop-star idol. Maybe next time, kiddo.

I get it, Candy is cute. Petite with pin-straight black hair and dark eyebrows and lashes. She wore skirts as short as our Catholic school dress code would allow, and cute blouses that showed off her developed cleavage while still leaving plenty to the imagination.

She was a senior, older even than Anthony, and clearly way out of his league.

Toward the end of the year, after watching this interaction again and again and wondering why I could never get Anthony to act that way with me, I started to wonder. Was that the kind of girl he wanted?

Petite? Not me.

Thin? Not exactly me …

Black hair? I could dye mine.

I wore skirts too, but maybe they didn't exactly have the same appeal on me as they did on her. Both of her legs together were still skinnier than one of mine.

That summer, I forced myself to eat boiled zucchini from the garden and to work out daily. I knew I needed to transform myself from a chubby Italian girl to someone he would want to stop and talk to in the hallway. After all, he would be graduating this year. I had one school year, ten short months, to make him "my future husband" notice me, fall in love, cancel his college plans, and propose marriage. At least I could count Candy out as competition.

I had my work cut out for me, but I was on a mission. As my Zia Teresa would say, "Old curtains today ... new pants tomorrow."

Between working with my family in the garden, my boiled zucchini lunches, and an hour every other day on the treadmill, I actually started losing weight.

On my way out for a jog around the neighborhood on a hot day, half-walking, half-skipping out the door to Lisa Lisa and the Cult Jam, I noticed my dad in the front yard.

"Going out for a run!" I called to my dad, sliding a headphone off one ear.

"Really? Okay, be safe." He stood and inspected Mary in her blue bathtub shelter, not catching my stink eye. What did he mean, "really?"

As soon as I turned down the sidewalk, I noticed some boys in the neighborhood. Mike Capone and Tommy Romano in their tank tops and work pants, looking as if they were on their way to their landscaping and construction jobs. They weren't anywhere near as cute as my Anthony.

I was about to wave when they both quickly crossed the street. What happened? Turning around, I saw my dad standing on the sidewalk in front of our house, arms crossed, watching them. Yep, that made sense.

With two daughters in the house, my dad liked to intimidate all the boys in the neighborhood. This was not the first time I'd seen boys cross the street so they wouldn't have to walk in front of our house.

It wasn't a coincidence that my dad liked to swing a baseball bat on the front lawn during the weekends and a lot of boys would avoid our neighborhood.

I shrugged and moved on, a bounce in my step, before I forced myself into a slow jog. The only thing that helped me to jog all the way around the block was imagining how good I'd look on the first day of school. As I rounded the last corner onto our street, my jog slowed to a walk. My little brother Vinny and two neighborhood kids his age stood in a circle up ahead. As I got closer, I heard what the kids were saying. They shouted and pointed at Little Vin.

"Whatcha gonna do now?" one of the kids said. The red remote-control race car that Vinny got for Christmas last year lay in pieces at his feet.

"Gonna cry about it? Cry about it to your mommy? Little cry baby," the other kid jeered.

"Gonna pee your pants now?" They kept going. One of them even shoved him. My jaw dropped.

That was it.

I took off into a full-on sprint.

I rammed into one of them as hard as I could, pushing him to the ground. I grabbed the other kid and put him in a headlock.

"Don't mess with my little brother!" I yelled as the kid tried to get away as I pinned him. "Didn't your parents teach you any manners? Never talk to my little brother like that again!"

I finally let go of the flailing kid. He sprinted away and his friend followed.

The look of terror in their eyes was priceless. I looked around, in case anyone had seen, but nobody else was outside.

Breathing hard, I hugged my little brother. He was crying, sweet little Vin.

"Are you okay?" I asked.

He nodded into my shoulder. I was only a few years older than he was, but sometimes I felt more like little Vinny's mom than his sister. I was his protector, ever since we were little. If he was the family prince, I was his protector. "C'mon, let's go home."

"I have a feeling those jerks aren't going to bother me anymore," he said.

"Ya think?" I shot him a look. Holding his hand, we walked back to the house, sure that our dad would make those boys replace my brother's toy.

~~~~~

Summer vacation meant family beach days. Not just my parents, brother, sister, and me, but my grandparents, my other grandmother Annunziata, my aunt, uncle, and cousins, as well as *Comare and Compare*—my godparents—and their family. And this was still considered a small gathering for Italians. My other cousins, who lived a few towns away, would probably meet us at the beach too.

My mom, Nancy, and Nonna had spent hours the night before preparing the food: cheese, crackers, tuna salad, chicken salad, eggplant parmigiana, a big tossed salad, and cannolis and apple cake for dessert, all ready to go in Tupperware containers in coolers in the back of our car. There was enough food in there to feed several Italian families.

My mom like to tell a story about a new immigrant family from our neighborhood who packed up their car to go on a beach trip. They spent the whole day driving around, trying to find the beach, stopping every three hours to eat. They had a map, but nobody knew how to read it. When they gave up at sunset, they still had leftovers to bring home. They never saw even a sliver of the ocean.

A car horn blared twice out front. Dad was getting impatient.

"Mary Lou!" my mom called again.

"Coming!" I yelled, trying to yank my bathing suit top down as I ran out of my room toward the front door, dodging furniture along the way.

The zucchini diet had done only so much so far. I had faith that if I kept it up all summer, it would pay off. This tiny hand-me-down bathing suit wasn't helping either.

"That bathing suit looks a little tight on you," Mom said as I got in. "Maybe we should see if any of the cousins have any extras that might fit."

Hand-me-downs and hand-mades were all I could hope for from my family.

At my mom's comment, everyone turned to look at me in my bathing suit. Even my dad twisted around to look. He was behind the wheel, wearing sunglasses and a sunhat. He shook his head. Dad hadn't even turned on the station wagon yet.

"What?" I said. "Sorry, it took me a second to change. I had to put on my bathing suit."

"We all did that an hour ago," Nancy said, pausing from her Nancy Drew book.

"That's right," my dad said, "when your mother said to. Listen to your mother, Mary Lou, like Nancy does. When the bell rings at sunset, go inside, or you'll be eaten by the wolves."

Um, excuse me? One of my dad's confusing parables, emerging bright and early as they always did.

Nancy gave me a little proud-of-herself smirk before settling back in with her book. I sighed. I could never do anything right. Never as good as Nancy.

He leaned over to my mom in the passenger seat. "Why doesn't she wear a one-piece? Girls would never wear two pieces in Italy."

But we live in America, not Italy.

Finally we were all buckled up and ready to go, no thanks to my "tardy" behavior. My grandparents sat in the middle row. Nancy, Vinny, and I were in the third row in back.

"Now we can pray," my father announced.

Here we go.

"*Bene*," Nonno said with a smack of his gums. The only thing he said during the whole car ride.

Little clacks of rosary beads hitting each other filled the car as my dad got them out from the car console and wrapped them ceremoniously around his hand. These were his "car beads." We had a different set in every vehicle.

A quiet peace fell over the car. Nonna and Nonno bowed their heads and closed their eyes. So did Mom and Nancy. Vinny kind of just went along with it, eyes open, head up, bobbing his head to a music beat in his mind. I pretended so I wouldn't get myself into even worse graces with my dad, just in case he sneaked a peek. Three prayers, three amen's, he put the car in reverse and we hit the road.

I sat fidgeting uncomfortably in my seat, pulling at the seatbelt as it cut into my shoulder. I wondered what my friends were doing this summer. I hated summers. I hated breaks in general. Not to say that I loved school, but I loved socializing at school. My friends and I hung out at each other's houses, did "homework" together (really, we just painted our nails and read magazines or went to the mall) and did fun, American-girl things that my parents did not approve of at all.

Growing up, I lived with one foot in each world. I had my old-world family of Italian immigrants at home, who tried their best to preserve their culture and ways of life away from their homeland, and then I had my modern, Rick Springfield-loving, McDonald's-eating, scrunchie-wearing, culturally American friends. Of course, before I got to high school, all my friends were from families and upbringings just like mine—immigrant families living in crowded three-family homes, where maybe their grandparents lived above or below them, and they probably shared a walkway with strangers on the second floor. My friends and I bonded over how traditional our parents were, how annoying they were about bargains, and how obsessed they were with never wasting any food, ever.

I was obsessed with being American and studied pop culture as if it were my homework. Ms. Joe said if I new my Latin like I knew my rap music I would be the valedictorian of my class. American music, American actors and actresses, American movies, American style, American magazines, American dance moves—I loved it all. Even though my eccentric Italian family could get on my nerves, I loved my traditions and my big, crazy, Catholic Italian family.

Nonna stared out the window, her chin resting on her fist, elbow on the arm rest, watching the modern world pass her by. Her tall, proud forehead pressed against the glass, her brows set low over her eyes, which sparkled in her long, narrow face. What was she thinking about?

America must have felt like a different planet to my parents and grandparents, after living in Italy so long. The world had changed a lot since they were young, especially for Nonna.

She turned away from the window and twisted in her seat to look back at us. "Should we play a game?" she said in Italian.

"Yeah!"

"The poem game?"

I loved this one. Nonna would recite a poem in Italian, and my siblings and I would try to memorize it. If we could recite it back to her with no mistakes, she would open up her plastic purse and distribute Tootsie Rolls as rewards. Nonna tapped her finger to her chin in thought. After a few minutes she took a deep breath and a beautiful, lilting Italian poem rolled off her tongue. We spent some time in the car learning Nonna's poem until each of us had gotten it right and earned a Tootsie Roll.

It was a thirty-minute car ride to the beach. There came the time in every family car ride when my dad started philosophizing. He went off on a tangent, telling a story about something that happened to him when he was little or something that happened to someone else. Eventually, he got around to some obscure nugget of wisdom packaged in a riddle. We all grappled with his newest "lesson" for the remaining twenty minutes of the car ride. Nobody seemed to have come to a definitive meaning by the time we parked. Whether this pleased my father or frustrated him, I am still not sure.

When we got to the beach, we unloaded the food, beach chairs, fold-out table, umbrellas, towels, beach toys, and every necessary beach item.

From the parking lot, I heard the sound of the waves breaking on the sand, the high-pitched cries of seagulls, the fresh scent of salt. As soon as I stepped outside, I started sweating, but the sun's heat felt good on my skin.

By the time we'd set everything up on the beach, you'd have thought we were planning on camping out for a few days and nights, not just a few hours. The table was covered buffet-style with all the food Nonna and Mom had made, with space left for whatever our cousins were bringing. There were stacks of plastic cups and bottles of red wine, all homemade, of course. The beach chairs were set up in rows as if we were all going to watch a movie, and we had so many towels that we could hand some out to people on the beach and still have a few to spare.

Quickly, I slathered myself in sunscreen and plopped down into my beach chair, digging my toes into the sun-warmed sand.

A couple paused on their beach walk and stood watching at the edge of our Italian beach village as if we were a pride of wild lions. After a minute, they walked up to the table where the adults were standing around.

"Are you having a party?" the man asked.

Nope, we're just Italian.

My parents laughed. "Sort of. Just a family beach day," Dad said.

"Big family," the woman said.

My father invited them to help themselves to the food.

Nonna played with me and the kids in the sand, helping us build sand castles, moats and sand sculptures. My other grandmother, Annunziata, sat fully clothed in the shade of her umbrella, her shiny black shoe hanging off her toes. She peered out from behind her big bug-like sunglasses and sipped wine through pursed lips with the other adults. My Nonna was the odd one out, more kid than adult, I guess.

Our cousins and godparents finally arrived and increased our "party" size to fifteen. My Zio Mimi, my favorite uncle and godfather found me and gave me a big hug. He wore his uniform of white socks with brown flip-flops, blue short shorts and a white tank top t-shirt.

"I brought you something," he said, his big, bushy mustache moving over his lip. He pulled out a little souvenir of the Empire State Building from his pocket.

"Don't tell your brother or sister. This is just for you." He kissed my head.

"Thanks, Zio." I kissed his cheek while he was still kneeling down. Now, where to hide this?

Now that all the cousins had arrived, it was really a party. The adults all sat around under the umbrellas, rubbing sunscreen on the kids, eating and sipping wine out of plastic cups.

A good half hour after we finished lunch, my dad called us together to pray the rosary before we went swimming. No jellyfish, no cramps, no rip tides, amen.

As soon as we finished saying "amen," Vinny and I took off as fast as we could for the ocean. I was sweaty and hot and just wanted to plunge into the Atlantic to cool off. I raced my brother to the tide, the cold water splashing up my legs, before I launched myself into a wave. The sudden cold took my breath away. Gasping, I broke the surface.

Rubbing the water out of my eyes, bobbing on the blue-green sea, I turned to look back at my dad as he stood in the water up to his ankles, wearing his bathing suit, his tan stomach hanging out. The gold cross he wore around his neck caught the sun and gleamed. He opened his arms wide, like Jesus on the cross, and tipped his head back to the sky. I knew he was praying again. I rolled my eyes and ducked just as Vinny splashed a wave of water at me.

I shrieked and kicked water back in his direction.

Catholicism was like the sun my family revolved around. God, a little bit of guilt, and tradition.

For two weeks in the third grade, I was convinced that I wanted to be a nun. Yep, I thought I would renounce boys and scrunchies for the habit and veil, become a woman of the cloth, saying Hail Marys more times a day than my dad. That phase passed, and I never looked back. My dad provided all the religion I needed in my life. He was a biblical force to be reckoned with. If he chose, he could giveth, or he could taketh away. I watched my dad walk back toward the beach chairs and umbrellas. Mom sat in the sun, her sunglasses on her head. Dad sat in the chair next to her. I saw him lay his hand on top of hers. She leaned her head onto his shoulder as they watched us from the shore. My mom, Rose, is in many ways the perfect companion to my dad. When he spoke, she listened. When he commanded, she acted. While he worked, she tended to the home and garden. While my dad is hot tempered and excitable, my mom is clam, steady and stable. When he was serious, he was light hearted and loved to laugh. For every one of my dad's obscure wisdoms, my mom had a concrete and straightforward piece of advice I could understand. My parents were, and still are, the perfect pair.

~~~~~

When the first day of school finally came, I made sure I had the best first-day outfit any girl in the 80s could have imagined.

I picked out a skirt that reminded me of something Candy would wear: flouncy, plaid, preppy. Then I coordinated the rest of my outfit around it, including my blazer, scrunchie, and eye shadow. I must've spent an hour that morning on my hair alone, teasing it up to the perfect height, arranging my bangs so they fell just right across my forehead, and making sure the back was smooth and shiny. I finished off the look with a good spray of Aqua Net. I think I may have overdone it, because when I got in the car, my hair scraped the roof of my car.

~~~~~

The girl sitting behind me in third period Spanish looked familiar. I think we were in a class together last year. But something about her seemed different. Had her hair been so blonde? Maybe it had gotten lighter over the summer.

"Excuse me," I whispered as I quietly turned around from my desk. "Do you know what time it is?"

"It's 9:20," the petite blonde whispered back.

"Thanks. How much longer do we have to sit through this boring Spanish class?"

"Girls, I want it quiet over there." Mrs. Tarantello paused indignantly in her writing of the conjugations on the blackboard.

She muttered something in Spanish as she turned her back. I'd probably have had an idea of what she'd said if I'd paid any attention to her lectures. Especially since her muttering was always sarcasm and probably about me. I didn't care enough to worry about it. I quietly ripped a piece of paper in half and scribbled on it to continue my conversation where I left off.

How much longer until the torture ends? I wrote, followed by a smiley face.

As soon as my teacher turned around again to walk toward the board, I slipped the note back onto the blonde girl's desk, then I heard a snicker. She tapped me on the shoulder and dropped the note onto my desk.

Twenty-two more minutes and counting ... Carla, she wrote. I decided to keep the note going, since it was making the time go by faster.

I think you're in my math class too.

That's my twin sister, Julia. We have another sister too, Samantha. She's a senior.

I might need a bigger piece of paper. A sister who was a senior? Anthony was a senior. Could she know him? She had to. Sacred Heart High was a small school. They must have a class together, or had in the past.

You have a sister who's a senior? I wrote in huge letters. Not very subtle.

Yeah, what's the big deal? She scribbled back in even bigger letters.

She probably thought I was crazy. Didn't matter. I had to get to the point.

Do you think she knows Anthony Knight? Funny, how I suddenly didn't want this class to end so soon.

We all know him. He comes to our house often. Why?

I nearly swallowed my pen. This was my first real connection. I needed to become better friends with—with … wait, what was her name again? I looked over our notes. Oh, yeah, Carla. I needed to become better friends with Carla. I was onto something here.

I wrestled with the next question. There was no way I would let this golden opportunity pass me by. It wasn't that I didn't want to ask. I just didn't want to hear the answer, but if I was going to get anywhere with this new friendship, I had to.

Does he come to your house because he likes your sister? I wrote in tiny letters, as if it would change the answer.

It seemed like an eternity. It was a yes or no question. What was taking her so long?

Maybe Carla liked him. Maybe they were dating. Maybe they just broke up. Maybe she's caught onto me and doesn't want to be "used." People are so sensitive about that. Should I tell her that I just figured I'd ask and hoped I didn't somehow offend her? Ah! Why wasn't she writing me back?

As soon as I looked up, I knew why.

There she was. Mrs. Tarantello, standing there in her long, plaid skirt and purple shirt. I wondered if they had actual "teacher" stores filled with dark-colored patterns and bad outfits. She was leaning beside our desks, her right hand stretched out, palm up. "Hand over the note, girls."

She unfolded it and read it out loud.

I wished I had swallowed my pen. It would have been less painful.

"I will see both of you at the end of class. Or should I say, at the end of *torture?*" She stomped back to her desk. During the last few minutes of class I barely moved.

When the bell rang and class was over, we listened to our lecture from Mrs. Tarantello. I think it was something about expecting better from us and not to let cute boys cloud our vision or something. She obviously hadn't met Anthony Knight.

"Can you believe she humiliated us like that, Carla?" I asked as we walked out of the classroom.

"It could have been worse. She could have given us detentions."

"Does he really come to your house?"

"Who, Anthony? You need to calm down, girl. You sound like you just ran up twenty flights of stairs. You're acting like he's some sort of movie star. He's cute and all, but he's not my type."

Okay, but what about her sisters? One down, two to go.

"That was the second bell. I have to run," Carla said. "I gotta get up to the fourth floor before the third bell. I'll catch up with you tomorrow. What did you say your name was?"

"Mary Lou."

We waved bye.

"Mary Lou Knight," I whispered to myself as I walked in the other direction.

~~~~~~

Nancy and I went to separate private Catholic high schools, in the same town and we couldn't have been more different. Come to think of it, we went to rival high schools. Funny thing was, she helped me in ways she never knew. I once "borrowed" her family tree project, crossing out her name and the B she received before I handed it in. I added my name, turned it in, and received an A.

So what if I was a high school family tree plagiarist? I needed to spend more time trying to date Anthony and less on homework and class projects.

In return, I took Nancy to all my school functions. I took her to the dances and games. Because of me, she had more friends at my school than she did at her own. It always boosted my ego too when I introduced her to people. Looking popular to her made me feel as though I looked popular to everyone else. I could almost hear the line of classmates screaming, "Touch my hand, touch my hand," when I walked down the hallway. Of course that's not what happened. I imagine that if it was, Anthony would have certainly noticed me by now.

My imagination has gotten so used to running wild. This habit of exaggerating my relationship with Anthony in my head has got me in split realities. One of which is, unfortunately, not real. I suppose I've become quite the fantasist. I prefer to call myself a dreamer. Either way, the point is that I would introduce my sister to people I knew as we passed by them. I'd say it was a more than fair exchange on my end for "borrowing" her homework. Plus, in order to go out, I always need a "yes" from my father, and if Nancy came along, I always got it.

In theory, we may have made a good team. We filled in each other's blanks socially and academically and counteracted each other's flaws. It did work, in some cases.

~~~~~~

I had pretty much memorized a color-coordinated mental map with Anthony's classes, lunch table, parking spot, and all preferred routes and paths. Sure, I was bordering stalking, but it's not as if anyone knew except Carla. We were quickly becoming friends and talked every day after Spanish.

Walking along the senior lockers, I scanned for Anthony's number. Carla followed a few steps behind me.

"Mar, I don't know if this is a good idea. You better hurry up. Everyone knows only seniors have lockers in the cafeteria. Are you sure you even have the right locker?"

"Carla, please. I have only seven months and ten days to make him fall in love with me, ditch college, and propose. I'm on a mission, and I know what I'm doing. His locker number is 228. Combination: 16 right, 2 left, 36 right and … open, Sesame." The door swung open on cue. "Did you think this was the first time I've broken into his locker? Please, girl. I've done it a million times."

"You realize you're basically stalking this guy, right?"

"Girl, it's not stalking. It's just running into him in a premeditated way."

Carla looked at me as if she didn't know whether to laugh or call the principal. "Why do you keep doing it? What are you looking for?"

"I don't know, anything. A pen, a note. Oh, check this out! Doesn't this smell good? It's a bottle of Egyptian Musk Oil. Have you smelled it before?"

"Yeah, it smells just like Anthony."

I sniffed it and sighed. "I know. I love it. I put it on so when I'm in class I can smell my wrists and daydream about him."

"You are one crazy girl." Carla laughed, putting on some of the musk oil too. "Do you think he knows?"

"That I like him? Or that I riffle through his locker every day?"

"Good question."

"I don't know. I think he's starting to catch on, though."

"Has he ever talked to you?"

I returned the musk oil to Anthony's locker and gently shut the door, quiet enough that I wouldn't draw attention. "Kind of. Well, not really. But I am getting closer. Last Tuesday, I broke into his locker and borrowed his sweater."

"You mean stole his sweater?"

"It would have been stealing if I hadn't put it back. I just wore it to a few classes and then slipped it back into his locker."

"This is insane" she said as we headed toward math class. "You could get in a lot of trouble."

"I know, isn't it exciting?"

I was always one to push the limits, at home and at school. Especially in school. Especially with Anthony. I knew what I wanted, and I would do pretty much anything to try to make it happen.

"I found out some information for you over the weekend," Carla told me when we returned to school the following week. "I bet you don't know that Anthony works at a restaurant."

"How did you find out?"

"He came by my house and told us Saturday night after his interview."

Two seconds later, I concocted a plan. "Maybe I could come over after school on Friday. We could all go out to eat. Do you think your sister could drive us?"

"I'll ask her tonight and let you know."

"Okay, but Carla, don't say a word to Anthony. I want to surprise him. Do you know what kind of restaurant it is?"

"Well, it's called Sea Loft so ... seafood. Do you like it?"

Mrs. Joe stepped out of her classroom just ten feet away, so I lowered my voice. "I would eat a live lobster if Anthony dropped it on my plate. What time do you think we should go? What should I wear? Oh, and when you introduce me to him, make sure you tell him that I'm a sophomore, just in case. Oh, and one more thing. Do you think you could mention something like, 'You know, Anthony, if you need a prom date, my good friend here would love to go.'"

"Prom is in April. You know what I think, my good friend? I think you have lost your mind."

Even if she thought I was completely crazy, she still asked her sister about driving us and got the green light. Friday night. It was happening.

I spent the rest of the week not doing my homework, daydreaming instead about what it would be like to have Anthony wait on me at a table. A true fantasy scenario.

I closed my eyes and imagined Anthony approaching the table, wearing a pressed white button-down with a black tie and apron. He pauses when he sees me in my red evening dress and heels—it's a fancy restaurant, after all. My dress glitters like something Whitney Houston would wear to the Grammy Awards. Anthony can't take his gaze from me, as if I actually were Whitney Houston, until he wrinkles his forehead and says, "Hey, aren't you Mary Lou?" I wink and say, "The one and only."

Blink.

"Mar! Dinner!"

"Be there in a sec!" I shout back to Nancy.

The last one to the dinner table, I scrambled into my seat. When I'd finished off the last bite of my first round, I set down my fork. "Mom, Dad?"

Their eyes turned to me.

Nancy looked at me as well. I hadn't shared with her that I planned to put in a request at dinner tonight.

Requests had to be worded carefully with my parents.

"My new friend Carla invited me over to her house on Friday after school. We might go out to dinner too. Can I please, please go?"

My parents looked at each other. My mom gave the slightest of shrugs. My dad looked back to me.

"What's her last name?"

Of course. I came prepared. "Borelli?"

"From the neighborhood?"

"No, she's a new friend. From Sacred Heart. Her family is Italian but they've lived in America for a while. I asked." This sat well with my father.

I totally made up a last name for Carla. With her fair skin and freckles, I'm pretty sure Carla must have been English or Irish, but what my dad didn't know wouldn't hurt him, right?

"Borelli. Good," he said.

My mom stood and reached for the meat dish, serving spoon ready. "Seconds, anyone?"

And that was that.

I saw Anthony a few times in the hall that week, but I played it casual and didn't call too much attention to myself. Our big encounter would soon come.

After school on Friday, Carla's older sister, Julia, drove us to their house in her wood-paneled station wagon. If only I had a cool older sister who could drive. Instead, I had a socially anxious, license-less Nancy, who had reminded me to be home by our ten o'clock curfew tonight.

Julia and her friends Samantha and Alan were at the house with us, and we spent the afternoon playing Twister in Carla's huge, plush-carpeted basement until it was time to get ready for dinner.

I brought a change of clothes, a black skirt with a cute red blouse. I wanted to work at least a remnant of my sparkly red dress fantasy in there somewhere, and makeup, of course.

This was it. The first time Anthony and I would "hang out" outside of school.

He'd probably talk to us at dinner, and then maybe he'd get off kinda early and we could all hang out before I had to go home. I just knew that if I could get him alone, and if he saw me hanging out with people he likes …Anthony and Carla's older sister were good friends. Being seen with them would have to help my chances.

"Have I told you I'm excited?" I said as I put on mascara in Carla's huge, beautiful bathroom mirror. My whole family, including Nonna and Nonno, could have brushed our teeth at the same time in here.

"I think you've mentioned it," Carla said. She was sitting on the fuzzy covered toilet seat, reading Cosmo while I finished up.

I capped my mascara and speed-brushed my hair until it shone, but still nowhere near as smooth and shiny as Carla's. "Ready."

"You look great," Carla said sweetly. She had spent about thirty seconds on her look. Her blonde hair was naturally sleek. Lucky.

"Thanks, you too. Let's go see Anthony Knight."

Was she getting sick of my Anthony obsession? I couldn't tell. She rolled her eyes a lot anyway, right?

We all piled back into Julia's station wagon and drove to the Sea Loft. When we got there, the parking lot was packed. My heart started pounding. What if we couldn't get in? "Maybe we should have made reservations."

"Don't worry. If we have to wait, we'll wait," Julia said.

I opened my mouth to say of course I'd wait, when Carla interrupted, "I already know. You would wait all night."

"You guys okay back there?" Julia asked from up front as she pulled into the last free parking spot.

"Oh, yeah, fine!" I said.

"She just really wants to try this place," Carla added, smiling at me.

I headed the group into the restaurant, despite Carla saying, "Mar! Slow down!" but just in case Anthony was at the front desk, I wanted him to see me.

"How many in your party, please?" the stocky hostess with the raspy voice asked us.

"Five," I said as the others stopped behind me.

"Would you like a booth or a table?"

"We would like a booth or a table that Anthony will be waiting on, please."

"Anthony who?"

How could she not know him? "Anthony. Tall, dark, handsome ..."

"Oh, that Anthony. He's our new dishwasher."

"Dishwasher?" I turned to Carla and Julia, who shrugged. Anthony was far too handsome to wash strangers' dirty dishes. "Well, anyway, could you tell him we're here, please?"

"Who's 'we'?"

"Samantha, Carla, Julia, Alan, and Mary Lou. We're from school."

"Of course you are," she said, rolling her eyes as she turned to grab five menus. "I will let him know you're here, but we're extremely busy tonight, so I don't know if he'll be able to come out to the dining room. Right this way."

She led us to a table, not a booth, off to the side of the main dining room. I had dressed up and still felt underdressed, so I couldn't imagine how Julia, Samantha, and Alan must have felt in jeans and t-shirts.

I glanced through the lengthy menu. "Wow, I didn't know it was this expensive. What are you going to get, Samantha?"

"The only thing I can afford is a Coke and maybe an order of fries." Samantha turned to Alan. "How about you?"

"Can we split the fries?"

All I could think of was what my mother would say. Her voice rang in my ear, as if she was sitting next to me at the table. *Do you know how many bags of potatoes I could buy and fry for twelve dollars?*

"Act civilized, guys," I said. "Here comes our waitress."

We gave her our order: two fries, onion rings, and five Cokes—and more free bread and butter. Her annoyance showed in her narrow-eyed gaze.

"Excuse me," I said when she came back with our second basket of free bread. I sat there twirling my hair nervously. "Could you please let Anthony know we're here?"

"I think someone already did." she said in a snippy tone as she left in a whirl.

"We shouldn't have come here," Samantha said. "I'm embarrassed."

I shoveled another piece of warm bread and butter in my mouth. "My father says you should feel embarrassed only if you lie or steal."

Alan eyed my hand as I reached for more bread. "If you order another basket of bread, that would cover the stealing part."

We laughed until Anthony came out of the kitchen's swinging door. For a moment, he was framed by the fluorescent kitchen lights, stark against the soft mood lighting of the romantic restaurant. As he stepped into the dim light and started toward our table, I could barely breathe. I was mesmerized. I had never seen him outside of school before. He looked even more charming outside of his typical school attire. So what if he was wearing a dirty apron with soggy food all over it? He was perfect. At our table in an instant, he placed a note on the white cloth. Without a word, he turned and zoomed back toward the kitchen.

"Where's he going?" I whispered to Carla.

"Anthony, wait!" At her loud call, heads turned our way.

He froze, slowly turned, and marched back to our table as if he'd been ordered there.

"We're sorry if we embarrassed you. We didn't mean to. Oh, and Anthony ... this is Mary Lou," she said, giving my shirt a tug.

I froze. Did she just do that? Call me out? And tug on my shirt? Was she trying to make more of my cleavage show? What was she thinking?

Anthony politely extended his hand. He had to recognize me, right? But maybe he was just being polite. I looked from his hand up to his face, calm, expectant. As I pulled myself up from beneath the table, I extended mine too.

Then our hands touched for the very first time. I swear, sparks flew. He had to of felt it too.

"Wow," I said. "I mean, umm, hi, um, yes, umm …" I had to pull it together, or he'd think I was an idiot. I now know what a lightning strike felt like.

"Your dad is a mechanic, right?" he asked as he tried to pry his hand from mine.

"Why, yes," I said, "he is."

"She goes to our high school," Carla said.

"Yes, I know. I've seen her in the hallway. I think we may even have the same yellow sweater."

Carla choked on her Coke.

I started sweating. At least he remembered me.

Back at the kitchen door, another silhouette appeared. Anthony glanced over his shoulder. "Hey, I have to get back to work, but I get done at eleven. Why don't you guys come back then, and we can hang out?" My heart sank down to my shoes as he retreated to the kitchen.

"What's wrong, girl?" Carla rolled her eyes. "Shouldn't you be, like, beyond happy right now?"

"I would be if my curfew wasn't at ten."

"Call your parents and tell them you're going to be late."

"What planet did you just land from? Italian parents don't know the meaning of the word late."

"So, tell them you're sleeping over at my house."

"That definitely won't work. They'd have to know your

parents, grandparents, aunts, uncles, social security number ..."

This was it, my big chance. I could hang out with Anthony, outside of school, late at night. And I had to pass it up because of my overprotective Italian parents with their overprotective strict rules. It was so unfair.

"Here, you keep the note." Carla rubbed my arm, seeing my disappointment. "That way you'll have something to remind you of him."

Trying to smile, I picked it up and read it out loud. "'To whom it may concern: You guys are silly. Why didn't you go to Burger King and have five sodas, two sides of fries, and onion rings? Love, Anthony.'"

Love? For all of us? I pretended it was just for me.

We pooled enough money to pay the bill, which was still shockingly expensive. Then we got in Carla's car and got drive-through McDonald's. As I bit into my Happy Meal, there was my mom's voice in my ear again. *Is it better than my homemade Happy Meals, made with love?* Yes, it is.

After another hour or two of driving around town, blasting music, and gossiping about who was hooking up with who at school, I realized the time: ten minutes before ten. "Shoot, guys, I gotta head home. My parents will kill me if I'm not back soon."

Samantha she turned the car around and headed to my neighborhood on the other side of town. No way would we make it back there in ten minutes. I leaned my head against the window and played with my hair. I brushed my fingers against the folded note in my pocket.

"You okay, Mar?" Carla said.

"Huh? Oh, yeah. If I'm not at school on Monday, it's because my parents killed me. Keep an eye out for my obituary."

"Relax. What, you've never gone out on a Friday night

before? Your parents don't let you out of their sight?"

"What? No, of course they do. They're just overprotective."

In truth, I hadn't been out late on my own much at all. I usually went out with my family or with friends from the neighborhood. I'd never hung out with kids outside of Waterbury. It was only my second year in a school that wasn't exclusively Italian. Ever since I started at Sacred Heart, my parents seemed a little crazier. More Italian, if that was even possible. Specifically, asking me to be more Italian.

"This is it," I said as Julia pulled up to my house.

Glancing at the clock on the car's dashboard I noted the time. Ten fourteen. Fourteen minutes late. "This was so fun. Thanks for the ride home, Julia."

"Of course!" Julia said from the front as she fiddled with the radio dial.

Carla and I hugged goodbye in the cramped car.

"Bye, Mar! I'll tell Anthony you say hi tonight," she said sympathetically.

The car zoomed off down the street, leaving me alone at the foot of our walkway. I mentally prepped myself for what I might face on the other side of the door—which should have been locked. When I got there, it was open.

The hallway light was on, but nobody hovered by the door, waiting for me. Sitting at the kitchen table, stark in the light, was not my mom, not my dad, but Nancy. Sitting there in her Lilac night gown, her dark hair in a braid, she glared at me as if I had just burned her encyclopedia.

"You're late."

"What's it to you?"

"You know curfew is ten, not ten fourteen. How could you disobey Mamma and Pappa like that?"

"I got home as quickly as I could. I was out having fun with my friends. Don't be jealous just because you didn't have plans tonight."

"I'm not jealous. I just can't believe how little respect you have for your family. They're worrying about you in their room right now. You should go tell them you're home." She stood and whirled out of the kitchen so fast, her scrunchie fell off her braid. Nancy could pout and whine all she wanted. I was the one who had gone out with a cute boy tonight. Or, almost.

Prom, Purple Rain, and a Fog Horn

With prom looming on the horizon a mere month away, I decided it was about time I made things clear to Anthony.

I'd spent the better part of the year getting to know his friends instead of him, but we'd finally all started to hang out at times when I could leave my house. I knew they all hung out at Julia and Carla's house late at night, after Anthony got off work. I fantasized about what it would be like to go to those parties. Did they drink beer? Or wine? Did they watch movies? I knew Alan and Samantha were dating, sort of. I had to wonder if Anthony had anything going with Julia or Carla.

Carla swore there was nothing with her and him. I believed her. She's an excellent wing-woman and has been my biggest advocate in getting to know Anthony. Julia, though … Carla said they're just friends, in the same graduating class. But, of course, I was nervous about every hangout I wasn't there for.

After that night at Sea Loft, Anthony opened up a little more. We started talking in the halls, real conversations. More than just me asking him questions and pointing at him. We started to get to know each other, and even had inside jokes. The yellow sweater one was our favorite. As our friendship built steadily, so did my feelings for him. Being around him, catching a whiff of that Egyptian musk when he touched my arm and laughed at my jokes. I was starting to have a hard time controlling myself.

All I wanted was to run up to him and confess, *I love you, I love you.*

I wanted to share my love with him, and I wanted him to accept it and love me too.

In the week leading up to my self-proclaimed declaration day, I rehearsed what I would say and how I would say it at least twelve times every half hour every day. After all, the prom was just around the corner, and I still hadn't found a dress. Prom was only for juniors and seniors, unless they ask a sophomore or freshman, but I was already dreaming about my dress.

I suppose the whole "being asked" factor had delayed my outfit hunt. My sources told me he hadn't asked anyone yet, so it looked promising. But time was running out. I still needed to get a dress and shoes, or my mom and Zia Teresa would end up making me a prom dress out of old curtains.

And so, I decided to slip a note through the vent, into his locker.

"Why don't you just open it right up? It's not like you haven't broken in before, just to put on his cologne," Carla said one day as prom drew near.

I pretended not to detect her sarcasm.

"I can't. What if he sees? I don't want him to think I'm a stalker. I have to be shy, yet confident. Sneaky, but sophisticated."

Carla laughed. "You weren't saying that a month ago when you were memorizing his schedule. What does the note say?"

I opened it and handed it to her.

"Ooh, what's that smell?" She lifted the edge of the paper to her nose.

"I sprayed it with some Giorgio perfume. Too much?"

I watched her grinning as she read the letter.

Dear Anthony,

It was nice to see you at Sea Loft on Friday. You looked so handsome. I'm sorry I couldn't go out with all of you that night, but let me know if you ever want to go to a movie, dinner, or maybe ... the prom ...?

At the bottom I'd signed it with a pink heart above my name.

"What do you think?"

The bell rang.

"I think it's great! Smooth." Carla handed back the letter. "We better get to class."

I stared at the paper, my heart pounding in my head. My hands trembled. Taking a deep breath, I steadied myself, folded the note, and slipped it between the grates of his locker.

"Whew!" I whistled, adrenaline pumping through my body. Now all there was left to do was wait.

"You did it," she said matter-of-factly. "See ya later."

She started toward the stairs to her second-floor class. Then she turned around. "Hey, Mar," she yelled down the stairwell. "Save a seat for me at lunch. I can't wait to see if the glass slipper fits your foot."

I supposed she was half-genuinely excited about it and half-thought the whole thing was a form of personal entertainment. I was surprised she didn't have a bucket of movie theatre popcorn ready whenever Anthony and I were in the room together.

I imagined her sitting on her couch and picking up the remote. On the TV is a still of Anthony, turning the corner of the hall. She hits play on the remote and time resumes as Anthony walks down the hall toward me, Mary Lou, starry-eyed and in love.

Squeezing my eyes shut, I tried to block out the image. I didn't like to think Carla was my friend only because my obsession with Anthony amused her. At this point, I tuned out her jokes and sarcasm and put them in a mental safe, to which I purposely forgot the combination. At least she was a fun friend—a friend, period.

Walking away, I thought about the letter sitting in Anthony's locker. I hoped he would respond by the end of the day. I couldn't focus on any of my classes, not that I usually could anyway.

I felt as if I was standing on a tennis court with a racket in my hand. I'd just hit the ball to the other side, and now I was afraid to sit down or walk away, in case the ball landed back in my court. I had to be ready. I had to be focused. But the school day ended, and I hadn't heard from him. In a state of perpetual anxiety, I left school for the night.

~~~~~

The next day, at my locker before second period, Samantha came running up to me. "I have a note from Anthony," she said as she pulled back her long, curly, blond hair and twisted it into a purple scrunchie.

What? A million thoughts flooded my mind, some positive, more negative. My palms were sweating. "Can I have it?"

"Yeah, hang on. Now where did I put it?"

"What do you mean, where did you put it?" I felt ready to snap. But even though the tension was high, I coached myself stay cool. She was one of his best friends. He'd obviously given the note to her personally. She rummaged around, first in her backpack, then in her coat pockets.

"I think I left it in my locker. No wait, it might be … Yep, here it is!" She dug her hand into her gray skirt pocket and pulled out a crinkled mess of brownish paper, taped at both ends.

I slipped it into my biology notebook.

"Wait, you're not going to read it?" Samantha stammered.

"Later. I have to prepare myself." I had to read it in private, just in case.

When she had left for class, I took the note out of my notebook and contemplated opening it. I held onto that piece of paper with the strength of Hercules. I wanted to read it but I didn't want to read it. If he said no, my entire world would be destroyed. This could be fatal.

In algebra class ten minutes later, the teacher scrawled equations on the board while I sat there with a blank page in front of me, tapping my pen on my desk. After about three minutes of that, Billy Weir sitting next to me glared and said, "Sh!"

I stopped and pretended to look at the board, but my mind was on the note. If he said yes, I had better come up with a good reason why he couldn't pick me up at my house before the prom. Either way, this over-thinker didn't do such a good job on this particular mission.

I slipped out of class without Mr. Brown noticing and slunk into the nearest restroom. I steadied myself on the brown tiled wall, leaning up against the hand dryer for extra support. There I delicately unfolded the note, as if it were part of the Dead Sea scrolls and was on the verge of disintegration.

Dear Mary Lou,

The answer to your question is easy. Yes, I like you very much. You are one of my few good friends. I care about you and hope we'll be friends for a long time. At this time in my life, I need true friends like you. This is only the beginning, and there is so much time for you. I know you're probably thinking you want to be more than friends.

All the blood rushed from my broken heart to my feet. I slowly slid down the wall.

But I am the type of person who wants friendship, not love relationships. I'm young and so are you. I want to make as few mistakes as possible. I hope you understand. And please don't think there is anything wrong with you, because there is not.
Love you (a deep feeling of fondness for you),
Anthony

I read it again. And again, and again.

Sweat dripped down my sides as my heart pounded. I scrunched my eyes and read the note as if it was messy and hard to read, but really, it was hard to understand. Was he saying no? He didn't like me? It sounded, overall, like a no. My heart crumbled like an old pillar. He didn't want me? He didn't feel the same?

For the first time in my life, I understood rejection. Through my tears, I read it one more time, just to be sure.

There were so many mixed messages in that note. Yes, he likes me. No, he doesn't. I felt as if I was picking the petals off a daisy. He loves me; he loves me not. He loves me; he loves me not …

A wave of sadness swallowed me whole. I disappeared, and all that remained was my heartache, like a sinkhole deep in my core. That was it. There were no more chances. He had written me off. What else could I do?

I could hear my heartbeat in my ears. Tears slid down my cheeks. At least I managed to hold in the sobs and cry in silence.

The bathroom door creaked open.

A teacher came in to use the bathroom and found me on the floor. All I could see of her were her heels, her stockinged legs, and then her powder-blue cardigan. Next thing I knew she was on her walkie-talkie. "Code blue. I repeat. We have a code blue in hallway 321, location: ladies restroom."

I somewhat didn't care. I was just sitting there, the tears still coming, the sinkhole still sinking ...

Within ten seconds, the bathroom was bombarded with three male teachers and the school nurse. I lay there like a wet noodle, partly in sheer embarrassment, partly because of my broken heart. I floated in and out, there and not there.

Wait, was that the principal's voice I heard?

Fading in and out, I heard, as if underwater, "Should we call 911?"

I had to pull myself together, or they'd drag me out to an ambulance, complete with the oxygen mask, in front of the whole school. Well, that wouldn't be so bad if Anthony saw that happen, would it? Maybe then he would take me to the prom.

"I'm okay," I finally said, heaving myself off the floor to sit up against the wall. "I feel a little dizzy and lightheaded, but I'm somewhat better."

Somehow nobody had noticed me clutching the note. It was even more crumpled now. I folded it up and discretely slipped it into my shoe.

"Do you think you can walk to the nurse's office?" The nurse, Mrs. O'Malley, asked.

"I feel better now and should go back to class." I started to get up, very slowly.

"Not an option, until after I check your blood pressure."

I sheepishly agreed. I had never visited the nurse's office before. I'd once stood outside it for a good forty-five minutes to scope Anthony out, but overall, I was a healthy kid. There's a first time for everything.

I lay down on a cot and let her take my blood pressure, the inflatable band tightening around my arm. My fingers tingled.

"Seems a little low to me," she said. "90/60 … Maybe that's why you felt faint."

If she had taken it twenty minutes sooner, right after I'd read the note, I'm sure I would've popped that little dial right off the meter.

"I don't think it would be a good idea to send you back to class. You need to go home, drink lots of water, and get some rest," Nurse O'Malley said.

What was I going to tell my mom?

Stomach ache, I decided. It wasn't so far from the truth. My stomach hurt, my head hurt, my heart hurt. I sounded like a country western song. At least at home, I could relax and watch TV for the rest of the day. A Get Out of School Free card. "Thanks, Anthony," I mumbled to myself.

The only shows on TV during the school day were soap operas. I'd never watched one before. This might have been the first time I'd ever come home sick from school in the middle of the day. I never got sick. "Strong as an ox," my dad would say, but I didn't like that comparison. I'd overheard my aunt and Mom talk about soap operas on at least three different occasions. They made them sound exciting, dramatic, romantic, and that sounded like just the right medicine for my broken heart.

When I flicked on the TV, I was surprised to hear a man's deep, sensual voice.

"Like the sands through an hour glass, so are the days of our lives …"

I laughed. Did the writers of this soap know my dad?

Grinning as the opening sequence played, I guessed *Days of Our Lives* would do it.

Despite his letter, my heart and mind still wandered in Anthony's direction. They weren't easily persuaded once they were set on something, or someone. Watching this show, the relationship between a beautiful, sexy woman and a muscular, toned, dark-skinned man with a gravelly voice and stubble, made me wish I could fast forward to the day when Anthony would finally become interested. I daydreamed how my life would be when I married Anthony someday. It would be as romantic as *Days of Our Lives*. We would lounge around in our pajamas all day and have a beautiful mansion filled with adorable children and a nanny. Just like these two characters.

Did American people spend their days lounging around? Italians definitely did not. Not my family, anyway. We kept busy. My mom was in the kitchen right then, sewing our Easter outfits on the dinner table.

Some yelling and fussing on the TV screen brought me back to the drama.

"Marlena, wait! Don't leave me," Beau said, grabbing for Marlena's hand as she stormed toward the door. What had I just missed?

He caught her hand and she turned to him.

"Beau, we've been through this a million times. You don't love me … you never did." Tears welled in her eyes.

"But, Marlena, you've been so cold and vague lately. I've realized I can't live without you. I love you. I promise, if you give me one more chance, I will never break your heart again."

"No, Beau, I have already given you a million and one chances. I have moved on."

"I miss you. Don't play hard to get, Marlena. You know that just makes me want you more."

Transfixed by the screen, I watched her reel him back in, despite the fact that she'd just been saying no. *Play hard to get.*

"That's the secret," I whispered.

Thank you, Marlena and Nurse O'Malley. I owe you one.

I woke up extra-early the next morning after strategically planning to execute my next mission. This would be an experiment. I'd never worked this angle before. Playing hard to get meant passing him in the hallway and not even acknowledging him, right? I learned yesterday that I can't be at his beck and call. I can't keep letting him play with my heart like a little piece of soft, pink Silly Putty.

Mission Hard to Get starts now. I am armed and ready.

We passed each other in the hall a few times the following week, and I managed to play it cooler than ever. I didn't even look at him. No smile, no wave. I iced him out every time. And even though it felt like the last thing I wanted to do, I reminded myself how well it had worked for Marlena. When I ignored Anthony's friendly gestures, he was clearly confused.

By the end of the week, Samantha came and found me at my locker again. "I'm going to have to start charging you for mail delivery."

"What?" I said, startled. She showed up out of nowhere, seeming to move on silent feet. Her bright blue eyes and big blonde hair always surprised me.

"I have a card for you from Anthony. What's going on with you two, anyway?"

"Nothing." I knew the smirk on my face didn't disguise anything. "We're just friends."

I hoped that didn't sounded too rehearsed. I had practiced saying it out loud to myself at least a few hundred times within the past two weeks. A card? Is that nothing? It was a step up from the usual scraps of ripped paper I used to beg for. "He wrote a card for me?"

"Not just a card. A sparkly blue and pink Care Bear card. I was there when he signed it."

I could barely contain my excitement. What did it say, what did it say, what did it say? I took the sealed blue envelope from Samantha and sped away to class with it on top of my books. He had written "Mary Lou" in nice lettering on the front.

I sat at my desk and gingerly peeled open the envelope.

I care about you.
How will you know it
If I don't send a card like this to show it?

I had to read the front five times before I realized I wasn't dreaming.

Good morning. How are you, sunshine? You looked
fantastic yesterday. How come you don't talk to me
anymore (hardly)? I miss you. I hope our friendship
hasn't ended. I will go crazy.

I stared ahead, dumbstruck. "Sunshine"? "Miss you"? And there he went with that word "friendship" again, which made me think I was still not playing so hard to get. I should have avoided and ignored him harder. From now on, I'd make sure to be in the same hallway with him at school and then blatantly avoid him. It would be a tricky, carefully orchestrated dance. But if it would send him running into my arms by the end of the school year, then call me Irene Cara.

~~~~~

Monday morning, I walked into school feeling like a rock star, walking into a stadium for my own sold-out show. An invisible fan seemed to blow against me as I soared down the hallway. My hair blew effortlessly in what I was pretty sure was some sort of artificial wind. Okay, maybe I dramatically flipped it once or twice, but I felt like a rock star, remember?

As Anthony approached me, he smiled. Even though I wanted to smile and act flirty, I reminded myself: *hard to get*. I cooled my smile to a tight-lipped smirk.

As we passed, he touched my hand for a few short seconds, pressing a note into my palm. Physical contact sent a wave of heat through my body. I hoped he couldn't feel that. I passed myself off coolly, holding it together for a few more paces, before letting my excitement overtake me.

This had to be it. Prom was Friday, and tomorrow was the last day of ticket sales. I covered my mouth with my hand to hide my smile. At this point, I was sure I would scare someone as I walked into class. I don't think it's normal to look this happy.

I sat down and unfolded the note.

Mar,
Give me a call later, after school. Have a good day,
and talk to you then.
Anthony

It wasn't the note I'd been waiting for, but maybe this was better. Maybe he just wanted to ask me over the phone, a little more personal. That was sweet.

I practiced in my mind for my "on-the-spot" acceptance to his

82

question.

Mary Lou, will you go to prom with me?

Yes, Anthony. I would love to be your prom date.

I caught myself lip syncing my response on the way to my next class. Good thing it was only Carla walking by my side. She was probably used to me talking to myself at this point, or at least she was used to my crazy imagination.

If only I could fast forward time. It wasn't even noon yet.

I managed to contain my excitement all day, through school, chores, and dinner. I asked to be excused as soon as I finished eating and raced to my room while my family finished up dinner table conversation. I left while Nancy was talking about the A she'd gotten on one of her papers, so I knew she'd be down there for a while.

I salvaged the ounce of privacy that I could and sat against the closed door in our bedroom. My hand trembling, Anthony's number memorized and poised on the tip of my finger, I picked up my banana phone, punched in the numbers, and listened to it ring.

My heart pounded in my throat, anticipating the question, but once again Anthony kept me waiting.

He answered, and we talked for a minute, but when the big pause came, I inevitably thought, *Here it comes*. But he asked me to meet him tomorrow at school to talk instead.

Okay, so that wasn't the big phone call. Obviously, he wanted to ask me in person. How sweet of him.

We verbally set up a place and time while I mentally set up my outfit, my reactions, our wedding plans, and the names of our unborn children. He wanted to meet under the bleachers during lunch. Private, secluded, possibly romantic. The seniors all went there to make out and fool around. Is that why he wanted to meet there? I couldn't help fantasizing about our first kiss under the bleachers, right after he asks me to go to prom with him.

~~~~~

I got to school early that day. As soon as I sat down in first period math, I realized I'd forgotten my homework in my math book. I'd forgotten my math book in my backpack, and I'd forgotten my backpack at home. It was sitting on the floor, leaning up against the wall in my bedroom. I did manage to remember my lip gloss, earrings, breath mints, and a swatch of the satin fabric I'd been eyeing for my prom dress. Lunch finally came. I headed outside to the soccer field, the dress swatch tucked under my arm.

Anthony waited on the first step of the bleachers, not underneath them as I'd imagined. He stood there wearing my favorite yellow cardigan. Would he want to wear a yellow tie for prom? Maybe I should get yellow fabric for my dress. As I got closer, he waved. My heart quickened.

We walked under the bleachers, side by side, our hands almost touching, the dress swatch still tucked out of sight under my arm.

"Can I ask you something, Mar?"

My heart doubled its speed. Maybe I should have brought two swatches so he could choose a color to match.

He stopped. I stopped too. He turned to face me.

Suddenly it felt as if we were very close. Was it just me or was he leaning in? My heart beat out of control. *Just stick to the prom response. Just say what you practiced.*

I almost didn't even hear him when he asked if I would … wait, would I what?

I'd been too busy planning my prom response. What exactly had he just asked me? I stood so still he had to ask again.

"Does your father sell cars as well? If so, does he sell American cars too? Or just foreign models? Does he have any for sale? Think you could put in a good word? Oh, and could I get the phone number to your father's garage?"

Really? I'd shaved my legs for this?

I recited the numbers to him so numbly, I'm not sure I said them in the right order.

"Cool. Thanks, Mar. And here, I have a note for you too."

I perked up. At least there was more.

Okay, so, that wasn't the conversation … but maybe this was the note.

I walked to class and placed the note on my desk. My math teacher was already irritated with me for not having my book or homework open to begin with. The fact that this note was the only thing on my desk didn't help.

"What's this, Mary Lou?" Mrs. Tarantello came up to my desk, obviously referring to the folded note. "Is that your homework? Would you share your answers with the class?"

I gawked at her in pleading disbelief. She knew it wasn't my homework. The only thing worse than having Mrs. Tarantello read a note out loud was her making me read the note from Anthony out loud to the class. A note I hadn't even read yet.

The only thing keeping me from preemptively jumping out of the window or running to the nurse's office was the fact that this would be the note in which he'd ask me to the prom.

Dear Mary Lou,
Prom's this week. Has anybody asked you? I figured
a girl like you would certainly be asked. Anyway, I'm
going with Michelle. Maybe I will see you there. Talk
to you later.
Love, your friend,
Anthony
PS, Save me a dance.

"Michelle?" I said out loud, shocked. "Who is Michelle?"

I looked up at Mrs. Tarantello, as if she might know. She shrugged. I stared back at the note. Ten solid seconds of mortifying silence followed.

"Thanks for sharing that." She clicked away on her heels, satisfied, to the front of the classroom.

I sat there, stunned. If I hadn't just read that out loud, I wouldn't have believed it had happened.

Have I been asked? Um, no. You were going to ask me, Anthony!

I wracked my brain, trying to remember if I had ever heard him talk about a Michelle. Now that Candy had graduated, maybe Michelle was his new crush. Ouch.

It had seemed so obvious that he was going to ask me, not her.

I looked up to the actual world around me. Why was everyone still staring at me? Had I been muttering out loud to myself again? I needed to work on that.

As class resumed, I noticed Bobby, a family friend, sitting in the back corner of the room with the other jocks. He was awkward but popular and cute—black-brown hair, clear skin, light eyes. I'm pretty sure he'd always had a crush on me. We'd gone to the same school since kindergarten.

After class, Bobby approached me. At that point, I was sure my disappointment was no secret.

"Hey ... um, Mar, my name isn't Anthony, but I know someone who would love to take you to the prom," Bobby told me as he stood there tapping one foot and ringing his hands.

"Who?"

"Me. I'd be honored if you'd still like to go."

"Of course I want to go." Even though he wasn't Anthony, I'd at least get to go to the prom, maybe make him jealous. Plus, he asked me to save him a dance. I was practically obligated to go, right?

"Great!" Bobby's face lit up. At least someone's day had been made. "Pick you up at six?"

"Sure, sounds good," I said. "See you Saturday."

I walked away from Bobby feeling a little bad because I was still thinking about Anthony. Actually, I was fuming about this Michelle. I knew I should be happy. I had been asked to prom after all. I tried to justify it, but even so, I couldn't get Anthony out of my head, and Bobby barely made an appearance.

The rest of that week I played the hardest I've ever played to get. I didn't even look at Anthony in the halls. I walked right by, as if he were a ghost. All in the name of love. I was determined to make him miss me that week so when we finally saw each other at the dance, he'd have to come over and say something. He owed me that dance too.

That Saturday, as I finished getting ready for the big night, I barely thought of being Bobby's date. I was too busy imagining my entrance into the Continental Room to see Anthony. My mom made me a beautiful powder-blue evening dress. We went to a store to pick out the fabrics—blue silky base with a layer of sparkling gauze draped over the skirt, and some sparkles and embellishment at the straps, neckline, and bodice. I paired it with pretty silver heels, not too high, and beautiful silver and diamond jewelry my mom let me borrow.

I imagined myself entering the ballroom, a huge, sweeping room, crowded at the edges with students, dimly lit and elegantly decorated with silver, pink, and yellow balloons. A live band would play romantic swing on the stage, the dance floor still wide and unoccupied. I'd see him standing on the floor, in plain sight, somehow caught alone. Anthony, in his tuxedo, a glass of non-alcoholic punch in his hand. He'd turn just in time for my entrance, and he'd look at me as if I was the most beautiful girl in the room. I could see myself in his eyes, the way he saw me or the way I hoped he saw me: beautiful, perfect and cute, everything a person could want in another person. He'd be sorry he hadn't asked me to the prom.

The sound of a foghorn jerked me out of my fantasy. That would be Bobby.

"Are you ready?" my mother yelled.

"I'll be right out," I yelled back. "Just putting on lip gloss."

Is it bad that this is the fifth time I've reapplied in the past ten minutes?

"My goodness, she's been getting herself all dolled up for you for a while now." My mom's voice carried from the front door.

Right. Just for you, Bobby. I popped my lips in the mirror.

When I came out, I noticed the oversized corsage Bobby held proudly in front of him. "My mother was going to make one herself from our garden, but she just couldn't resist this one from Lee Bouquet Barn. She thought you would love it."

I worked to pin a little matching bouquet onto Bobby's lapel. That close to him, I could smell the bitter smell of his aftershave. Nothing like Anthony's Egyptian musk. I couldn't help but feel a twinge of sadness.

I slipped on the wrist corsage he held out for me. The bouquet was so big that the flowers crept all the way up to my elbow.

As we walked out to Bobby's car, a Cadillac Eldorado, my father pulled into the driveway from work. In his usual mechanic jumpsuit, he was hardly dressed for a photo shoot. We got a few with just me and Bobby, and then a few with my mother in her apron and my father in his work suit flanking us, all next to our bathtub lawn Madonna shrine.

After the photos, my mom kissed me on the cheek. "Have a good night. And remember Mar, you're a Christian."

I controlled my eye-roll, but I couldn't control my blush.

Bobby cordially opened the passenger side door for me.

I literally slid across the seat. Bobby probably wondered why I was all the way on his side by the time he walked over to his car door. He must have been waxing these mustard leather seats all week.

"You look beautiful tonight, Mar."

I moved back to my own side, as close to the door as I could get and kept a tight grip on my seat. This was not the time to slide closer to him accidentally.

"And you by far will have the biggest corsage there. It'll surely attract the most attention." He said it as if it was a good thing.

"You're right about that." I wondered if he detected my sarcasm. Did he really think the size of this wrist bouquet made it so measurably impressive? Impressive in terms of gaudiest, maybe …

I contemplated telling him my plan to dance with Anthony, but I figured I'd keep it on a need-to-know basis.

We arrived at prom, and the time came for my grand entrance, the one I had imagined a hundred times. The ballroom was about what I'd been imagining—tables on one side, DJ and dance floor on the other, blue and gold balloons and tablecloths in our school colors, a photographer snapping posed prom photos of kids.

Ignoring Bobby, I headed straight for the dance floor, gliding, graceful. Until I glided a little too literally, slid, and fell. So much for my grand entrance.

From the ground, I looked up and saw Anthony watching me from the edge of the dance floor. Found him.

Before I knew it, Anthony, not Bobby, stooped down in front of me and offered his hand. With as much grace as possible, I positioned my heels underneath me and stood.

Was my clumsiness charming? Or could it be the small garden on elastic around my wrist?

"You look stunning," Anthony said.

Perhaps he was smiling at my expense. I didn't expect him to flatter me. I mean, I had just spent the past few seconds crawling at his feet.

"May I have this dance, Mary Lou?" he asked, just as the band switched over to a cover of Purple Rain, one of my favorites. It was even more amazing than the original, actually, because it involved Anthony, in real life.

I glanced over at Bobby at the food and drinks table by the entrance, watching me.

"Where's Michelle?" I asked.

"She's talking to her friends over there." He nodded his head in her direction.

I didn't bother looking. My eyes were locked on him.

Anthony and I danced the entire night. After the first few songs, I stopped checking on Bobby. I felt a little bad that we didn't spend more time together, but I couldn't help how overjoyed I was to spend so much time with Anthony.

During the last song, I finally asked what had been on my mind all night.

"Anthony, why didn't you ask me to the prom? We've practically spent the whole night together anyway."

The song ended. He didn't say anything. He kind of gazed at the top of my head as if in thought, and then looked back down at me and shrugged.

The song ended. Five seconds later, the bright fluorescent overhead lights clicked on. Romantic mood ruined. Anthony and I hugged goodbye and returned to our respective dates.

I found Bobby hovering by the entrance. He didn't look at me. Without saying anything, we walked out to the parking lot. My head was full of the last few hours, how close Anthony and I had been, his smell, the feel of my hand on his shoulder, his hand on my back.

I almost slipped across the seat again when I got in but managed to stay on my side.

Bobby turned on the radio and didn't say a word. He drove me straight home. When we parked, he reached across me to open my door and said, "Mar, don't ever speak to me again."

I'd been a lousy date. But I was too happy to feel guilty. I shrugged off his goodbye and raced back into my house to think of, dream of, and talk about my night with Anthony. I sang "Purple Rain" to myself as I walked up the driveway.

Don't Fall in Love with Him

Sunday morning, I called Carla. I leapt out of bed, grabbed my phone off the nightstand, quietly closed the door, and got back under the covers. Nancy always woke up early, even on the weekends. She was out of the room.

"What happened? I thought he asked Michelle." Carla said through the shoe.

"I know. I don't know." I was ecstatic, elated, still dreaming. I couldn't quite believe how great last night had been. The only thing that could have made it better was a kiss.

"So now what? Are you guys dating? Did he tell you he likes you?"

"Not exactly." *Come on, Carla, let me have this one.* "I'm not sure what happened. I mean, we danced, and we were close, basically hugging, but at the end of the night, we just said goodbye."

It didn't matter. It was still a good sign.

Anthony and I were becoming friends. Good friends. And girlfriend and boyfriend both had the word *friend*, didn't they?

Friends were at least the first step, right?

I couldn't help but see him as my husband, my future, my everything. I wanted him in my life so badly, but I kept trying to remind myself to play it cool.

Ever since that night at the Sea Loft, we'd spent time together in groups on Friday or Saturday nights. Now that Anthony and I'd had our magical night at prom, things were better than ever. I couldn't wait to see what happened at our next gathering with Carla, Julia, and the gang.

"Want to do something this weekend?" I asked.

"Wanna go to a drive in?"

"That could be good," I said. Dark, quiet, semi-private, potential for hand-holding. "Could we go to the one in Meriden?"

"I guess. Why so far? There's one right outside of town."

"I think it could be fun to get out of town, out of our comfort zone. We could pretend to be totally different people there."

"Are you scared of your parents seeing you with non-Italians?"

"Let's just go to Meriden," I said, ignoring her sarcastic tone. "Please."

Carla sighed. "I'll start a note and see if everyone can go."

~~~~~

That Thursday before the movie night, just after we'd gone to bed, Nancy turned to me. "How'd you do with my recycled family tree for your project?"

"You're not gonna believe it." I rolled over in bed to face her. "I aced."

She slapped the comforter. "I only got a B on it!"

"Thanks for letting me use it. Best sister ever." I couldn't keep the hint of sarcasm out of my voice.

"Sure. What are you doing this weekend?"

"Going with friends to a drive-in movie tomorrow night." Why did she want to know?

"Mom wants me to come with you."

If Nancy came with me, we could probably stay out until eleven. And she could meet him and tell me what she thought. If I was gonna marry Anthony someday, she'd have to meet him sooner or later.

The next night, we hopped in our mom's Camaro, and Nancy drove us out to Meriden. "Isn't there a drive-in right outside of town?"

"Yeah, but, I don't want anyone to see me out with Anthony."

"Who's Anthony?"

All this time, I hadn't shared my life-altering crush with Nancy. "He's basically the most beautiful boy I've ever seen. More beautiful than Michael." Nancy knew the extent of my crush on Michael. I ogled him before I went to sleep every night. "I might be kind of a little bit in love with him."

"If he's so beautiful, why don't you want to be seen with him?"

"It's not that I don't want to be seen with him. But if it gets back to Dad …" I couldn't bring myself to tell her he wasn't white and wasn't Italian.

"What, because Dad scares away all the guys who are remotely interested in us?"

"Not exactly."

When we got there and I introduced her to Anthony, she gave me a look that said it all.

We hung out and talked for a few minutes before the movie started. Anthony asked if Nancy and I wanted to watch the movie with him and Kyle in his car.

I looked over at Nancy, on the brink of telling her to stay with

Carla so I could try to get some alone time with Anthony. But it would be mean to leave her alone with them, so she came, too.

We watched *Back to the Future*, laughing, joking, commenting the whole time. I knew Nancy hated when people talked through movies, but lucky for me, she was outnumbered this time.

After dinner, we got milk shakes from Roscoe's, an old classic diner spot. One of those places with a jukebox and booths with squishy red seats and signed pictures of famous people all over the walls. After *Back to the Future*, we felt inspired to get a taste of the fifties.

Sitting at a booth, sipping our milkshakes through red straws out of tall glasses—it all seemed perfect. Anthony was on one side of me, Nancy on the other. They talked to each other, getting along. Maybe this dream life of mine could blend into reality, after all. I could hardly have imagined anyone in my family meeting Anthony at all, and now here was Nancy, laughing at his jokes and listening intently to his stories. Like Nancy, Anthony was an A student, so it was no wonder she liked him.

"So you had a good time?" I asked Nancy on the ride home.

"I hardly noticed it was after eleven. Your friends are fun."

"And Anthony?"

"Anthony," she said. "I get it, he's cute. Smart, and nice, too. But why are you falling in love with him? He's black. Dad will kill you."

Both my parents, and all my relatives, had eyes and hearts only for Italians. I loved how Italian my family was, but I wished, just sometimes, they could be a little more open. I wished my dad could see what a beautiful thing it was to have so many different types of people in one place. It's what I loved most about my new school. Even though it was still Catholic, which met my parents' standards, not everyone was white and not everyone was Italian. There was this little thing called diversity.

Nancy talked about it as if I had a choice. I couldn't change my heart, and I didn't want to. It was fixed on him, and I had no choice but to follow it.

I knew Nancy was right, but I still hoped she would be wrong.

~~~~~

The rest of the school year flew by. Before I knew it, it was the last dance of the year, and then Anthony would graduate. Nancy came with me to the dance and laughed at all of Anthony's jokes again. Afterward, we all went out for milkshakes. Nancy helped extend our curfew.

That spring, when he left for the Air Force, my heart sank. I knew he would be leaving, and I would not be going with him. We spent some time together before he left, but still nothing more than strictly friend-zone things. Just movies or dinners with groups of friends. Never alone. No kissing. No hand-holding. Quick hugs goodbye. He had been signing his letters "Your Friend" the past few times, which made me think he wasn't so interested anymore. But it was confusing, because I also felt as if we were better friends than ever, closer than before. Now we sat next to each other in almost all our group hangouts, we traded notes at school, and sometimes we even talked on the phone. I was as obsessed as ever.

The last time I saw him before he left, he put his hand on my shoulder. The physical contact was crippling.

Of course, playing it cool as always, I couldn't help but cry.

I fought through my sadness, unable to look at him. "I guess I'll just have to get used to you not being here."

"Mar, when you graduate and go to college, you'll set out on a big adventure of your own. Maybe you'll understand then." He pulled me into a hug. His tone was babying, almost condescending. I ignored it. "I'm going to miss you."

"Me too," I said into his shoulder, my tears soaking his shirt. "Will you at least come home and visit sometimes?"

"Of course. And we can keep writing. I'll send you my address. Yours will stay the same, right?"

We'd pulled back by now, looking into each other's eyes. When he asked me that last question, he fixed his brown-eyed gaze on me and seemed to search my face for an answer. I yearned, so badly, for a kiss goodbye, something to show I was just a little bit more than a friend to him. Here we were, standing close and face to face again. This was torture. After a long test of a moment, I closed my eyes. I knew I should play hard to get. Try at least to keep some kind of mystery or allure. I wiped my eyes and played with a piece of my hair.

But what did I have going for me? He was about to travel the country, the world, and start a new life. I would stay here in Waterbury for the next two years to finish high school. Not much excitement there.

My favorite part of school was leaving. What would I do without him?

Bye Bye, Anthony

Anthony left for the Air Force the day after the fourth of July, 1985. We hugged goodbye—a tight squeeze, his muscular arms around me, the smell of his Egyptian musk combined with his leather jacket—and then he was gone.

I wrote him letters every day. At first I tried to act cool, but with each letter I wrote, I felt more and more panicked about losing him forever and began professing my undying love and how I couldn't wait for him to come home. Not the coolest, but I couldn't help it. It was compulsive.

The days passed. And then the weeks. Still no mail, but I kept writing. I sat on my front porch and waited for the mailman every day.

That summer was a hot one. I swam in our above-ground pool with Nancy and Vinny and kids from the neighborhood. It felt good to cool down in the humid Connecticut summer. Nancy and I would be floating in the pool when all of a sudden, we'd hear a "plop!" and there would be a Tootsie Roll, floating in the water, Nonna's grinning face peering out the open third-floor window. She had really good aim.

When I wasn't cooling off or doing things with Carla or my neighborhood friends, I spent time with my Nonna. Nonno had passed away earlier that year, and with his loss came the realization that someday Nonna would go, too.

In bed at night, I lay awake, wondering how Nonna was doing two floors above me, now by herself. Was she lonely? Did she miss having Nonno sleeping next to her? When he died, she'd wept, but she'd become calm and quiet quickly after. She didn't smile as much as she used to.

"Nonna?" I called, knocking at her door. It was a hot day. I'd broken a sweat just climbing the stairs. Holding onto some blank papers and pen, I used them to fan myself while I waited.

The door swung open on Nonna, her Einstein hair white and fluffy as a cloud.

"I thought that was you," she said in Italian, moving aside to let me in.

Her window AC unit managed to keep the attic-like room at around 70 degrees. I guessed it was better than nothing. The apartment felt different since Nonno died.

While she poured us cups of tea and brought the plate of saltines, I started in on another letter to Anthony.

"What are you writing?" Nonna settled onto the couch next to me.

"A letter to the boy I love."

Nonna took a moment before saying, "I see."

As I finished a sentence, I glanced over at her. She was watching me intently, a hand pressed to her cheek.

"What?"

"You remind me of someone," she said, tilting her head a few degrees.

I took a sip of tea and went back to writing Anthony about upcoming plans for a family beach trip.

We're having an Italian family beach day this weekend. It's going to be a huge event. All of my family will be there, my aunts, uncles, cousins. It's kind of embarrassing, going to the beach with them, because we always make such a huge scene. I would love to go to the beach with you someday, on a warm, beautiful island. We could even drink piña coladas. I miss you so much, Anthony, but I hope you are learning a lot and having a good time in the Air Force. Write me soon.
Love, Mar.

When I'd capped my pen, Nonna was waiting for me. "Who is he?"

"A boy I met at school. He graduated this spring and went away to the Air Force."

"A man in uniform. It's sweet of you to write him letters." She paused. "Does he write back?"

"We used to write notes at school, and he always wrote back then, kinda. Since he left, I haven't gotten any letters from him. He's probably busy, but I stay hopeful."

Nonna raised her eyebrows. "If he has eyes to see what a special girl you are, he will write back."

She could always make me feel better, ever since I was a little kid.

"Writing letters," she went on, "such an old fashioned thing. Now with phones, people can call each other, talk to each other right away, but when I was growing up, letters were all we had. All we could do was wait to hear from each other. Sometimes months, sometimes years." Her eyes were far away, remembering. Nonna had spent most of her life in rural Italy, coming to America when my parents were adults and married and had enough money to support her and Nonno here.

"Tell me more about him," she said. "What does he look like? What do you like about him?"

How much should I tell? My Nonna and I had a special relationship, the kind in which I could tell her anything and never worry about her sharing my secrets. Knowing how my parents felt, I wasn't sure if she would feel the same. She came from an Italian family that was even stricter than mine, if that was possible.

"Well, his name is Anthony."

"A good Italian name. Your father would like that."

My dad's name was Anthony too. Antonio in Italy, everybody here called him Tony.

My dad might like his name, but I wasn't sure he would like *him*. I decided to omit the key detail—that Anthony was black.

"Anthony is a stand-up guy. He's polite, smart, well-dressed, kind and unbelievably beautiful." I sighed. I couldn't help myself.

"Are you two dating?"

I laughed. "I wish. We're just friends. I'm writing him letters, hoping he'll realize he's in love with me, too."

"Mmm." Nonna sipped her tea.

"I love him, though," I said, in spite of myself. Sometimes it felt good to give in to the yearning. "I can't help it. Whenever I think of him, my stomach gets all bubbly and my heart starts pounding. I daydream about our future as if he has already proposed. I'm in so far over my head with him, Nonna, but I'm not sure I'm the kind of girl he would ever love. He used to sign his letters 'Love, Anthony.' I don't know why he stopped."

Nonna hesitated. I tasted the tea.

Something in her sweet eyes made me want, more than anything, to tell her all about Anthony. I knew I could trust her as I had all my secrets. "Nonna, the boy I love—he's different. My father will never approve of him."

Then I dropped the bomb. "He's not Italian."

Suddenly, my grandmother's face turned pale—so much that it scared me a little. Then, after a moment, she came around. "You really remind me of my someone" she said, dropping her gaze. "my mother, she was in love with a boy when she was young. She wrote love notes to him, even though her parents did not approve."

That got my attention. "Why didn't they approve?"

Nonna sighed as if she knew this conversation would open a can of worms. "The families were rivals. Their properties bordered each other, and they fought over the resources of the land. Namely, walnuts."

I remembered the walnut trees at her home in Italy.

Her parents did not approve, and they did their best to keep an eye on their only daughter. The children met when they were both out collecting walnuts, helping with the work, you know. Miraculously, they both knew how to read and write, which is not always the case for children in the country. In Verona, Florence, the cities, everyone could read, but for the most part, education was available only in the cities. My papa taught me how to read and write."

"What happened? With your mom?" I realized I was sitting at the edge of my seat. Could my great-grandmother's story help me with my situation?

"She wrote love notes to the boy next door. Slowly, secretly, they fell in love."

"He loved her back?"

"I know he did."

Apparently, my great-grandmother had been one step closer to marrying that man of her dreams than I was.

"One would leave a note for the other at the big walnut tree that marked the boundary. But when my mother was old enough to marry, her parents knew that if they did not act, they would lose their daughter to their rivals. They forbade her to see him and arranged a marriage for her with a man her parents thought more suitable."

I dreaded asking, but I had to know. I had a feeling this was not the ending I hoped for. "She didn't marry the walnut tree boy?"

Nonna's mouth turned down into a light frown. Maybe the girl ended up with the man she loved. If she could do it, so could I.

"No." The single word came out like the blade dropping on the guillotine. "She did as her parents said. She was a good, obedient daughter."

"Right. Obedience. I guess that makes a good kid, doesn't it?"

Nonna shrugged. "There is also something to be said for following your heart, even if it goes against your family."

I looked up at her, leaning back in her chair now. "Please tell me more. Tell me the whole thing."

She paused, seemingly in the middle of an internal debate.

"Can you keep a secret?" Nonna whispered.

"I'm, like, the master of keeping secrets."

"Wait here." She went into her bedroom and came back with an old leather-bound diary. She set it on the couch next to me. "Today, we need spumoni with our tea."

Before supper? That must have been some diary.

Nonna opened the door to her green metal cabinet, pulled out two bowls, and plopped three good-sized scoops into our bowls.

I dug into mine, but she just played with hers. "Look at this ice cream," she finally said. "Chocolate, vanilla, and strawberry. Three different colors, three different flavors. Look how beautifully they swirl together. They are like people. They all look different, but in the end, they're all the same."

I scraped the last of the chocolate spumoni from the dish. What was she talking about?

"This," Nonna said, holding up the diary, "this my grandmother's diary. Her story. I want you to hear her words."

In complete awe, I ran my hand over the smooth texture of the leather cover. The pages inside looked well-handled and yellowed with age.

It had to be one of the oldest things I'd ever seen.

She tapped the book. "This secret would bring hurt and sorrow to our family."

There was someone else in our family with a secret. A big secret. I had to hear this.

She opened it to the first page. Looked at me.

"I promise," I said. "Cross my heart."

We exchanged a look of agreement.

Nonna began reading out loud. My eyes closed. Her voice took over my mind. I imagined I was there.

~~~~~

When will she stop wanting to braid my hair? I knelt on the swept floor of our little summer shack, the wooden floorboards hard on my knees. Mama always braids my hair. She says I never do it properly myself. If it were up to me, I'd wear my hair flowing and loose, but Mama says it looks better and neater to have it combed and braided.

While she worked, I stared out the little window above me and watched the colors of sunset paint the sky orange, yellow, and white. A large walnut tree, its leaves in full spread, grew proud and wide at the top of the hill. It stood out in dark contrast against the bright sky. Mama sat behind me in our one chair, pulling the horsehair brush down and down through my hair. Crunching, ripping sounds came from behind me every time she hit a tangle.

"Ow," I let out, and Mama tugged more forcefully on my hair.

"Stop fidgeting." She began winding my hair into separate strands, the twisted hair pulling at my head. I withstood this because I knew how beautiful my hair looks when it is taken care of properly.

My hair is beautiful. Papa tells me, Mama tells me. When I go into town to pick up groceries with Papa, I hear the farmers and shopkeepers tell him how beautiful it is. It's thick and dark, like Mama's, but with lots of waves and natural shape, like Papa's. Whenever I overhear anyone talking about my hair, I swell with pride. It seems to be all anyone notices. Yes, I soothe myself, I have beautiful hair. Someone will want to marry me. I will make a good wife.

"Keep still." Mama always scolds me when she brushes my hair.

The door swung open and Papa stood there, holding a pail of water from the stream that flows down the mountain toward the village. His silhouette was handsome in the western light.

"Don't hurt the girl too much. She's our only one." He set the bucket down, careful not to slosh out any water, and kissed Mama's head, and then mine.

We'd already eaten supper, a delicious roast of vegetables and potatoes. All that was left for me to do that night was to let Mama set my hair. Then I'd be ready to wash up for bed.

She began separating my hair and twisting the strands so they pull tight at my scalp. As her fingers braided, Mama and Papa talked about the work to be done this week and this fall. The walnuts were coming to maturity, and soon they would start falling and falling, plentiful as rain. They decided how many pounds of walnuts we needed to harvest and sell this season. Mama complained that I'm not a boy, that I can't work as hard or carry as many walnuts as a boy, that she picks up my slack. She cursed herself for giving birth to me instead of a son.

Papa made a hissing noise to stop her. "At least we have her and her help."

"But my back aches, and my arms ache. Even my belly aches."

Her complaints are endless.

She finished the braid. I felt the tightness, the weight of it, hanging off my head and down my back like a rudder to a boat. My hair is so long, it falls almost all the way down my spine. She squeezed my shoulders to let me know she's done.

"Thank you, Mama."

"Try not to ruin it while you're sleeping." She turned away without a look in my direction, without even admiring her work.

Standing up, my knees aching, I moved to sit with Papa on the bed. I climbed over him and curled up on the inside, back leaned up against the wall, hugging my knees to my chest to make myself small.

Papa lay down, his head propped up against the pillow, eyes closed. The room darkened as the light left to follow the sun, like a hound that's fallen behind to sniff a smell and then runs ahead to follow its master. The heat of day left, but the late summer evening was still humid and soft. Mama lit candles in their little metal holders around the room.

As Mama tidied up, rinsing the plates and pots from dinner with the water Papa brought home, I closed my eyes and listened to the sound of water moving, the sounds of her scrubbing the pan with a little cloth, her occasional exasperated sighs and huffs. She dumped the excess water out the window. It made a hard, packing sound as it hit the ground below.

I lay down on the bed and stretched out next to him. "Will you tell me a bedtime story?"

"You're too old," he said in a tired voice.

He told me stories only when he was in a good mood and had energy. I'd heard them all before, but I never tired of the tenor of his voice, the sound of his words. When I was younger, I happily went to sleep to the sound of my Papa talking business with his friend from town or talking to Mama about Emelio's harvest.

Mama finished the dishes. She turned her back to us by the candlelight and pulled her dress over her head. Her back looked smooth as cream. Moles and freckles dotted her shoulders. Her arms were thin and wiry with muscle. She picked up her nightshirt from her little stack of clothes and slipped it on.

I crawled over Papa and went to my bed, a tiny cot at the end of theirs. Lying on the corn-husk mattress, I tried to get comfortable as Mama blew out the candles and got into bed.

Their breath soon leveled off in even rhythm, leaving me awake. It quickly became so dark I couldn't tell if my eyes were open or closed, so I squeezed them shut and tried to let my mind relax. I thought about tomorrow, about working in the waning warmth of summer, gathering walnuts all over our land, hiking up into the foothills of the mountain in search of harvest. I dreamed that night of the green hulls of walnuts, of holding them, of lying down beneath one of our trees on a bed of walnuts and looking up into the sun-cracked ceiling of leaves.

~~~~

It's early in the harvest season, and not many walnuts have fallen. Papa and I went out at dawn and combed the green mountainside, zig-zagging from one walnut tree to the next. The little green blades of grass poked up between my bare toes. Sweat beaded on my forehead and at the back of my neck, under my braid. When the wind blew, it cooled us. Good thing Mama's braid was so tight.

Papa walked ahead of me, the two burlap sacks hanging empty off his shoulders. Mama had chided that he wouldn't need both bags, since it was only the start of the season, but Papa was optimistic. When my mama frowned, he smiled and kissed her frown. But usually the frown was still there when he pulled away.

We climbed the grade of the foothills toward the next tree. It was taller than any other tree, the trunk so wide it might've taken four people to span it with their arms. The leaves were healthy green, and the expansive branches cast a wide umbrella of shade.

I narrowed my eyes against the bright sunlight and peered up into the branches, looking for the round, green hulls of raw walnuts. I saw a few big ones, ripening to maturity, plenty of small young ones, and it gave me hope. Soon the ground below the tree would teem with green bulbs.

When I stepped into the tree's shade, the temperature dropped—the leaf cover overhead was that thick. I inhaled the crisp mountain air through my nose, and it cooled my throat. I leaned against the tree and sat down against it.

Just a pace or so ahead, I saw my first walnut of the day. I reached and picked up the green ball, let it rest in the palm of my hand, felt its weight.

Noce, walnuts, grow in green hulls on the tree, and once the nut inside is mature, the hull falls from the branch. When they're ripe, the hull is soft. I pressed my thumb into the green skin. It was hard, no indent, not ready to crack yet.

I tucked the walnut into my sack and stood to look for more. I collected five or six from that tree, none of them ripe enough. It was only late summer, after all. Fall was the true walnut season. We sold or traded so many walnuts in the fall and winter that we made enough lira to last us through the rest of the year. Everyone who lives in Colle, our tiny town nestled in the mountains, is here for the walnuts. At the end of this harvest season, we will move back down to our other small stone house in Campo Basso, our town at the foot of the mountain, just as we did every year. We'll lug the harvest down the mountain to town and sell the nuts straight out of the barrel. Sometimes Papa accepts barter—thirty walnuts in exchange for a shank of beef, a rack of lamb.

We spent the winter in our insulated stone house, socializing with the other townspeople, selling our goods and going to our little town church. I liked being in town because it was less lonely there. There were other children to play with and talk to. I had a friend, Sophia, whom I missed while we were away. Up in the mountains it was just me, Mama, and Papa.

Around noon, Papa's voice carried across the hills. I looked around and saw him a ways away, by another walnut tree on a rise. He stood there shaking his fist at another man, who stood on the other side of the tree.

I ran to him, empty burlap bags flying behind me, my braid bouncing on my back with every stride. By the time I got there, my heart was pounding in my ears, and I was covered in a fresh sweat.

I stopped a few paces behind Papa and realized the man he was yelling at was not a man at all, but a boy.

He stood back from Papa, a little burlap collection bag of his own slung across his body, his face and arms tanned from working outside. A spray of dark hair fell over his forehead. He stood in a posture of deference and respect, head bowed. Down the hill beyond the boy, in a grassy valley, was a small hut just like ours.

"This tree is on my property," Papa barked, sounding meaner than usual. "That means the walnuts that fall from it are mine."

"*Mi dispiace, signore,* my father asked me to collect from this tree. He says it's on the border of our land, and that we have the right to collect the walnuts that fall on our side."

"Your father is a stupid man. He's wrong. The tree is on our property, not yours. Now scram!"

Just then, another man, perhaps the boy's father, emerged over the crest of the nearest hill. His fist came up and started shaking before I could hear his voice.

A roaring match commenced between Papa and the man. The boy wisely edged away, letting his father take the fight for him. He stood off to the side, somewhat in line with the spot where I stayed put.

The boy watched our fathers fight and then seemed to notice me standing there. From so far away, it was hard to see his eyes. The sunlight beat down almost directly overhead and cast shadows on his face. He waved.

Who waves at the daughter of his father's enemy?

I nodded to him, unsure how to respond.

Papa called my name. He knelt by the trunk of the tree, rapidly grabbing as many walnut hulls as he could, while the man on the other side of the tree did the same thing. I ran into the shade and scooped up the only walnut I saw on the ground before Papa started yelling at the man again.

"Stop that! Stop! Don't you dare collect any walnuts from this tree!" Papa's face had turned a bright tomato-red as he stood upright.

"I'll take all the walnuts that fall on my side. Just you try to stop me. If they fall on my property, they belong to me."

Papa swore the most swears I'd ever

heard him say in one sentence. Then he stormed toward me, grabbed me by the arm, and led me back down the hill toward our shack, leaving behind the rest of the walnuts. I glanced behind me and saw the boy and his father talking and gesturing.

"I didn't know we had neighbors," I said on the walk home.

"They're new," Papa grunted. "The land fell to them last year, and he was wise enough to stay away from our tree then. He's grown foolish over the winter and summer."

"What do we do if they keep taking them?"

"We go hungry." Papa's face crumpled in anger in the heat of day.

When we got home to show Mama our harvest, she pursed her lips and spat.

"The season is young. There's plenty more to come," Papa said, lowering himself to the bench we had built just outside the door of the hut. He leaned back against the house wall.

"You better hope so," Mama said, her eyes narrowed like a cat's. Arms folded, she slipped back inside.

I ducked into the shade of the house. The floorboards felt cool and almost damp compared to the heat outside. I grabbed a large wooden bucket and tipped my sack into it. The walnuts rolled out and thunked to the bottom of the bucket. The first of the year. It made me giddy to see them in there at the start of my favorite season.

Harvest had always been my favorite time of year because I loved coming to our mountain shack and I loved spending all day with Papa.

I wandered out into the hills, moving slowly and aimlessly. I imagined the breeze directing me without my realizing it, guiding me. I felt the prickle of grass on the soles of my bare feet.

After a while I laid down on my back in the field, and gazed up at the blue sky with its puffed, mountainous clouds. I closed my eyes, the sunlight bright and burning even through my lids. I saw the color yellow, the color red. The grass pricked the backs of my arms and legs. The mound of braid pressed into the back of my *head.*

I dozed off, dreaming of a little girl who lived in a cloud castle and threw walnuts down from the heavens for us to collect. As I filled my sack with the walnuts, I looked up at the little girl, too far away to see. She waved down at me, a curt, brisk wave, as the boy had done when our fathers were fighting.

When I woke up, the sun had waned, the air cooler. I pressed myself up and looked around at the green foothills of the mountains and upward to the main peak, covered with trees. In the wintertime, snow gathered at the mountain's peak, but it had all melted through the summer. The snow would return soon enough.

Standing up and brushing the dirt and loose grass from the back of my dress, I looked around to decide what to do next. The gnats hovered, illuminated in the sun's late light, little golden spots moving aimlessly through the air as I imagined the stars did in the heavens. I'm sure they must float, suspended, as if the night sky were some thick stew, and the stars little shavings of vegetables, or maybe walnuts, far, far-away walnuts, burning through the dark.

Mama was probably wondering where I was. I usually helped prepare supper and tidy up the house at this time of day. But when I lifted my gaze, I saw the great walnut tree at the edge of our property. I skipped over to it, flying between each step, until it swallowed me up in its dense shade.

I studied the patterns of the ripples and folds on the great trunk and noticed that, in some places, it looked like a braid—the mounds bending and flattening, one beneath the others.

"I like you," I said to it, and then tried to embrace it. "Thank you for giving us your walnuts."

"I didn't give them to you."

At the sound of the strange voice, I yelped and leapt back, my heart suddenly pounding at the base of my throat. I whirled around, my braid whipping behind me, scanning the empty field.

"You just took them," came the voice again.

I ran a circle around the tree.

Then he laughed. "Up here."

Ten or fifteen feet off the ground, a boy sat perched on a thick branch, leaning up against the trunk, one foot dangling. I could see the sole of his foot, lighter than the dark skin of his leg. It wasn't just a boy, I realized. It was the boy from the other night. It had to be.

"How did you get up there?"

"Easy. I climbed."

Lowering himself from one branch to another, he crept down to the lowest branch, still out of jumping distance above my head, and landed with a thump on his feet in front of me.

He was surprisingly tall. He didn't look so tall from far away earlier today. He had looked small, being yelled at by my father.

He was hardly a boy at all.

Up close, I could see his eyes, more green than brown, and his dark hair, cut to fall evenly around his head.

He wore nice but simple clothes: burlap pants, a white linen shirt, bare feet, just like mine. I caught a new smell, pungent and a little sweet.

Goosebumps sprang up on my arms, and my heart started doing a strange new dance. I didn't know why. Still, I swallowed against my nerves.

"Maybe you should stick to climbing your own trees," I said with an upturned nose and wrinkle between my brows, my best impression of my mother.

"This is my tree."

"My papa says it's ours." This boy had some nerve.

He started pacing around me, as if we were about to duel.

He didn't scare me. "My father said when this tree was just a baby, it grew on our side. But as it got bigger and healthier, its limbs spread over both of our properties and started dropping walnuts on your side too. So the tree is on our land, but the walnuts fall on yours. Who gets them?"

The boy stopped circling me now and started pacing back and forth instead. Then he faced me. "I think we should share them. Half for your family, half for mine."

"My papa won't agree."

"Mine either." He smiled. The skin around his eyes crinkled so they turned into tiny smiling half-moons. "Our fathers don't like each other."

I bit my lip. I wasn't used to talking about my parents with other people, but this boy seemed to think it was fine. "No, they don't."

Then he introduced himself: Alessandro. I like that name.

That smile again—mysterious, relaxed. He looked at me and didn't try to hide it, as if he wanted me to know he was looking.

At first it made me feel strange. What was he looking at? Did I have something on my face? I self-consciously brushed a hand over my mouth and cheeks, and then he finally stopped looking.

"My papa said you're new here," I said, "and that you haven't been coming here long at all."

"Not true." For a moment, I thought he was calling my papa a liar. He must have seen my expression, because he quickly said, "He may not have seen me before, but my family and I have been coming here for a long time. Usually in the summers. My grandfather used to take care of the property, but he passed away last winter."

I tried to imagine how it would feel to lose a grandparent, but couldn't understand. I didn't have any.

"I'm sorry," I said without sorrow, because it seemed polite.

Sadness spread across his face like a cloud over the sun. But it passed, and his expression became pleasant and open again. "We take care of the house and the land now. My pop told me it'll be mine someday." He said it proudly and looked up at the walnut tree with almost as much love and gratitude as I did.

Just then a voice rang out over the land, a woman's voice, low and singing the syllables of Alessandro's name like an opera song.

"My mom," he said. "I've got to go."

He backed away from the tree, off in the direction where I thought his house must have been. The ground rose into a hill and then fell away out of sight. I had never explored past this tree before, never bothered to find out what lay in the valley past the hill.

He waved again, brusque and curt, smiled and then he left.

I fought the urge to run up to the hill crest and watch him make his way down to a little shack, just like mine, but I stood in the shade, breathing fast as if I'd just run all the way from our house.

Alessandro. My neighbor.

Walking home, I wondered how I had never seen him before in the twelve years I'd come up to the mountain. I knew I had never seen him in the village, which meant his family lived somewhere else, further away than Campo Basso. Since the harvest had just begun, we might see each other again.

I quickly committed to memory his face, tan skin, dark hair, beautiful eyes, and wide, angular jaw. Alessandro, who are you? Will I ever find out? My thoughts burbled in my head like water from a brook, splashing out messily and uncontained. Was he lonely? Did he have a lot of brothers and sisters? Or was it just him and his parents, just like me and mine?

I knew not to tell my parents, especially my father. He would not approve of us speaking and Mama doesn't approve of anything.

When I got home, Papa was sitting on the front bench with what had to be *la Bibbia* open on his lap. Mama appeared in the doorway and then disappeared into the darkness inside.

When I came in, Mama hit me on the back of my head. "You didn't help in the garden at all today. And you made me prepare dinner all by myself, ungrateful girl."

She let me eat the homemade pasta with delicious vegetables and tomato sauce. The food was so warm and nourishing that, even though we ate before sunset, I felt ready to go to bed. I woke up in the middle of the night to Mama and Papa's snores, the strange dancing feeling back in my chest, but now in my stomach, too. I couldn't stop thinking of Alessandro's bare feet dangling from the branch over my head.

I couldn't get him out of my head. He

was so beautiful.

~~~~~

I interrupted my Nonna. "That sounds just like me," I said. "I can't get Anthony out of my head either! What did she do next?"

Nonna closed the diary and leaned her head back, closing her eyes. "Let's take a break there."

"Aw, okay." I didn't even try to hide my disappointment. "Thanks for reading, Nonna. Can we read some more tomorrow? I need something to distract me from the fact that Anthony isn't writing back."

I tried to laugh, making light of my situation. These diary entries were a great distraction, but I couldn't completely deny my dread. Why hadn't Anthony written back? It had already been a whole week.

Nonna barely cracked a smile. Her eyes sparkled from under her low brows. "If you want to hear more, I will tell you. Tomorrow, then."

I collected my papers and pen, stood, and kissed Nonna on the cheek.

"*Ti amo, grazie,* Nonna," I said on my way out. "And don't worry. The secret is safe with me."

I folded the letter I had written to Anthony, slipped it into an envelope, and addressed it from memory. I licked the envelope shut and grabbed a postage stamp from the kitchen drawer, where my mom kept all the handy stuff. Then I walked to the end of the street and deposited the letter into the blue tray of the mailbox there. Another one out of my hands.

~~~~~

That night as I went to bed, I found myself thinking of the diary, of Italy, of forbidden love. It was so romantic. But I didn't understand how she didn't end up with him.

The next day, I sat in Nonna's living room again, stringing buttons to make bracelets. After only a few buttons, Nonna brought the diary back out.

"Story time," she said with a cute, excited little smile on her face. She was obviously enjoying it too. Flipping to the page where we left off, she settled in to begin.

~~~~~

Weeks passed. The days grew shorter and cooler, and the walnuts fell more and more bountifully from the trees. Papa and I spent our days moving from tree to tree, cluster to cluster. Usually we made two trips out, coming home for lunch, when we each lugged two nearly full burlap sacks on each shoulder. By the time we got there, I was sweating and trembling, back aching. But I tried not to show it. Papa carried the weight with no problem, and his bags were fuller than mine. The walnuts were so many and so heavy, the weight of the straps made big red welts on both my shoulders. I sat in the grass, not bothering to empty the walnuts right away.

My shoulders hurt badly, so I bent my

neck to examine one side and stared at the deep red mark.

"What's the matter?" My mother came out from the shadows inside. "Tired?"

For a moment, I thought she might do something sweet and motherly, like rub my shoulders for me, or scratch my back.

"The bags are heavy, that's all," I said.

Once I'd heard her tell my father that if she'd had a boy instead of a girl, her life would be easier.

Turning around, I saw that she had ducked into the shack, but she returned in a moment. She laid a sandwich in my lap—slices of mozzarella, tomato, and lettuce, simple and delicious. My mother touched my shoulder lightly with her fingertips.

"Thank you, mama," I said, barely a moment before sinking my teeth into the bread.

Not only was I tired, but I was starving too. Sometimes, when I was out collecting, I tried to crack the tough, green shell of the walnuts against tree trunks or under the weight of my foot or the sack, but it rarely worked.

I went back to the big tree several times that fall to fill my sack, but I didn't see Alessandro again. I tried to go as many times as I could, but sometimes Papa set out in that direction before I'd had a chance to choose, and I'd resign myself to the other trees, wondering if Papa would catch Alessandro or Alessandro's mother or father at the tree. Whenever I went, I hoped to see a pair of feet swinging from a low branch or a young man kneeling down to collect the nuts. But each time I was disappointed. I collected the nuts, thanked the great tree, and went on. Until one day, when I noticed a note wedged between a small crevice in the bark of the walnut tree where I first laid eyes on my Alessandro.

I unfolded it. He'd written my name, followed by a drawing of a flower. I said my name out loud, still smiling. I ran my fingers over the letters, imagining him writing my name. I smiled, tucked the piece of paper into my bag with the walnuts and skipped home. So he does think of me, too.

~~~~~

After we'd picked up everything in sight, we needed to wait patiently for more walnuts to ripen and fall, and to let the tree rest. I wandered out into the fields as I liked to do, but this time I had my calligraphy pen, paper, and ink bottle tucked under my arm and held tight in my fist.

Glancing over my shoulder to be sure Mama and Papa weren't following, I continued a little farther until I found a patch of open grass surrounded by tufts of late-blooming wildflowers.

At first I tried to draw the flowers. I had mostly been using the pen and paper for writing, but it occurred to me that there were other ways I could use them too. And so I sketched the flowers, and they emerged from my hand more lopsided and different than they really were--the flower heads too big or too small, the stems too thick, the leaves not spaced apart properly.

Alessandro appeared in my mind, as he often did. Many times since our meeting, I had imagined what would happen when we met again. And each time the scenario played out a little differently.

Sometimes I showed up skipping and joyful at the tree to collect walnuts, the partially filled sack bouncing against my hip. I'd see him there doing the same, gathering green walnut hulls into his bag, and before I'd get too close, he'd look up. I'd see the glint of green in his eyes from that distance, and he'd stand and give me that curt, shy wave. He would be happy to see me. I'd hurry closer, I would go right up to him and say, "Hello," and we'd talk more. In these daydreams, our words don't matter as much as our actions.

We'd sit together, and our knees would touch and drift apart. Even though it's only in my imagination, I still feel the spark of it, the nervous dancing in my belly, the clenching and unclenching of my heart. It's only the touch of our knees, only in my imagination, and still ...

Other times, our knees touch and stay touching, and I see myself trying hard not to look at him, because we are sitting right next to each other and parts of our bodies are touching and it feels awkward, like something that shouldn't happen, isn't allowed. But it's happening and no one's there to say it's not allowed. When I finally summon the courage to turn my face, he's already looking at me, and he lifts his hand to brush my cheek, just the way I brushed my cheek, blushing, when he stared at me that first time.

I blinked and came back to the field, the flowers drawn on the page. On my belly, bending my knees, kicking up my feet, heels together, the sun warm on my back. I began to write.

Alessandro,
Thank you for your note. I didn't know you could read and write. I'm glad you do. When will see you again?

I signed the short note and marveled. How lovely the letters looked side by side when I wrote them fancy and curly-cued like the writing in *La Bibbia*.

~~~~~

Papa and I set out for the first walnut harvest of the day. They were fewer now, *but it was still worth going back out to the trees to collect the last ones.*

Today was a cool day, so I slipped my new knit sweater over my head, the cream-brown colored fabric trapped the heat against my body. Empty bags slung over my shoulders, a ten-pace head start on Mama and Papa, I waved in the direction I was going: the tree at the border of our property and his.

I stopped at other trees along the way, a few green nuts here, a few there. Then I went to the tree and saw Alessandro.

He was sitting against the trunk. When my gaze landed on him, I stopped, and my body turned to ice, as if winter had just arrived. A chilly breeze blew. The yellowing leaves on the tree shifted and rustled above him.

He looked up and noticed me almost as if he could sense my presence. I remembered my legs and told them to walk. I looked over my shoulder to make sure Mama and Papa were nowhere in sight.

He stood there, shaggy hair hanging over his eyes, his stance slouched, slight, but appealingly so. He reminded me of a scrappy street puppy I had seen at Campo Basso. As I got closer, I noticed he held something in his hands, tenderly and delicately.

"Here," he said, as shy as I had ever seen him. "I made this for you."

Eyes cast down, he offered me a small wood carving of a bird with a round chest, wings shaped into a comfortable nesting position, the tips meeting over the tail. The little head and beak sat atop the body, and he had carved shallow indents for the eyes.

My cheeks burning, I took it and held it as delicately as he had, cupped in my palms. He'd made this for me?

"It's beautiful," I said, finally.

He beamed a huge smile that he tried to make smaller.

I hugged the little bird to my chest and stroked the smooth wood with my fingertips. "You carved this?"

He nodded, going into his customary pacing. "I've made a few small things. I like working with wood, carving and making things. It comes easy to me."

A humble brag. The bird was beautiful. He was skilled and he had made it just for me. For me. I felt the rush of having his attention again. It occurred to me he might even have been waiting here, hoping to see me.

I turned the bird over and examined its underside. He had carved an elegant "Q" across the face of the bottom.

"Q?"

"Quirici. My family name."

I nodded.

"So you can read," he said.

I blushed, unsure if he would approve or disapprove. "My papa taught me. I found your note."

"I thought the wind must have blown it away."

"I wrote you back." I handed him the little note I'd folded up in my pocket, seizing the opportunity.

He opened it in front of me.

"I anticipated seeing you again, too," he said quietly, almost embarrassed. "Let's keep leaving notes for each other. It will be our little secret."

I agreed.

"How has the harvest been for you?" he went on quickly.

"Good. Very good." I paused. Surely this wasn't some kind of secret ploy to assess the competition. "For your family?"

"Also good. We've collected buckets and buckets, enough to last us the winter and plenty to sell. I'm sad to go back down to our village. I've liked it here. The peace and quiet, the time with my parents."

"I love it up here too. Which village do you live in?"

"Boscona."

Papa sometimes rode there to buy and barter goods. The trip there and back took three days. "You come back here every fall, yes? Maybe we will see each other next year too."

He looked at me with almond-shaped eyes. This close, I could see light freckles on his nose and cheeks after a summer of sun. My heart pounded faster, and sweat broke out on my upper lip and under my arms beneath my sweater. I stood there in awkward silence, still clutching the little wooden bird, nervously stroking and playing with my braid. He leaned against the tree now, looking at his feet. Was he nervous? What was he thinking about? His face remained calm and unreadable.

"We're leaving in a few days," I said.

"May I see you again before you go? Tomorrow?" he asked, now looking me directly in the eyes.

May he? I nodded. "When?"

"Same time. Late afternoon, before dinner."

It was decided.

Was this happening? I ran home in the twilight, cradling the bird to my chest as if it was my baby. I got home just before sunset, carefully tucking the bird under my sweater so my parents wouldn't see. Instead of taking it inside, I hid it in my burlap collection bag outside, under the bench.

My parents sat talking by the light of the candles on the table.

"Where have you been the last few hours?" Mama snapped. "We have to start packing tomorrow."

Back to reality.

"What were you doing?" Mam's voice sounded harsher than usual.

"I went on a walk around our property," I said. "A long walk."

"Apparently."

"Did you see anybody out there? Like that neighbor?"

Why did Papa ask that? He had never asked me anything like that before when I'd been out on my walks.

"No," I said quickly. "No one."

They exchanged glances as if I had just told them the truth.

The next day Mama held her word. She made me work for hours, cleaning in the shack, scrubbing the floor, packing up our belongings, and loading them into the cart Papa would guide down the mountain. We didn't own a horse to bring up with us for the summer.

As late afternoon approached, I grew sadder and sadder. I looked out toward the field, in the direction of the tree. I'd kept busy all day so my parents wouldn't get suspicious. I tried to keep my face expressionless.

When I was sure Mama and Papa were not watching, I knelt down and slipped my hand inside the burlap sack under the bench and feel for the bird to make sure it was still there.

All day, my mind buzzed. Alessandro would be standing at the tree, waiting for me. For how long I did not know. But all day long, and that evening also, I felt Mama's constant eye on me. It never left.

Determined to make it to the tree one last time, I woke up early on the morning we were to leave. I willed myself awake before the sun rose and crawled out of bed, holding my breath. Then I slipped my sweater over my head and boots onto my feet and opened the door, miraculously without a creak. Dio willed it so. I managed to grab a piece of paper, the ink and the quill off Papa's desk too.

The early morning air was brisk. The season had nearly changed, and it was time to leave. My shoes crunched on the frosty grass. I sprinted across the fields under the lightening sky. The deep blue night sky had begun to fade to lighter shades: blue-gray, bird's egg, and just the first touches of white and butter yellow, the sun's gold emerging. The stars still shining at one end of the sky. It was that in-between time of pre-dawn.

Squinting in the half-dark, I searched for signs of Alessandro's presence, other wood carvings he might have left, or a note. Looking with my hands, I felt around the tree trunk until my fingers came into contact with something smoother than the bark, a distinct shape. It was the shape of the first letter of my name! My fingers traced the carving over and over and over. He had carved this for me. It had to be a sign of love.

The light was gaining now, and I could make out the features of the tree better. I searched for some kind of crevice or fold, and found, in the roots, a perfect kind of nook. My fingers slipped into my sweater and went to the secret pocket, closing around the paper, pen and ink I had stowed there.

Against the bark of the tree, I managed to write.

I will think of you all winter, Alessandro.

I folded it up as small as I could and wedged it into the little crevice formed by the root against the ground and the tree trunk. I hoped he'd find it. I felt bold, signing it "love," but I couldn't deny my heart. I had to listen to my heart.

Dio, let him find it. Dio, per piacere. . .

I carried our secret with me. I liked having something all to myself, that Mama and Papa knew nothing about. I liked it, but at the same time, I knew it was wrong. Wrong to keep anything from them at all. I lived for the family. I served the family. But this one little thing, this was just for me.

The Walnut Tree

"Nonna, you can't stop there!"

Nonna leaned back in her chair and yawned, the pages of the diary splaying open. Once the longest yawn ever had ended, Nonna laughed a little and then settled back in.

"This story is killing me." I'd strung about five bracelets out of my grandmother's buttons before giving up and giving myself completely to the story, hanging on every word.

"What time is it?" she looked around absently, as if we weren't in the middle of a heart-wrencher.

Who cares? Hiding my impatience with slow movements, I checked my watch. "Three-thirty."

"Oh, good, we have time before dinner."

~~~~~

The next summer, we had been back on the mountain barely a day before I had to check the walnut tree. I hoped he would be there, but the tree stood quietly and peacefully alone. It looked just the same as last year, and when my eyes landed on Alessandro's carving, I felt a familiar flutter of excitement.

Walking around the tree, inspecting every knob and nook of bark, I could not believe my eyes. I found it, hidden deep in a crevice by the roots. A small piece of paper neatly folded up. My heart quickened, I kneeled to read it.

Mia Bella,
Is it fair that we get to see each other only three months of the year? Why can't the trees produce year round?
My heart longs to see you again.

I read it and re-read it and then practically leaped for joy. A powerful wave of relief washed over me—he had been thinking about me all winter too.

I folded the letter carefully so not to wrinkle it, and then slipped it into my shirt. When I got back home, I'd hide it with the bird carving and his other note for *safekeeping.*

Oh, Alessandro! I thought of all the wonderful times ahead this summer and fall. If Mama and Papa knew what Alessandro and I had already done behind their backs, they would be furious. Why they so despise our new neighbors I'm not sure. Maybe the competition for the walnuts scares Papa. These walnuts are, after all, all we have for money. Without them, we would starve in the winter. But Alessandro seems so nice, generous. If he and Papa could talk this summer, maybe Papa would hate him less, and maybe Mama would hate him less too.

It has been a strange winter, but a good winter. A strange but good spring too. One full of giddiness and daydreams and impatience. A spring came into my step the first day of summer. Mama and Papa noticed.

"Spring fever," Papa chuckled to Mama. She narrowed her eyes at him as if to say, That's not allowed.

Without meaning to, I began spinning between my turns, humming made-up songs, even asking Mama if I could help with her work. She didn't mind the extra help, but she could tell something was different.

While I helped her mend some torn clothes, she said, "You seem happy."

As if my happiness was a rarity. Perhaps it was. I was surprised by Mama's interest—she usually didn't care about me as long as I got my chores done and was home for dinner.

I shrugged. I pinched the ripped fabric together and looped the needle through.

"A boy?" There was no charm in Mama's voice. It sounded like a threat.

"No, I'm just happy it's summer. I like going to the mountains."

I looked up from stitching and saw Mama watching me with the intensity of a hawk.

"What? Why are you looking at me like that?"

"You're my daughter. I can look at you however I want."

I nodded and went back to the stitching, "Yes, Mama."

"*You are getting older. Men are noticing you now.*"

My fingers fell still. I stared down at the ripped knee of Papa's pants, half-stitched up, half still gaping.

"*And as more men start to notice you, the day may come, sooner than you think, to marry.*" Mama had not stopped her stitching. She methodically finished her mending and tied a knot in the thread with three quick swooping movements of her hand. She held up the pants to examine her work. "*Papa and I were just wondering if there might be a young man interested in you already, and if that's the reason for your good mood. A little friend of yours, hmm? But if you don't want to tell us—*" here she set the pants down on her lap and gave me her most pointed *never keep anything from your mama* look "*—don't tell us.*"

I thought right then that I should just admit that I thought about Alessandro. The boy next door on the mountain who was very nice and even offered to help with our collection this harvest. But she would not approve, and neither would Papa. I had no one on my side. Papa wanted to see me marry someone wealthier than we were, and there was nobody in Colle like that. Unless Alessandro and his family were from the city, he probably wasn't up to Papa's standards. He always talked about men of industry, new technology, all the change happening in the cities. "That's where the money is, not in farming—it's the way of the past."

The thought of Mama and Papa already wanting to give me away in marriage made me feel cold. They are my family. They are all I've ever had—my best friends and my worst enemies. I could not imagine life without them, away from them. Until then, I'd thought felt the same about me.

Marriage had always loomed on the horizon, some distant day in the future. I still thought of myself as a little girl, more tom-boy than girl, really. I worked hard like a boy, and was an only child. It was unusual, everyone told me, to be an only child and a girl.

On the mountain, on a clear, warm, beautiful late summer day shortly after we'd arrived, Papa and I sat on the front bench side by side, each reading our own copy of *La Bibbia*.

"Papa?" I closed the book, keeping my place with a finger tucked between the pages. "Why am I an only child?"

Papa glanced at me from the corner of his eye, turned back to his line, and then, when he'd reached the end of the sentence, he closed the book and sighed. "You are our only child because you are the only one the Holy Father felt we deserved."

"But what will happen to you and Mama after I'm gone?"

"What do you mean?"

"After I'm married. You and Mama will be all alone. Who will help you?"

Papa peered at the distant mountaintop, as if thinking. The sheer rock faces jutted up out of the grassed hillsides in steep angles, way high up. Higher than I'd ever gone. The summer heat had melted off all the snow. The stone face of the mountain stared back at us from far away.

"Well," Papa began, his voice lingering tiredly, "we will keep going. We will have to work harder, but we will keep working."

A long silence rested between us.

"Do you think I could stay with you? Instead of getting married?"

Sitting next to him, I could see the lines in his face. The deep grooves in his forehead, the deep lines carved from the corners of his nose to his lips. His beard and mustache were thick and black and were starting to sprout gray hairs.

"I don't think so. Girls get married. Young people get married. You are too beautiful not to be married."

I blushed and looked down at my closed book and my eyes slowly filled with tears.

I knew I had a duty to my parents to marry well, to marry someone they chose and approved of. That's what happened, that's how things were done but I had already met Alessandro, my soulmate. What kind of cruel trick is it that my soulmate is forbidden, that our families are rivals, that my heart has chosen the impossible?

~~~~~

That summer felt like a dream. Every time I went to the tree, even if Alessandro wasn't there, I walked away with a fuller heart than before. My collection of love notes grew almost every day. Though they were short, they meant the world to me. I had Alessandro's love, so pure, sweet and untouched. We hadn't even held hands. We'd barely touched. We just spoke of how beautiful we found each other, how beautiful life was together, how beautiful, how perfect.

I never let Mama or Papa see the notes. The wooden bird Alessandro had carved for me last year was safely stored away in my bag of personals—books, clothes, gifts— along with Alessandro's letters. I put them all at the very bottom of the bag, but I wanted to keep them near.

I suspected Mama and Papa were on to me. They had to know, or at least surmise, that I wasn't off sitting in a field by myself all day long. I did while away some hours by practicing writing, exploring, climbing new trees, scouting around for the first hulls of the season. But I also spent plenty of time with Alessandro.

~~~~~

Coming home from a secret visit with Alessandro, I saw Mama hunched over in the garden. All day, every day, she tended the garden, our only source of food on the mountain unless we traded walnuts for more.

"Do you need help, Mama?" I ran to her, stopping just outside the garden bed.

She looked over her shoulder at me, sweat dripping down her face. She wiped it with her arm. "I needed help hours ago."

I shifted to move away. But just then, the love note Alessandro had written for me today fell out of my collection bag, a little beige paper bright against the grass. Mama's eyes immediately went to it.

"What is this?" Before I could reach down to pick it up, she beat me to it, her lightning reflexes snatching the note. She unfolded it, stared at the markings on the page, grimacing in anger.

"What does this say?" She thrust it into

my face. "And don't lie."

I never believed in love, until I met you, it said. I looked up, trying to think of something.

"It's from that Quirici boy, isn't it?"

Before I could come up with anything to say, her hand connected with the side of my face, so hard it knocked out my earring. I opened my mouth in pain but managed not to make a sound.

"Don't talk to him anymore," she said in a voice hard and cold as steel.

"Yes, Mama," I said, hoping it would save me from another smack.

"What's happening out here?" Papa emerged over the nearest hill, and in moments had reached us at the garden.

"She didn't help me at all today," Mama snapped. "And now she comes home, trying to hide things from me. Here, what does this say?" She stepped over to Papa and showed him the note.

Papa, I knew, would understand.

He read it. "It's gibberish. It says nothing."

Thank you, Papa.

Mama stared in furious disbelief. "That's not what it says."

"You ask what it says—I tell you what it says." Papa didn't look at me at all. He crumpled the note in his hand, crammed it in his pants pocket, and stalked silently toward the house.

I glared at Mama. She stood there with her arms crossed, frowning. She knew, even though she couldn't read. At least Alessandro hadn't signed his name on the letter. For all Papa knew, it could have just been a little doodle I'd drawn myself. I made sure, from then on, not to put the letters in my bag anymore. Now they went in my shoes, if I was wearing them, safely under my feet until I could take them out and hide them.

Sometimes by chance and sometimes arranged, we spent hours at the tree or wandering around the fields, always careful to avoid my father's property.

"They're not too fond of me, are they?" he said after asking me for the third time to see my family's land.

"Not at the moment. They don't dislike

you, exactly. They just don't know you. They think you're just our pushy neighbor's pushy son."

He nodded, his gaze faraway. "My parents aren't your biggest admirers, either." He said it as if to make things even. We nodded. Common knowledge.

"Do you think—" he paused "—they could ever come to see me differently?"

I wanted him to reach out and touch my arm or grab my hand and interlock his fingers with mine.

"I hope so."

He looked over at me, hope dancing in his eyes.

"I would like for them to know you. I just have to think about how to introduce you ..."

"I'll leave that up to you." Silent for several moments, he seemed to retreat back into himself. "I would love to meet your mother. Try to make a better impression on your father ..."

"You say you want to meet her." I shot him a glance that said, *but you don't.*

He laughed and dropped the

conversation. I couldn't bring myself to say anything else. We walked on in silence until I said goodbye and made my way home in the twilight.

When would Alessandro try to kiss me? I wanted him to try.

As our house came over the hill into view, I could see the candles already burning in the window. *No ... How would I explain where I'd been this time?*

I quickened my pace and jogged the rest of the way home. Dropping my bag under the bench by the front door, I noticed a large sack outside, made of shiny, tightly woven material, with tools sticking out. Hammers, scrapers, measuring devices, mallets.

Curious, I pushed through the door.

In our tiny house, stationed at our small kitchen table, my parents sat with a strange man. A handsome man.

"There she is," Papa said.

Mama twisted in her chair and flashed me a severe look. *Where have you been?*

I stood there, stunned.

Papa introduced me to the man.

155

He stood—so tall and broad his head almost touched the ceiling—and moved gracefully around Papa's chair to reach forward and take my motionless hand from my side. He proceeded to gently bow and kiss the tips of my fingers. It sent a shiver up my arm and a pang of cold dread through my belly.

"A beautiful name," he said. His eyes were kind, simple, a flat brown, his hair jet black, trimmed in an interesting style I had never seen on a man. He turned to my parents as if complimenting them on their naming.

"He is one of the workers making on the road system better farther up the mountain," Papa said.

"Is that so?" I looked around the room. My Papa looked beyond impressed, Mama looked irritated.

The young man said he could stay only a little while longer, but Mama stood anyway and prepared a plate of cheese and bread and wine for us all. She insisted I take her place.

Papa and the man talked and talked

about all the industries beginning in the cities, about automobiles and "the industrial revolution," as the man called it. He leaned forward in his chair, listening intently and asking questions.

The young man answered each of Papa's questions thoroughly and seriously. He was authoritative, gentle, but serious. I mostly stayed quiet and listened, slowly sinking into my own dreadful thoughts about what this visitor might mean to me. Every once in a while, the man looked over at me while Papa talked. His eyes skimmed down my body, and then back up to my face.

He shook Papa's hand in goodbye and bowed again to Mama and me. I heard his tools clinking outside as he lifted the bag and set off. Oppressive silence filled the house in his absence.

I didn't dare ask them what that visit was about. It could mean only one thing. But maybe, if I didn't talk about it, they would forget about it, or somehow understand to let it go. That I wasn't ready.

No one said anything about the visitor.

In silence, I helped Mama clear the table and then went to bed.

"He is a very hardworking man," Papa said the next morning on our walk out into the fields.

"You like him, I can tell."

"But do you?" Papa looked down to me.

I stared ahead and shrugged. "He seems fine."

This answer didn't satisfy Papa. He squinted.

"He is a smart man," he said. "He is investing in the future. I'm sure he gets paid well." Papa glanced down at me as if looking for my reaction.

I had none. I didn't care about the money. I liked our life in our tiny town.

He sighed. "I want a better life for you than what we have here."

"I don't," I almost shouted, on the verge of tears "I like this life."

I stopped walking and crossed my arms, turning away from him to cry. My head spun as if I might be sick. Just yesterday, all I'd had on my mind was my next love note to Alessandro and how many walnuts I'd collect the next day.

Papa let me cry and then gently touched my hair. "Why don't you want this?"

"Because I like it here with you. I don't want to leave my home. I don't even know him ..." *And Alessandro. I couldn't leave him.*

"But you wouldn't have to leave, necessarily." Papa stroked my hair. "He is here for work but he told me he is interested in purchasing land in Colle. I don't want to see you go far, trust me."

If he didn't want me to go far, why couldn't I just marry our next-door neighbor? But I could already imagine what Papa would say. *Not our neighbor, our nemesis. Our rival.*

The idea of living in Colle made the arrangement slightly more tolerable.

For a slow, burning moment, I thought of just coming out and asking him: *What about Alessandro? Is he so bad? Is there any way ...?*

I knew the answer. Papa would never allow us to be together. The rivalry between *our families was silly, foolish even, but Papa was stuck in his ways, his thoughts, almost as stubborn as me. And Mama was stuck in hers too. If I challenged them, they'd either beat me or arrange a marriage for the next day.*

"We know what is best for you, daughter," Papa said softly. "Mama and I see where the world is going. He will give you a good life."

My stomach dropped. Had it already been decided?

I bit my lip. "But Papa—"

"Don't argue with me." His tone shifted to the edge. "And don't argue with your mama either. She'll only give me grief."

I had to see Alessandro.

Somehow my determination to see him dried my tears. I kept walking, leaving Papa behind. He let me go.

I had started keeping a little pad of paper, a pen, and ink in my bag now. When I reached the great tree by Alessandro's house, I knelt there and wrote on a paper scrap:

Meet me here after your parents are asleep.

I folded it small and tucked it between the roots. *Please see the note.*

I ran away.

That night, I crept outside on silent feet. I dove into the chill of the night, racing to the tree as fast as I could. I ran hard, breaking into a sweat.

The note was gone. He'd seen it.

He was coming.

I waited there, pacing, circling the trunk, even venturing a little way toward his house, which was completely dark, before thinking better of it and going back to sit at the base of the trunk.

The man from earlier kept fluttering around the edges of my mind. The way he'd stared at me when Papa was talking, that piercing look. It was *that* look, the look of wanting that I had seen on other men. But on him there was something else to it. An entitlement, maybe, as if I was already his.

I blinked. It made me nervous.

He was older. A stranger. I didn't

know him at all. His demeanor was serious, cold. I didn't know what life with him would be like, and I didn't want to know.

Alessandro would know what to do, I desperately hoped. He would come up with a plan, an escape—something. I was sure he would be heartbroken to hear of the possibility of me having to marry someone else.

"Psst!"

Alessandro ran up the hill, around the trunk of the tree.

I hastened to my feet and whirled right into his chest.

We each took a step back.

"What is it? Why did you need to see me?"

Already the space between us closed again, his hands landing lightly on the outsides of my arms. He slid them down to my hands. I marveled at him in the moonlight, at the sensation of his hands on my skin.

"Alessandro." I gave in to the yearning.

I stepped back into his chest and let him wrap his arms around me. I pressed my face into his shoulder and inhaled deeply of the scent of wood, fresh-cut grass, *home*. He felt so strong in the embrace.

My face still pressed into his chest, I said, "My parents are about to give me away."

We stood there, holding each other, feeling each other's warmth. Swaying. The breeze ruffled the tall grass, and walnuts fell.

I hoped he would say something like, *I have an idea. Let's get out of here. Tonight. We'll take my uncle's horse in Colle and ride for a new land.*

But he just stood there, saying nothing.

Finally he let go of me. I stepped back and gazed up at the pained look in his eyes.

"Do you love him?"

I shook my head vigorously, "I don't even know him."

I searched his face. Was he about to ask if I loved him? I wanted him to ask.

The question seemed to be on his mind, and on his lips ... but after a moment, he closed his eyes. His slim form stood still in the moonlight. Why wasn't he more upset?

More forceful? I'd thought he would cry, beg me to run away, beg me to marry him.

Instead he said nothing.

Eventually he turned away, pushing his hand through his long hair over and over again as if in thought. Walking around with both hands on his head, elbows out, sighing.

I slumped down against the tree. I was tired. Disappointment settled around my heart. Why had I asked him to meet me here tonight?

I wanted him to tell me I couldn't marry someone else, because he loved me. But I knew that, in our parents' eyes, it was wrong. The one match that could not be made. Of course he knew this too.

"I wanted you to know I don't want to marry him." I looked right into his eyes as I said it.

"Can I see you tomorrow night?"

At least he had asked that much.

That night I couldn't sleep. My mind raced and reminisced of thoughts that were out of my control. Alessandro's foot dangling in the tree, dappled sunlight, the exhilaration of writing notes and leaving them in secret at the tree. The suspense of waiting for a response. The sweetness, the relief of finding a note in return. Our moonlit meetings always left me walking home on air. I wished they would give him a chance. I wished I could change their minds. I wished my choice didn't have to be so hard, that I could choose for myself instead of others.

Sadness clouded my thoughts and my stomach twisted up with nerves. My mind raced.

Why were they doing this? Why was Papa doing this? Didn't they need me?

As I thought in bed, tears sprang to my eyes again.

How could I live without seeing Papa every day? Without his stories, his gentle and loving touches, the silent gift of his company? This must be Mama's idea. Maybe the man had offered to pay them a dowry. Maybe it was about money.

I reminded myself that Papa seemed certain that the man would buy land in Colle.

But what if it wasn't right away? What if he didn't buy land in Colle at all? Did he even have enough money to buy land? Papa seemed to think so. I wondered if Alessandro's family was wealthy. Their mountain house seemed humble but nice. It was hard to tell.

The handsome stranger loomed in my mind, dark and serious. I felt his lips on my fingertips again and trembled. Turning over to face the wall, I tried to empty my mind.

~~~~~

The next morning, a knock came on the door. Mama and I were mending in silence that morning. I wove the needle and thread in and out, trying not to say anything, because I knew if I opened my mouth, no matter what came out would offend her in some way. I had nothing good to say to her.

Papa answered the door. It was the man.

I could see his face through the slat of space in the doorway that my Papa wasn't blocking.

It wasn't a good sign that he was back.

Papa stepped outside, closing the door behind. Their muffled voices carried through the walls as they were walking away.

I set down my work and looked out the window to watch.

They walked side by side, heads bent, hands moving every now and then in conversation.

No. Tell him I can't go. I pleaded with Papa in my mind. Please don't make me go.

"He's to be your husband." Mama's voice, close behind me.

I turned. I couldn't say anything.

"You're finally growing up," my mother said without an ounce of compassion in her voice. "He is quite handsome. You're lucky your father found such a good match for you."

My heart pounded until I felt faint. I turned away from her and the window and staggered back to the bed, where I picked up my mending and set to it determinedly. I tried not to think about what it all meant.

When Papa came back, he looked tired

and sad. He didn't look at me. He just came in to get something to drink, exchanged a few quick, curt words with Mama, and then went back outside.

In a burst, I threw down my mending and charged outside after Papa.

"Where are you going?" Mama called, but I was already out the door.

I finally caught up to him—neck bent, hands in pockets, feet dragging.

"Papa!" I yelled. He turned. I ran the rest of the way and came to a stop right in front of him. "Papa, please. Please don't make me marry him."

He did not look me in the eye.

"Would it make a difference if I told you I love another?" My heart pounded so hard in my ears, my legs might give out underneath me.

"It makes no difference."

"Papa, I'm begging you." Helpless, I babbled on. "Give me more time, another year with you and Mama."

Papa pressed his thumb and first finger to his eyes, rubbing them. "Why, so you can run off with Quirici boy?"

He did know. I went cold.

"He's not so bad, Papa. He's respectful, a gentleman, sweet and kind—"

"It makes no difference." He repeated, louder, harsher.

"Please, Papa, Alessandro and I—"

His hand came up and slapped me across the face.

Stunned, I pressed my hand to my cheek, exploding with pain. I stood there in front of him, heartbroken. Papa always protected me.

"Don't argue with me." His voice was low and cold, but also resigned. He said the words as if he was reading them from a paper. "Just listen. Do as we say. You will marry who we tell you to marry. Now go home."

He turned his back. "It is done."

~~~~

I went back to the tree that night. Alessandro was there, sitting against the trunk, waiting. He stood to greet me, his form outlined by silver moonlight.

"What's wrong?" He touched my elbow.

"I'm getting married."

Alessandro's eyes softened. He looked away from me, as everybody else had that day. I stared at him, begging him, pleading with him in my mind to ask me anyway. This was our chance, our last chance.

Eyes wide, watching me, he brought the back of my hand to his mouth. Then he closed his eyes and kissed my fingers, a long, lingering kiss.

I watched his slim eyebrows furrow, felt the brush of his breath on my hand.

When he lifted his gaze, he had a new intensity, a determination in his gentle eyes that looked foreign on him.

"I'll take you away. Tonight." He breath caught, quick. "My uncle has a horse in Colle, and I'll take some walnuts to sell. We can do it, if you're ready."

The touch between our hands burned hot. There seemed to be a magnetic pull between our faces. I couldn't keep away from him. His fingertips skimmed up my arms to my shoulders. He guided me closer, stepping closer, and touched his lips to mine. Lightly at first, testing, and then more firmly, passionately. The kiss felt like heaven. We sat down against the tree and leaned into each other for what felt like forever and a second. Time seemed to stop. The rest of the world dropped away. We were all that existed, and all that mattered.

Could I do it? Could I forgive myself for leaving my family? For blatantly abandoning and disrespecting them that way? Could they forgive me? If I went with Alessandro, I wouldn't have to face the uncertain future of marrying a stranger. But the future with Alessandro was just as uncertain.

"Meet me here tonight, after your parents go to sleep," he said after a minute. "I'll be waiting with a bag. We can go from here."

I hesitated. "I should go."

He kissed me one more wonderful time.

My very first kiss. Our last kiss.

Walking away, I glanced over my shoulder. He stood there in the shade, watching me go. I brushed flying strands of hair from my face, to see him better. A small wave. My heart broke.

That night as the sun sank and Mama and Papa discussed when he would come back for me, I lit a candle and stared at the flame, my heart in pieces, torn and strewn about the hills of Colle. I felt paralyzed, completely caught. How could I be sure I would make the right choice? I—we all— had so much at stake. There was no right choice. Either way, I lose. So does one of the men. Sinking my chin into my hands, I watched the flame flicker and dance, grow steady, waver.

That night I tuned out everything. I went to bed early and lay there not knowing what to do.

The moonlight filtered through the window. I wasn't sleepy, or even tired. I was just lying there, imagining Alessandro at the tree with a bag sitting by the trunk. He was probably there, right now, waiting. Calming himself, assuring himself I would come, any minute now.

I hated doing this to him. I hated that I was a coward. Truly, I was afraid. Afraid to leave my parents, afraid to be so far from them, unable to talk to them, unable to communicate with them. Although, I reasoned, Papa and I could send letters in the post. Who knew how long it would take them to travel, though?

If I left, my parents might stop loving me. Papa might stop loving me.

I remembered the fresh sting of Papa's slap earlier that day, how quick and abrupt it had been, how the tears had sprung to my eyes, not because of the pain but because of the shock. Tears came to my eyes again, now, for letting Alessandro wait there.

It had to be over with us. I didn't want to see him again. I felt sick to my stomach, I hated myself. But seeing him, I figured, would only make everything worse.

I cried in silence all through that night, watching the moon travel across the sky. When it had sunk low enough that I could not see it, I closed my eyes and willed myself to sleep. To sleep and forget there had ever been a choice at all.

~~~~~

My last few days at the shack passed quickly. I tried to busy myself getting ready. I savored my last night's sleeping in our little shack, the slow peaceful days collecting in the field. I didn't argue with Mama or Papa anymore.

Papa and I read side by side in the sun on the front bench. Mama braided my hair the day before I was to go down the hill to Campo Basso and get married at the church. I guessed I would go to live at my husband's house after that, wherever that may be.

My hair hanging heavy and solid off my head, I walked on trembling feet toward the great walnut tree. I paused and squinted as it came into view. Nobody else was there.

I approached it like a graveyard. With solemn steps, I walked into its shade and gazed up at the many layers of branches overhead, filtering sunlight through leaves. I remembered Alessandro's foot dangling over me from the branch, the first day we met. The memory lit up my mind like lightning as I day dreamed.

I blinked, back to the present, and moved around the tree, examining all the

nooks and crannies in the bark and roots—
all our hiding places. No notes waited for
me now. I guessed he understood.

Standing before the carving in the tree,
I reached out to touch it. The rough bark
contrasted with the smooth, carved wood. I
had packed the little bird Alessandro
carved for me. I had a small suitcase full of
belongings to bring with me. My warmest
sweater, favorite shirts, a blanket I'd had
since I was a baby, *La Bibbia*, and of course,
all his love notes. I couldn't bear to leave
them.

Something caught my eye, tucked
between the roots of the tree. I knelt down
to inspect it. It was not a note, it was a
small carved wooden leaf on a necklace of
twine.

It was obviously from Alessandro. I
slipped it over my head and under my
shirt. The wooden pendant sat right in the
center of my chest. I could feel it against my
skin, inches from my heart.

I hoped I'd be able to come back to this
place soon, but I could not know when. The
pendant on my chest brought me comfort.

With its presence, close to my heart, I felt a close to him.

With heavy hearts, my parents walked me down the main street in Colle, where we met him. He greeted us all cordially and politely, looking very handsome. He has a nice smile, a genuine, kind face.

The marriage was fast and simple in our tiny church in Colle. His family was not present. It was mostly just him, me, Mama, Papa, and the priest. Some of the townspeople came too, familiar faces. After the wedding, we mingled in the church for a few minutes, eating grapes and cheese, drinking wine. Every person there kissed me on the cheek and wished us both well.

I prayed it would last longer, the service, the reception, but it all happened quickly. Too quickly.

The next thing I knew, we were loading his cart.

"*Congratulazioni,*" Papa hugged me tight and kissed the top of my head, tears in his eyes. He wiped them away quickly and stood there with an expectant, hesitant expression on his face, as if he wanted to say more. In the end, he said only, "I hope we see you soon."

"Good luck," Mama said. "Take care of yourself."

My new husband climbed into the cart beside me and grabbed the reins. Mama and Papa waved goodbye and grew smaller and smaller as he directed the horses down the mountain. It would be a two-week journey to his house in a town outside Verona. I had no idea how to act, what to say. What if I had to relieve myself?

We were alone, and it was completely overwhelming. I just sat there, trying to remain calm, as the cart bumped along the rocky dirt roads, the horse hooves clopping ahead of us.

The journey there was long, awkward, and uncomfortable. We had to sleep under blankets in the cart, no mattress. I couldn't wait to sleep in a house again, on a real bed.

"Welcome home," he said stiffly as he stopped the horses in front of a small house in a field of its own.

It was nicer than our house in Colle. It had three rooms, a fireplace in the bedroom, and a separate room for the kitchen. I had never been in a house so nice. "Did you build it?"

"With my father and a friend."

"It's lovely," I said. "I like it."

"I'm glad."

He closed the front door and set down my suitcase. He stared at me, intensely. I burned under his gaze. In five large strides, he closed the space between us. Suddenly, he stood right in front of me, his face, higher than mine, hovering close. My body remembered that night with Alessandro, the way he'd stood close like this, the feel of his fingers on my arm in the dark, his chest against my cheek, his smell.

My husband smelled like heat, sweat. But underneath it all was something smoky and piney, like cedar wood. He brushed his hands up my arms and let them both land on my shoulders. Then he touched my hair, running his finger down the braid, tugging lightly on the end.

"You're very beautiful. Did you know this?" he asked gently. He let go of my braid and pulled me close, but I felt nothing.

"Thank you," I whispered.

That night when we undressed, I realized I'd not taken off my new necklace.

He noticed. "What's this?"

My hand instinctively went to the leaf, to my heart. "A gift. From my parents."

"It's unique." He said. Planting a kiss on my cheek, and then my mouth. "It suits you."

My stomach churned.

Going to sleep in my husband's bed, under his fur throw, lying against his bare chest, I turned over. It felt strange to lie so close to someone sleeping. His body was hot, prickly with hair. Inching away to get some space, I glanced around the room. No window. No walnut tree. New bed. New person.

I closed my eyes and automatically thought of Alessandro. What might it have been like to press the skin of my body against his skin? I imagined him again, waiting for me at the tree that night, probably growing more despondent, more hopeless by the minute. Part of me wished, so badly, that I'd gone there to meet him. I wish I had listened to my heart. My broken heart.

~~~~~

My husband had news today. He was given a promotion. He was joyous—more money! We get to travel! But to me, it's the worst news in the world.

Brazil. He has been hired to direct a team of road workers building roads in Brazil. When he told me, I went cold. I felt as if I might have died.

"I thought we were moving to Colle," I said, my voice thin and small.

"Not anymore."

"How long will we be there?"

He shrugged. "Until the work is done."

We were to leave in one week. I was terrified. Every night in private, I read my love notes from Alessandro. Did I make the wrong choice? If so, I had resigned myself to a life of misery. Was it too late to leave now and run away with Alessandro? Would he even take me? I cried, thinking about how I'd hurt him. How I'd hurt myself. But still, I feel the same—trapped.

The choice was not my own.

~~~~~

The ship was larger than anything I'd ever seen in my life. I was terrified to go aboard. "Aboard" was the word everyone kept saying. I had never even seen the ocean before, I couldn't swim, and I was supposed to trust this massive, heavy object not to sink? As I looked up at it, it obstructed the sun, darkening the light and casting a giant shadow across the docks.

A crowd of people milled about, getting in line to board. Everyone looked different. People spoke languages that were not Italian, I couldn't understand. It was all shouting, waving hands and horns blasting. It was overwhelming. I miss the peace and quiet and I miss Alessandro.

We found our cabin, a room that would've been too small even for my bed from the summer shack. It had two bunks, one for each of us, and a little closet for our luggage. The bob and shift of the boat felt strange and disorienting down there. Everything leaned left, then right, then center, just so slightly.

We went up to the deck for the castoff. I looked down at all the people below, at the land, the coast stretching away in either direction. Blue sky above and an endless expanse of dark blue sea. A horn blared and the ship emitted a huge, white billow of steam, like a decaying cloud.

I held in my tears, my horrible hopelessness, as I left my homeland. The painful journey to Brazil would take one month.

~~~~~

The motion of the boat as it crashed over the waves was horrible. After only two days, sea sickness had already taken its toll. It came out of nowhere, because the subtle tilting back and forth was constant. Sometimes the salt air smelled crisp and fresh, and other times the smell made me heave.

Taking a walk to get some fresh air, in the hopes it might soothe my queasy stomach, I went out on deck. I looked out to sea, the cool wind on my cheeks, but it didn't make me feel better. Instead, I got worse. A bad feeling came up.

My life was ruined. I cried bitterly, missing Italy already, and my Papa. I missed Alessandro's face, voice and touch which was still so vibrant in my mind.

I did the right thing, I tried to tell myself. But I still felt terribly, terribly alone. I was a good daughter. I did as my parents wanted, so why did it all feel wrong? My heart was broken. I had lost my homeland, I had lost my family, I had lost my love.

Footsteps approached, and I quickly wiped my face. A handsome, portly man stood beside me. As I took in his blue dress jacket, gold stars, and white cap, I realized he was the captain of the ship.

"Why so sad, miss?" he asked.

"I am sad to leave Italy," I said, feeling oddly open. "I miss my family. I feel very alone."

Then, suddenly, his hand went to my waist. "Come stay with me in my stateroom tonight. Then you won't be alone."

He tried to press a key into my hand.

"Your words are flattering," I said, trying to hand back the key. "But I am married."

At his confused look, I broke down crying. "I don't want to go to Brazil."

Again his hand squeezed my waist. "Come with me, beautiful, and you don't even have to get off the ship. You can disappear. Go back to Italy, even."

Still crying, still holding the key, I turned it in my fingers. What he said was true. I could escape from my husband, escape from Brazil. But if I left him, I could never go back to my family. To run away from a marriage would be disgraceful, shameful for our family. No one would say our names the same again. It would ruin everyone.

I handed the key back to him. He took it.

"You're welcome any time." He gave me the number to his state room. It would be nicer than the cabins, I knew that, but if my husband ever found out about this, who knew what he would do? I kept it from him. What's one more secret to keep?

I'd made my decision, and now I had to live with it. Everything in life is a tradeoff. It was time to close this chapter of my life, for my own good, never to be heard from again. I couldn't keep going over my choices—were they right, were they wrong?

It seems all paths lead to suffering for me. No matter what I did, what I chose, I would still lose. I had to write this down, because truly my love with Alessandro felt so real, so vibrant, so once-in-a-lifetime, that I had to memorialize it somewhere. Now, to look over the notes, to write about it, to reminisce deeply hurts my heart.

I can't do it anymore. I made my choice, now I can't look back. I think it will be easiest if I just forget about it. If I pretend it never happened. My heart aches even to write these words. My tears mark the page. I must end this diary. I must settle for this life. I must close my heart.

~~~~~

Nonna fell silent.

Lying on the sofa, near tears, I expected there to be more, but there wasn't. I opened my eyes. "Wait—that's it?"

"That's it." Nonna nodded, tears on her cheeks. "Well, almost it."

"Tell me he died or left her or something, and she got to go home and find Alessandro waiting for her. This can't be how it ends."

But Nonna just shook her head, her mouth pressed into a sad, flat line.

"No, *Maria Louisa*, she married him and they stayed married. She never saw Alessandro again. She lived in Brazil and had a very hard life. She never got used to the climate, or the culture there. She was often ill. She suffered." Nonna's eyes still sparkled with tears. "But the saddest part is that she never got to see her family again. They died while she was in Brazil."

"No."

"*Sí*. It's true." She reached for a tea napkin and dabbed the corners of her eyes. She cried for a few minutes while I let the story sink in. It was a heavy secret. One she had been keeping. And now it was mine to keep too.

Why did it have to have such a sad ending? It made it so much worse that it was true. Nonna was usually one for happy stories. A happy woman. I thought it was going to end with some kind of upbeat advice, not show me how to give up on my dream guy.

Nonna's eyes were distant, as if she were still seeing the scenes from the diary. I started to wonder about Nonna's story now. How had she met Nonno?

"What happened to Alessandro?" I asked instead. "Did he stay in Colle?"

She pressed a hand to her cheek and shook her head slightly.

"What about the letters? Did great-gramma keep the notes?" It was pretty amazing to have this diary, but I wanted to get my hands on the notes too. It was practically part of my family history.

Nonna wasn't quick to respond.

"Nonna? The love notes?" I prompted.

She blinked. "I don't know where they are," she finally said in a sad voice.

Was she lying? "Your mom never talked about it with you?"

"*Maria Louisa*, you have to understand." Nonna stood and paced the length of the room, faster than I'd seen her walk for a while. At the door, she stopped and turned to me, her gaze burning into mine. "It was a secret, and a shameful secret at that time. Women did not cheat on their husbands. They did not think about it. They did not love other people. Italian people care about how their family is perceived. Once she was married, like I just read you, she put it out of her mind. She knew to keep thinking about it would bring pain and shame. She didn't talk about it."

She had that distant look in her eye again.

"What about you, Nonna?" I asked.

"Hmm?"

"You and Nonno. How did you meet? I know all about your mom, but now I want to know about you." I hoped telling her own love story might cheer her up. She and Nonno had seemed so content, the sweetest old couple.

But instead she raised her hand, shaking slightly, and said, "I'm tired now. No more stories today. I want to take a rest before dinner."

I ate the last flaky cracker off the plate and brought it and our empty tea cups to the kitchen. "Thanks for reading the rest of the diary to me. It's such a sad story, but a good story. I couldn't stop listening."

She didn't answer. Instead, she sat in her chair with her eyes closed, breathing slowly. I let myself out and closed the door on Nonna and her secret.

The Letter is Not in the Mail

The summer between my sophomore and junior years of high school dragged on. Maybe Nonna's story had put me in a bittersweet mood, but I couldn't stop thinking of Anthony and our letters. It gave me a little pride to write letters, just as my ancestors had.

Nonna and I kept up our dates—walking to the farm stand up the street, stringing bracelets and necklaces with her buttons, playing cards. Swimming in the pool, Nonna tossing Tootsie Rolls from her window. Once on a hot day, I filled one of the huge oak wine barrels with water and sat in it as if it was a kiddy pool. Ah, that cool water felt good. Nonna pulled up a chair and sat outside in the lawn beside me, handing me my drink every few minutes when I asked for it, as I told her the whole story with Anthony. How on-again, off-again he was, how much potential I thought we had as a couple, how badly I wanted him to come back to me, how achingly much I loved him. How amazing he was.

Three months and eleven letters passed. I checked our mail every day as if my life depended on it.

Opening the door and seeing the empty tin box reminded me of Alessandro, waiting lovelorn under the tree, for a lover who would never come. Still, I spent a good portion of my time practicing writing our names next to each other, and then the complete combo: Anthony and Mary Lou Knight.

If I sent enough letters, he had to write back eventually.

Finally, one day in September, as I flipped through the stack of letters, one stood out.

One for my dad, another one for my dad, *another* one for my dad, and then I read my name in Anthony's beautiful handwriting. Dropping the other mail on the kitchen table, I sat down, eyes locked on the letter. He hadn't forgotten me, after all.

Intently I ripped open the envelope. It looked as if he'd finally found the time to scribble some sentences on Air Force stationary. I was expecting, "I miss you" and maybe even "I love you." But instead it was signed, "Your friend."

Hi, Mary Lou,

Today I received a lot of letters from you. I wasn't able to read them until after dinner. I guess you're wondering what I do all day in the Air Force. Since I've been here, I got my blues, my real uniform. It looks good.

I got up early today for basic training. After that, I went to the BX, which is the general store. I have so many things to tell you. But I don't have enough time.

Don't be sad, but they cut off all my hair on August 9th and again on the 26th. So I hardly have any hair. I hope you're still smiling just like you were when you first opened the letter.

Your friend,
Anthony

Disappointment sat in my stomach like a heavy stone. *Your friend.* That wasn't exactly the signoff I'd been hoping for. Not even the girl in my Nonna's story had been stuck in this dilemma.

Trying not to be deflated, I reasoned with myself. At least he'd written back, even though it had taken him three months.

Just then I heard the doorknob turning. I slid the letter to my lap, out of sight below the table, but it was just Nonna coming in from upstairs.

I must have looked stunned, because she said, "Everything okay?"

I let out a silent breath of relief that it wasn't my father. If it had been him, I guess I would have crammed the letter in the waistband of my pants so I could smuggle the contraband mail to my room.

As Nonna sat down with me, her eyes asked questions. She glanced at my hands on my lap. I brought them up above the table.

"Better than okay. Well, maybe just okay. Anthony finally wrote back to me."

"And what did he say?"

"Not much. He told me a little about the Air Force, but it was a short letter. I hope he'll write more next time."

Inevitably, he would write me again. How would I intercept the mail before my parents got to it?

Watching Nonna's sweet, inquisitive face, I got an idea. School started next week. The mail came during the day, which meant I wouldn't be there to screen it. If my parents saw a letter from the Air Force, they'd surely be suspicious. I'd rather not have them asking questions. "Nonna, do you think you could do me a huge favor?"

She raised her eyebrows.

"I need you to check the mail for me when I'm at school. If anything comes with my name on it, will you pull it out of the mail pile and hide it for me? In the wooden nightstand?"

After a moment, Nonna looked up and nodded. "I am happy to help you on your mission of love," she said.

"Thank you, Nonna, you are totally the best!" I said. I loved my Nonna so much, I jumped up to kiss her cheek. Then I skipped off to grab some paper to write back to Anthony. I sent my response the very same day.

~~~~~

One crisp morning in November, we all sat in PJs and bath robes at the breakfast table, our morning hair messy. We blinked the sleep out of our eyes as we ate scrambled eggs and toast.

My mom cleared her throat. "I have some special news. We're going to have a new baby in the family."

"A gift from the Lord," my dad said, tears springing to his eyes. He leaned over and kissed her as if they were still young and newly in love, as if it were her first baby, not her fourth. My parents were so sweet with each other, it warmed my heart.

I was sixteen and about to have a new brother or sister? I couldn't wait.

"*Auguroni alla nuova arrivata!*"

"*Congratulazioni!*"

The news came with a move to a bigger house. My parents saved enough money for us to move out of the three-family house and into an entire home of our own. I guess recycling all those plastic bags paid off!

In the new giant house, Nancy, Vinny, and I each had a room to ourselves, and Baby Teresa would have her own nursery too.

Finally, a room of my own. I plastered the walls with posters of my favorite pop stars and movies and I played my cassette tapes as loud as I wanted, whenever I wanted, and danced around with nobody telling me to stop.

I brought the antique nightstand from Italy into the new house and placed it by my bed in my new room, right where it belonged. The little Christmas angel my dad had given me and my prized yellow banana phone sat on its surface, right by my head.

Nonna continued to be my best friend. In the new house, we had an entire guest suite over the garage, so Nonna got her own room too. We spent many hours in her suite, talking about life or, now that I had my driver's license, in my car.

Her favorite place was McDonald's. She might have liked it even more than I did.

We always told my mother we were going for a drive around the neighborhood, then we got into my blue Chevy Camaro and drove to Micky D's for chicken nuggets and apple "pine" as Nonna called it.

"It's *pie*, Nonna. No 'N.'" I always laughed. She never got it.

Over the next two years, I sent Anthony many letters. I'd say for about every five I sent, I received one back.

Can you blame me? I was in high school and nobody was like my Anthony.

Sure, I still had Carla and Tanya and all my other friends, but my heart remained fixed. Every time I uncapped the pen to write to him, I felt more sure that my words would reach him, that my love would reach him, that he would finally understand or decide that we were right for each other. The idea of him, of our future, of our beautiful life together kept me going forward.

Nonna, of course, became my biggest ally and confidante. Every day, when I came home from school, I found her sitting at the table, a stack of mail splayed in the middle. She'd catch my eye and wink, even if my parents or siblings were in the room. That's how I knew. Sure enough, there'd be a letter waiting in my nightstand. *Thanks, Nonna.*

And then there was Teresa.

Teresa and I are, as my father says, cut from the same cloth. Until she was born, I was the only black sheep of the family. Nancy continued to be more Italian than American—conservative, quiet, and obsessed with Italian language and culture. She read huge novels and books of ancient poetry still in their original Italian. Vinny could do no wrong, even if he did like American culture almost as much as I did. He loved Bruce Springsteen. I, on the other hand, always felt like the odd one out, the one who wanted to stay out late, see my friends. The social butterfly of the family, if you will. Of course, I spoke Italian at home, just like everybody else, and I loved our food and family traditions.

Family is my life. But my heart wanted to experience other things too. And I felt I had no choice but to follow where it led. And it led to Anthony.

When Anthony left, it was as if the path had dropped off the edge of a cliff. An entire ocean separated us.

I began to lose hope. We kept in touch during the years he was in the military, and we remained fairly loyal friends. We were never more than that anyway. I guess you can't miss what you never had.

After three years of fewer and fewer letters, I sensed we were growing more distant. Toward the end, my letters were as sparse as the plain white paper on which I scribbled the sentences. I stopped drawing hearts and stars on my perfumed stationery. They were probably boring to him, now more than ever. After several months had passed with no response since my last postmarked letter, I put the pen and paper away.

Feeling more and more like the girl from Nonna's story, I told myself it was time to move on. It was time I invested in my real life, not my fantasies. It killed me to do it, but I had to get real and face the evidence.

After I graduated high school, I started working at the local hospital. I began in the x-ray department, and then moved to the switchboard. Two women, Joan and Cathy, assisted me in fielding hundreds of calls per day.

"St. Mary's Hospital. Where may I direct your call?"

"I'm looking for my friend who worked at your hospital," the voice on the line said. "The last I knew, she worked in x-ray."

"Maybe I can help you," I said. "I worked in x-ray not long ago. What's her name?"

"Mary Lou."

Dead silence on the phone.

"Anthony? Is that you?"

"It is." I could hear the smile in his voice.

"It's been so long. It's so good to hear from you." As soon as I recognized him on the phone, the old familiar fluttery feeling and pounding heartrate were back.

We chatted for only a minute, since I was at work. I gave him my home number.

"Your address changed," he said.

He told me he was stationed in Germany but was coming home in September for ten days and would like to get together.

I couldn't believe Anthony had re-entered my life. Why did he want to see me? I stifled a nervous flutter in my stomach, but finally, after years of practice, was able to play it cool. "Give me a call when you get to Connecticut."

I remember hanging up that phone and saying to myself, "Wow, why would he want to see me?" To be safe, I went on assuming that when he did get here, he would be busy with his family and forget to call, or would leave my number in Germany.

Either way, I was elated that he even took the time to remember I was his friend.

September finally came. I hadn't forgotten that I was expecting a phone call, although I did coach myself to control my anticipation. I talked myself out of holding my phone at the stroke of midnight on the first of September. It wasn't as if he was going to call the exact moment August became September.

Within a week or so ... Okay, within six and a half days—of course I kept track—I heard from Anthony. He called me when he reached the States.

I couldn't wait to see him. Would things still feel the same?

Anthony asked if I wanted to go out to dinner and possibly catch a movie.

"Sounds great." I tried to sound as casual as my emotions would allow. This was no big deal, I reminded myself. Just old friends, getting together to catch up. That was all. Not only had he referred to me as a "friend" since he first became aware of our mutual existence, but he also signed his sporadic letters that way. Who was I to think an international plane ride may have changed his mind?

Regardless, I would soon find out. We scheduled plans for Friday.

I don't remember going to work that day. All I could think about was Anthony. I was sixteen all over again, even though some things had changed.

After work, I got into my blue Camaro. That was one new development—now I had my own car, and I loved driving. It had been the best eighteenth birthday present ever from my parents. As I drove to meet him, I couldn't help but laugh at this major change in my relationship with Anthony. Maybe I should call Carla. I hadn't heard from her in a few months, and she'd be thrilled at my news.

But really, what were Anthony and I going to talk about? Should we pick out the names for our children? Would we live in the same town as my parents? And then, of course, there was the matter of my family.

I turned the key in the ignition and shifted into drive. Trying to relax, I rolled down the windows and turned on the radio. Pedal to the metal, I sang along at the top of my lungs to "Ice, Ice, Baby."

Okay, that was better. I glanced in the rearview mirror. My hair looked great, my eye makeup looked perfect, even after a full day's work. Then, I imagined the fairytale ending—the one in which I'd ring his doorbell, he'd answer, and we'd gaze at each other like the long-lost lovers we were. Then we'd confess how much we'd missed each other, how much there is between us. Maybe this would bring the kiss I'd been waiting for. My first kiss.

Flashing red and blue lights behind me snapped me out of my zone. It took me a minute to realize the cop was pulling me over.

Great, now I'd probably be arrested for running from the police, or at least get a ticket for my initial failure to stop. My very first ticket. Perfect.

Before the officer even got out of his cruiser, I contemplated how—if this ticket affected my insurance—I was going to explain it to my father. So much for driving and singing to kill my nerves.

Luck was on my side that day. The officer let me off with a warning. I'd been going sixty in a forty-five. Oops.

I was full of nerves for the rest of the ride. I drove exactly the speed limit, in case more police had decided to lurk around the area. The closer I got to Anthony's street, the more I started to panic. Was this a good idea?

I parked on the street in front of his yellow ranch-style house. Teetering up the manicured walkway, struggling to keep my balance in my four-inch heels, I finally reached the large, painted front door. As I rang the bell, I am pretty sure that I had either a silent panic attack or a mini-stroke.

When the door swung open, I thought I might have died. But I knew I was still alive because my heart was beating so fast and so hard, he must have felt it from the doorway. For the first time in years, I was looking at him, and he was looking back at me, even more handsome than I remembered.

I imagine my nervousness was palpable, like a physical force radiating from my body.

What surprised me was that he seemed to reciprocate the same tension.

His deep brown eyes intensified, and he hesitated. Then he pulled me into a hug. "I have been gone too long."

He smelled amazing. That Egyptian Musk oil brought me right back to his locker, it still made me sway even though both feet were firmly planted. But even more, as he held me, I felt as if I were the one coming home, the one graced with an answered prayer.

When he pulled away, the heat remained in his eyes. But although my arms were empty, I didn't feel the loss. I knew somehow they'd hold him again. Soon. Often.

"Should we get something to eat?" Anthony asked.

Was this a date? Going out to dinner together, just us two? This had never happened before. But we were both older now, and mature adults could go out to dinner together even if they weren't involved. Still, I hoped it was a date.

He suggested somewhere right in town, mere blocks from my father's garage.

For an instant, I froze.

"How about Bianchi's in New Haven instead? It's a sweet little Italian place, although the food isn't as good as my mom's cooking." And it was about an hour from my house. No way would we run into anyone who knew my family.

At dinner, we talked about my job at the hospital and his in the Air Force.

"Do you still talk to your old friends?" he asked. "Carla and Samantha and Julia?"

"Not much. Nothing ever happened, we just kind of ..."

"Drifted apart," Anthony finished for me. He smiled softly, more to himself than to me.

I twirled my spaghetti around my fork. "What has the Air Force been like?"

He took a sip of his seltzer. I wasn't old enough to drink wine at the restaurant yet so, to be polite, he didn't order any alcohol either. "Amazing. I've been stationed in Germany, and I've traveled all around Europe. The training and work part is hard, and I don't like it as much as I thought I might. But we get the weekends off, and my buddies and I try to go somewhere new every chance we get."

I quickly remarked, "I love going to Italy, my whole family is originally from there."

"You know, in all that time we hung out, we never went to each other's houses," he mused. "We never met each other's families."

"Except for my sister Nancy."

He leaned toward me and the empty bread basket. "Tell me about your family."

Oh, brother.

"Well, they're nuts, but I love them. Mom and dad were born in Italy, so they're more Italian than American. At home, we basically act as if we still live in Italy. Speaking Italian, growing our own vegetables in the backyard, making our own tomato sauce, sausage, wine ..." He might as well know the rest. "They're also very religious.

We go to church every weekend without fail. Our house is decorated like a church. My dad prays at least five times a day, maybe more."

I glanced at Anthony. Was he freaked out yet?

"Sounds like a good man." His voice didn't change, didn't turn mocking or sarcastic as I might have feared. "I like church. I'm a Christian."

Anthony liked church? A lightbulb went off in my head. Maybe my dad would like him more than I initially thought. "Is your family religious too?"

He shrugged. "Pretty religious, I'd say. I grew up going to church. My mom always liked us to go."

"Are you Catholic?"

"Protestant."

Oh boy. That's going to be yet another whole other issue with my parents.

After dinner, we decided to go to a movie. The only theatre playing anything good was the one in my hometown. As I pulled into the parking lot, I scanned the area in case any of my dad's friends were in town.

I started across the parking lot at a near-jog. Anthony immediately caught up and then kept up. What was I thinking? Did I want someone to see me? Did I want to get caught?

I blinked and shook it off. I glanced over at Anthony, walking beside me. And in that moment, I didn't care if anyone saw us. I was with him, and I was happy. We weren't holding hands, and I hadn't taken his arm. Nothing about us would indicate a romance. Still, if we met up with anyone who knew me, all they'd see was Tony's daughter out with a black guy.

I decided to put it out of my mind.

Strangely enough, the movie playing was Jungle Fever. When it was over, I drove him back to his place.

Sitting in my car, the darkness broken only by the lights of the dash and street lights outside, we said goodbye.

There was a moment. A beat of tension. We angled toward each other, our eyes met. I couldn't look away from his mouth.

"Thanks for a great night, Mar," he said, reaching over to close the space. He wrapped an arm around my neck. The most awkward hug ever.

"Yup, thanks," I said, patting his back, my arm at a strange angle. "I had a great time too. It's good to see you again." With my eyes, I urged him to reconsider a goodnight kiss.

He looked out the window in silence for a moment.

When he turned back to me he said, "Want to get together again tomorrow?"

My heart soared almost as if he had kissed me.

"I would like that very much." I said it as coolly as I could, but I couldn't hide my smile.

This time we would spend the whole day together, if I could get off work. My co-worker had told me about a relaxing riverboat cruise an hour or so away. I mentioned the idea to Anthony, and he said it sounded like fun.

It seemed we would be spending more time together before he left, so I called my boss and asked him for the next two days off. Anthony had only three days left in Connecticut before his flight back to Germany. I wanted to spend as much time with him as possible.

The next morning, I picked him up at his house, just like the day before, and we drove an hour to the boat.

When we got to the river, the woman in the little ticket hut tipped her head forward, peering through her thick prescription glasses, and pointed to the boat. "You sure you want tickets for that boat?"

"It's the only one, right?" Anthony said.

"It's your money." She handed us our tickets, and off we went.

Once aboard, we discovered we were on a senior citizen cruise.

We passed waiters with trays full of glasses and tables piled with American food, but I didn't pay much attention to any of it. I was in my own little world. Until the ninety-year-old man started playing the banjo, we hadn't realized we were the youngest people on that boat and still would be if we added fifty years to our ages. We did have a great time, at least I did. We laughed a lot about the situation.

At the end of the day, we made plans to get together again.

"How about the amusement park tomorrow?" Anthony said with a sparkle in his eye. "Then maybe we'll be the oldest people there."

That night, as I drove home, I couldn't believe we'd be together three days in a row. Luther Vandross played on the radio, I reflected on how amazing the last two days had been. I still couldn't believe that, after two straight days together, he wanted to spend even more time with me.

Wow. Was this the start of something big?

I didn't want to mislead myself, and I didn't want more heartbreak. But here he was, the man I had dreamed of, yearned for all these years. And he wanted to spend time with me!

I needed to find out my blood type. Just in case they need that when we apply for our marriage license.

I couldn't get the notion out of my head that someday we would be more than friends. Our flirtation in high school had been light, minimal. He had never treated me as more than a friend, except for some of those letters, the ones he'd signed, "Love, Anthony."

Even if we were just friends now, I felt deep in my heart, my soul, that we would end up together. It's totally irrational, inexplicable, but that's love, isn't it? Who was I to deny it? I never stopped hoping.

In the two short days we spent together, he'd been the perfect gentleman, paying for dinner, the movie, and the senior citizen cruise, holding the door, opening my car door. But he'd never even held my hand. I needed to keep myself here on earth, but it was hard because I couldn't tell how much of the courtship was in my head and how much was real.

Was I confusing fantasy and reality?

But isn't that kind of what love is? A distortion of reality? A lens on normal life that makes everything rosy and sweet? I considered the juxtaposition of a realistic illusion.

Love, I figured, is the union of fairytale and reality. Love—at least as depicted in movies and literature—merges the two. But does that idea lead to unrealistic expectations? I thought back to the soap opera *Days of Our Lives*. How realistic was any of that? Not very. Was it possible, then, that the media sets men up for failure and women for disappointment? Perhaps men can't conceive of the concept of the fairytale. But then what do they base love on? How do they measure it? Is love the same to men as it is to women? Do men respond to the fairytale ideas of love in Disney classics, or to something else?

Was I wrong, or foolish, to expect fairytale love from a real-world man? Did he even love me? Each question in my mind led to countless more. Should I somehow sneak a copy of *Cinderella* into Anthony's luggage? Maybe I should make him a CD with subliminal messages, or in this case, a subliminal movie script? Life script?

My profound epiphany of love was getting me in way over my head. My head was actually starting to throb. Have movies led us to misinterpret the definition of romance? And if so, should I stop expecting my prince to show up and sweep me off my feet? Maybe it's Disney, maybe it's my parents' incredible relationship, but either way, I still thought I deserved that kind of love, that kind of relationship.

Hadn't the girl in Nonna's story suffered her whole life because she didn't pursue the love she wanted? That story was certainly no fairytale, but I took note of it, weighed the options, just as she must have done. *Everything in life is a trade-off.* Still, I wanted to choose my happy ending. His name was Anthony Knight, after all. A philosopher sat on one of my shoulders and a storybook prince on the other.

On Anthony's last day at home, we decided to go to Riverside Park.

"Want me to drive?" he said when I got to his house.

"Sure!" I knew he secretly just wanted to be behind the wheel in my Camaro. He opened the passenger door for me and then went around to the driver's side.

"How do you like it?"

He punched the engine up to seventy miles per hour as we merged onto the highway. He hooted in response. "You've got a sweet little ride here, Mar. She's got some pep!"

On the way we chatted and laughed, recalling high school memories. The dark rain clouds on the horizon didn't bother us. It was still blue skies overhead. Our reminiscing distracted us so much, we blew right by the exit.

"Shoot. Guess I'll have to get off and turn around." Moving into the right lane, he suddenly swerved and slammed on the brakes.

"Hey! Be careful!" I shouted.

"There was something in the road—"

I turned around and saw a mangled bicycle, a person underneath it.

"I think they're hurt." I suddenly felt as if I was back at the hospital.

He immediately pulled over to the shoulder and jumped out of the car.

I followed him over to the wreck. The bicycle looked bent in half. The person lying under the twisted frame lay limp, her helmeted head in a pool of blood on the pavement.

"Flag down a truck!" Anthony knelt beside the injured person.

As I diverted traffic around this poor girl, Anthony tried to calm her, telling her in his soothing voice that she'd be all right and that help was on the way.

Soon I was able to flag down a semi, and the driver radioed the ambulance. Anthony stayed with the girl until they came. I watched him tending her and realized what an incredibly good person Anthony was. Not only was he a natural leader, he also wanted to help people, and he was good at it.

Watching the EMTs load the girl into the ambulance, I realized intensity of the situation, and I think Anthony did too. In a haze, we walked back to my car, still parked on the shoulder.

Ever the gentleman, he walked with me to my side of the car, and we headed toward Riverside Park, but before we could reach it, he pulled onto a deserted side road and stopped under a canopy of oaks. Within moments, he'd gotten out, then he took my hand as I stepped out of the car. He kind of just stood there for a minute, frozen. I could feel his tension. He seemed on the edge of something, just about to move. And then, standing face to face, he leaned down, closing the difference between us, and kissed me.

The rain clouds had moved over us by now, and it was just starting to sprinkle, the clouds darkening the sky. But I swear, when his lips met mine, I saw sunshine.

We never did make it to the amusement park that day. It didn't matter. No rollercoaster on this planet could give me goose bumps like that.

It was just a quick kiss. The first one. My first.

I felt as if I were dreaming. The feeling of his lips on my lips was so much better than anything I'd imagined. It sent electric shock waves all through my body, out to my fingertips and toes. When he pulled away, all I wanted was to lean back in and stay that way forever.

He opened the car door the rest of the way, as if nothing had happened. I slid in, he slammed it shut. I melted into the seat.

"That was pretty intense," he said.

The kiss? The accident? The rain?

"Rain check on Riverside?" he asked. The rain was coming down harder now, pelting on the roof of the car.

I nodded, barely able to control my body.

We were quiet on the ride home. I replayed the events of the day over and over—the heart-stopping swerve, the biker, working together to help her. The way the rain started as soon as we got back to the car, and then, the kiss. The kiss I repeated most. The mood was strange, not exactly the romantic buildup I'd imagined. It had felt urgent. Necessary. The way he pressed his lips to mine, his body against me, felt so magnetic, uncontrollable. Even if it hadn't been prefaced with a dinner date, we'd kissed in the rain, and we'd tried to do good. That made it more special than anything I ever could have imagined.

When we pulled up in front of Anthony's house, he turned off the car. We sat in silence in the impending gloom of the rain storm.

He laid his hand on top of mine. "Drive me to the bus tomorrow?"

I barely slept that night, ecstatic with my secret. Maybe I should call Carla or at least share this with Nonna.

The next morning, I woke up early and got ready as if I were in high school again.

MaryLou Piland

The pouring rain didn't help my hair, but this was real life, not a fairytale. Anthony ran to my car, dripping wet, the water droplets standing out in his short hair. He looked so handsome in his military uniform. We didn't kiss hello.

The bus was late. We both huddled under a little black umbrella because the bus shelter was packed. My outfit was perfect, romantic, but not waterproof.

I loved that we were standing so close together. I knew it was to stay dry under the umbrella, but I hoped he just liked standing close to me too.

I knew we must have looked like a couple. I secretly wished for a photographer behind us or that the paparazzi had followed us for some reason. If I could've gotten that picture, I wouldn't just hang it. I'd blow it up, poster-size, and wallpaper my room with it.

The raindrops careened off the edge of the umbrella to land at our feet. With my arm wrapped around his, I wasn't ready for him to leave, or for these magical three days to end. Tears ran down my face, despite my best efforts.

He looked from my teary face to the approaching headlights. Wrong bus. It drove past the stop. Even though we stood right next to each other, I could already feel him pulling away.

A tap on my shoulder broke my flow of tears. I wiped my eyes, turned around, and tipped the umbrella to see who it was.

Oh, no.

Victorio and Christina, a sweet Italian couple, friends of my father.

The looks on their faces were almost comical: confused, maybe a touch concerned … bewildered. I could only imagine their thoughts. Their faces implied something along the lines of, "Why is she standing at the bus terminal, crying, under that little umbrella with this handsome stranger—who isn't Italian?"

Victorio finally spoke first. "How is your father? I ran into him at church on Sunday."

For one of the first and few times in my life, I was speechless---for a moment.

"Umm, he's good."

"Busy at the garage?"

"Always."

"Good to hear." He glanced around at the other passengers. "The bus isn't usually this late."

After ten minutes of, "I can't believe how hard it's raining" and "When is this bus coming?" the conversation eventually turned to my companion. Rudely, but intentionally, I had not introduced him.

"And who is this?" the old woman asked with far too much interest.

"Oh, this? Him? This is Anthony, an old friend from high school."

"You're in the military, I see." She gave me a slight, approving nod. I kept my eyes trained straight ahead, trying not to have a nervous breakdown.

Then they fired off more questions, like, "Where are you stationed?" "What do you do?" Finally, Christina got up the nerve to ask the dreaded question, "Is this your boyfriend?"

Before I could even process the thought, let alone reply, Anthony said, "Yes."

Wait. What? Did I hear that right?

I looked over to Anthony, who seemed totally confident and unperturbed.

Just then, the headlights of the bus appeared. As if it were moving in fast-forward, the bus pulled up, then Anthony, mid-conversation with Christina, hugged me goodbye, kissed my stunned cheek, and boarded the bus with his newfound friends. Christina and

Victorio waved goodbye through the window, and then turned back to Anthony to continue their conversation. I realized my mouth was hanging open. I closed it. I stood there under my umbrella in the rain, paralyzed.

The screaming inside my head was deafening. My lips stuck together as if someone had glued them shut. I couldn't move, even after the bus pulled away. I was stunned.

You decide now, in front of my father's friends, that you want to be my boyfriend? How was this going to work out? Had he been serious? He wanted to be my boyfriend? Now?

Since he was headed for Germany, I couldn't call him. I had no way to devise a plan with him to cover our bases, to cover up what just happened. I wiped my mascara off my cheeks and closed my eyes as hard as I could, trying to send him a message via mental telepathy. *Say you were joking, say you were joking, say you were just joking,* I urged in my mind until I reminded myself I didn't want it to be a joke.

Forget it. I'm dead.

The Bus Stop

Good news travels fast. Bad news travels faster.

I figured Anthony had a two-hour bus ride to the airport. I estimated that, in about two days, my life would be over. Christina or Victorio would call Dad. I hadn't felt this much anxiety since I got a detention for wearing the wrong color uniform shirt at Sacred Heart.

My father was going to kill me. I hoped we had a shovel at home so I could at least be buried in my own backyard.

Two days turned into two weeks, and I never heard anything about that rainy day at the bus stop. The holidays were approaching and I was steadily sending Anthony gifts and letters. I was finally his girlfriend—it was my job. He sent me cards and gifts back.

My Nonna continued to be the perfect accomplice. She was very smart, very spry, and a great informant. She was my partner in crime, my namesake, and the best grandmother anyone could ever ask for.

When I came home from work in the evenings, her raised eyebrows and the sweet look on her face always told me when she'd hidden a package. Sprinting up to my room, skipping every other step, I literally slid across the hardwood floor, stopping at my nightstand. Then I sat on the floor in my room, holding the package for a few minutes, trying to calm my breathing. I took my time and carefully peeled back the brown paper, my mind racing. What might it be? A new purse, a new jogging suit, a book, or quite possibly the engagement ring?

We had been dating almost three months now, and out of those three months we had spent a whole two and a half days together. I read the Happy Thanksgiving card to myself and then lifted the white tissue paper to reveal a new pink jogging suit. A German word was written in big white block letters down one of the pant legs. I noticed the size sticker. Medium.

I set the pants down and tweaked my mouth to the side in thought. Did he send this to the wrong girl, or was he trying to tell me something. Medium? Seriously?

I tried it on and checked myself out in the mirror. I looked and felt like an overstuffed bag of cotton candy. Still, Anthony had given it to me, so I loved it. Proud to display my new wares, I ran downstairs, where my mother was busy cooking dinner.

Scrunching up her nose while peering through the bottom of her glasses, chicken sizzling in the pan, she said, "Where did you get that?"

"What? Oh, this?" Like I didn't know what she was talking about, like she wouldn't notice all that pink. "Oh, at the mall."

"I can't make out what the big white letters say. Wees, Wis …" she said, trying hard to figure it out.

Second-guessing my decision to show off my new suit, I quickly said, "Wiesbaden."

"Wiesbaden, as in Wiesbaden, Germany? They sell pink jogging suits from Wiesbaden, Germany, in our mall?"

"Yes, why?"

"Because maybe you should go back and get a bigger size. This one seems a little tight."

A little tight. I ran upstairs and peeled the suit off my body before my father got home. Otherwise, I'd have to look for that shovel.

~~~~~

New Year's Eve has always been and will always be my least-favorite holiday. For as long as I can remember, I've cried every year when the ball dropped. Something always goes wrong. This year wouldn't be any different.

Actually, it would be worse.

My family always had a huge party with a different theme every year. It was 1990, going into 1991. This year we'd settled on a Hawaiian theme … Italian style. We decorated the huge basement of our new house with tons of streamers, beach chairs, and umbrellas. Huge sheets of brown and blue construction paper covered the walls to resemble the sand and the ocean, and then we painted in the sharks and starfish. I thought this would surely be an amazing New Year's Eve. I finally had Anthony in my life in a way that thrilled me, even if I couldn't share it with my family. So I was in a great mood this year.

The TV was on and the New Year's Eve countdown party had commenced. Dick Clark spoke into the microphone in Times Square, where a massive crowd gathered and bounced to live music on the stage in the background.

All of our cousins and friends were at our house, and our basement was loud, bustling, and packed. I only wished I could spend this night with Anthony. As I sipped my champagne, I talked to Nancy. I'd shared the new developments with her, and although she didn't exactly approve, she didn't exactly disapprove either.

"If only Anthony and I could share a New Year's kiss." I imagined us shouting the countdown together, bringing our love into the new year, sealing it with a kiss. Maybe he'd even propose on New Year's Eve …

"Yeah, but come on, Mar," Nancy said. "You could never bring him here. Everyone would say, 'Who's the black guy?'"

I looked around. Every single person in the basement was white and Italian. Half the room was speaking in Italian. If he were here, he'd stick out like a sore thumb.

"Yeah, maybe." I refused to concede to her completely.

Just then, my cousin Victor came pounding down the basement stairs, Lupo close behind, tail wagging. Dressed in a grass skirt with a purple lei around his neck and a black Hawaiian wig on his head, Victor scanned the room until he found me. As he drew closer, I could see the confused look in his eyes, even through his hula-girl costume. He whispered in my ear that he had been upstairs and heard the phone ringing in my room. "I hope you don't mind. I picked it up. There's a guy on the other end, looking for you."

"On the phone for me?"

"He said his name is Anthony."

He'd called! I took off, never responding to Victor, racing upstairs at full speed.

How romantic …

My feet couldn't keep up with my brain as I ran up the two flights of stairs. Breathlessly, I picked up my phone. "Hello, hello, Anthony?" I managed to squeak out while trying to catch my breath at the same time.

"Hey, how is your night going?" He sounded subdued.

"Okay, but I wish you were here. I miss you."

"Well," he said, his voice seeming to drawl, "I am—"

"You're in the States?" I couldn't take the suspense. "You're coming home soon? No, wait, you're already here? Please, please tell me you're right outside my door. I would die. Tell me quick. I can hardly wait!"

I waited for him to fill the empty space on the line, but he didn't.

"Anthony? You there?"

"I have to tell you something—"

"I have to tell you something first," I burst out. "I love you. I love you. I've loved you since the first time I laid my eyes on you."

The pause seemed like eternity.

"I'm seeing someone else. I just wanted to be honest with you …" He kept talking.

I stopped listening.

At first I needed a second to process what he'd just said. The words "seeing," "someone" and "else."

My anger began at irate, increased to incensed, and then finally escalated to downright fury.

He was still talking. Why was he still talking?

My words bubbled up out of me like hot lava. "Do me a favor, Mr. Anthony Knight. Do not call me, ever again. Do not look me up when you come home. Do not think one more minute that I would waste one more second thinking about you."

Click. Done. My heart pounded. My hands trembled. I sat for a minute, stunned.

I dragged myself downstairs, too shocked even to shed a tear. I also could not let my family see how upset I was because, as far as they knew, I didn't even have a boyfriend.

Suddenly everything looked different. Even Don Ho's song, "Tiny Bubbles" seemed to take on a sharply distinctive meaning. I was not happy, I was not feeling fine, and I didn't want to toast anyone.

I sat on the nearest folding metal chair, and my mom set Teresa in my lap. Surrounded by my family's happy faces, everyone singing, drinking and dancing, I felt more out of place than I would have if Anthony were actually here. Thinking his name sent a pang of twin anger and sadness shooting down to my belly. I blinked back the tears that unwelcomely welled in my eyes.

The fact that he decided to call me on New Year's Eve irritated me even more. What about the cards he'd sent me, the letters, the pink jogging suit? And all the presents I had just sent him? Now he'd be getting a million more loving cards and trinkets from me in the mail. Great.

Someone handed me a big glass of champagne. I gulped it down.

This was it. No more letting Anthony stomp all over my heart. I needed to be strong now and close my heart to him once and for all. I was the only one who could let him keep taking it and breaking it. I had no one to blame but myself.

I thought back to all the ups and downs, all the times in high school under the bleachers, where all the seniors went to make out. He'd leaned in so close as if to kiss me, only to turn away at the last second, or ask me some stupid question about Jell-O or the dance. And then our reunion, our amazing dates and the bicycle accident and seeing Christina and Victorio at the bus stop … I didn't understand. Did those things mean nothing to him?

It was time to drop the ball.

The room started the countdown chant. "Ten, nine, eight …"

Brushing back my sister's silky hair, I decided this new year would be the best year of my life. I promised myself never to mutter his horrible name again. It was time, I coached myself through my tears, to stand on my own. As far as I was concerned, it would be,

"Anthony who?" from now until the end of time.

The next day, I grabbed a trash bag from under the sink and took it up to my room. Meticulously I went around my room, through my drawers and book shelves, and collected every single thing Anthony had ever given me--everything that reminded me of him. In went the pink track suit. In went all the cards and letters. In went the shirt I'd worn the day of our first kiss. I almost threw away my banana phone but decided against it. Every time I looked at it, I thought of that terrible phone call, the heaviness in his voice, the time it took for those words to make their way across the phone lines all the way from Germany.

Stone-faced, I hung the black garbage bag over my shoulder like a sad Santa's sack of toys and carried it out the front door. I'd gotten up early and everyone else was still asleep. Good thing, or my parents would have been pretty suspicious.

What's in the bag, Mar? I could imagine my mother asking, just as she'd asked about the sweat suit.

I stood in front of the trash cans at the curb and let the bag drop to the concrete. As I stared into the empty bin, hollowness sunk into me.

Letting out a sigh, I swung the bag over my shoulder again and walked back to the house. Instead of going up to my room, I climbed the stairs to Nonna's suite over the garage and knocked at her door.

Nonna opened, eyes wide. "Are you okay?"

I burst into tears and dropped the bag. "You don't have to be the mail police anymore, Nonna."

"Come in, come in here." She ushered me in, her hand on my back. I dragged the bag along, and then I sat down on the couch, the trash bag beside me.

"Can I leave this stuff up here somewhere, Nonna?" With the

back of my hand, I wiped the tears off my face.

"Of course," Nonna frowned, concerned. "What is it? What happened?"

I told her what Anthony had said on the phone.

"Oh, dear," she said, putting a hand to her own heart, as if she could feel how broken mine was. She reached over and patted my knee.

"I can't bring myself to throw this stuff away. All the things that remind me of him," I finally managed.

She leaned in close. "I have just the place for it."

She opened her closet door and placed the trash bag of Anthony items inside.

"It will be safe here, if you ever want it." Back in the sitting room, Nonna placed a hot cup of tea on the coffee table in front of me. When she sat down next to me, I collapsed into her for a hug.

And said a silent *goodbye* to my romance.

~~~~~

I threw myself into work at the hospital, showing up early and staying late. I helped my parents with chores around the house as always. Life went on.

Would he try to call again, or call my work as he had last time? But the days passed after the new year, and then weeks, and then months. I left him behind.

I put all my thoughts of marriage and children and houses and dishware aside and started thinking just about me.

All through high school, I'd thought about how to get Anthony to like me. How to dress, how to look, how to act, what to say—all of it was crafted for him. Not to say I hadn't been "myself" in high school, but I started to realize all the things I could do with myself, for myself. The boiled zucchini diet returned, but this time it wasn't to impress. I started going to the gym four times a week after work. My friend Dave and I went together. We held each other's feet when we did sit-ups and pushed and pulled on the elliptical machines together. The weight started sloughing off me like dead skin. I felt light. I felt happy. I felt popular. I loved my coworkers and we even started going out for drinks and dinners together after work.

And then there was Teresa.

My baby sister and I were best friends from the second we met. My mom, cradling her in the hospital room, had said, "Meet your new sister."

Teresa's little eyes met mine and instantly, my whole world filled with color.

I spent as much time as I could with Teresa. The first thing I did when I woke up was tell her good morning and kiss her tummy. She laughed and grabbed for me. I swear she was my baby, not my mom's. I loved feeding her from the bottle, pushing her around in her stroller, taking her to the park or the playground, even changing her diaper. I leapt at any chance to take care of her, and Mom never complained.

My life felt full. Bright. It took a few months, but I bounced back and felt better than ever. I had crushes, and people had crushes on me, but nothing compared to my first love. I tried not to think too much about it, tried not to let it bother me. I was, after all, happy. I loved my family. I loved my job. I loved my life. Even though I continued to be somewhat of a black sheep in my household, my family still showered me, and each other, with love in all the ways we knew how. I felt grateful to have so much love in my life.

~~~~~

At work one morning the next spring, the switchboard buzzer went off. My co-worker buzzed open the door. I continued mindlessly scrolling through the database of patient names until footsteps echoed off the linoleum floor. I looked up.

The sudden collision of emotion I felt as Anthony approached my desk was unbearable. It was April 20, 1991. I hadn't heard from him since New Year's Eve, five months earlier. I didn't know if my heart was beating fast because this gorgeous man was standing in front of me or if my blood pressure had gone up because I remembered I was supposed to be mad at him. In a split second, I knew it was the latter. I felt my face transform from awestruck to neutral, cold. Closed.

He stood in front of me, more muscular and handsome than before, in a kind of defiant stance. Shouldn't he be hanging his head? Cowering like a bad puppy? Wasn't he here to apologize?

"Wow, Mar," he beamed, strutting toward my desk, arms spread wide, as if he were making some kind of grand entrance. "You look amazing."

He did too, but I wasn't about to say it.

"Thanks," I said. The confidence that swamped me, hearing those words, was unstoppable. "I've been going to the gym."

"I can see that," he said, leaning on my desk.

I couldn't believe that, despite everything he'd put me through, my heart still wanted him. My brain definitely didn't. So it had to be my heart. Or my body. "What are you doing here?"

"Well, I decided that, after six years of serving our country, I didn't want to re-enlist. I moved back home with my mom, and now I'm looking for a job. I'm here to apply. Isn't that great news?"

"Sure." I remembered when he told me he "didn't know where he'd be in five years," and yet here he was, back where he'd started. I wasn't about to wish him luck.

"Seriously. You look great. Better than ever. What gym do you go to?"

I could feel the games starting and, despite knowing better, I played along. But I kept my guard up this time. The guards, the moat, and the attack dogs.

"It's in Waterbury. The one on Lakewood, near my father's garage."

"Interesting." He turned to my co-workers. "Could I borrow her for a minute?"

My supervisor shrugged. It was okay.

Walking out to his car with him, I kept my answers short. I tried to, anyway.

"How have you been?"

"Great. I have a new baby sister," I said.

He stopped and looked at me as if I'd somehow changed in the time he'd been gone. "That's wonderful news, Mar. Congratulations. I want to meet her."

Yeah, right. "Are you home by yourself?" I asked, wondering about *her*.

"Yeah, who else would there be?" He flirted as if I'd been the only one on his mind all along. Maybe I had. Did this mean they had broken up? Could he have been thinking of me the whole time? No. I refused to let myself get starry-eyed.

He was merely playing with me. Irritated by his answer, I was eager to finish the conversation. "Thanks for coming by."

I extended my hand for a cordial handshake. He flipped my hand and leaned forward to kiss the top of it while gazing up at me. *"Ciao, bella."*

I smiled and rolled my eyes. Couldn't help it.

As I walked back up the steps, I dared myself not to turn around. *One more step. You can do it.* The door swung open … and I was in. Home free.

I was, for once in my life, so proud of myself.

Despite the flutter of excitement the kiss caused, I did not forget my irritation. Who did he think he was? Did he think I should wait breathlessly for his homecoming and forget everything he's ever done to me? That we would just pick up where we left off? Strolling back to the basement to the switchboard, savoring every second of that entire encounter—my feet didn't touch the ground.

Then I remembered New Year's Eve, and I pulled myself right back down to reality.

About an hour later, the switchboard buzzer went off again. It was Anthony, this time with a dozen red roses. My jaw dropped. Now he decides to be a prince?

"I promise I won't come back to see you again today if you promise to go to the gym with me after work."

"Today?" I managed, my head spinning.

"Why not?"

"But you don't—"

He raised a finger then reached into his pocket and pulled out his newly laminated gym card.

"Isn't this great? Now we can work out together." Stepping back, he looked me in the eye with that confidence, that command. "I'll meet you at the gym at 4:30."

I shook my head, wanting to say yes but knowing I should say no.

"Ciao, bella." He back-pedaled away from me and walked out the door.

Wow, maybe he is Italian ... I'd never thought to ask.

Did he really think that in one day he could come waltzing back into my life, sweep me off my feet, and make me forget the years of torture? Who did he think he was? Well, he knew who he was. He was Anthony Knight. Just as charming, confident, and handsome as he'd always been, maybe more now than ever. But this time, even this knight couldn't breach the wall I'd built around my heart.

When it was time to clock out of my shift, I intentionally left the flowers at the switchboard. My co-worker Casey gaped at me as if I was insane. "You're not going to take those?"

"I couldn't hold an arrangement that big while I'm driving." It was a lame excuse, and I knew it.

She raised her eyebrows.

"I'll just leave them here. They bring some color to the office, don't you think?"

She continued to gape like a fish out of water, and then closed up her jaw and shook her head.

I wanted to take them home. I really did. They were beautiful. But I distinctly remembered the last time I tried to pull a fast one on my mother with my tight pink Germany jogging suit. So this time I listened to my instincts and decided we would all enjoy the flowers at work, so nobody would ask questions at home.

I closed the door of my car, then I sat for a second. Should I go to the gym or not? My gym bag was in the car, but I didn't want to make it so easy for Anthony. Did I really want to run back to him the second he called? If he wanted me back, I was determined to make him work for it, as I'd worked for it since I was fourteen. I started the engine and drove off, straight past the turn to the gym.

The next day, Anthony showed up at the hospital, wanting to be buzzed into the switchboard room again.

"You heard back about the job so fast?" I asked as he approached.

"No. What happened to you yesterday?"

I took my time, shrugged, as if yesterday had been like any other day. I could practically see the sweat beading on his forehead. "I was tired after work, so I just went home."

His gaze moved over to the bouquet of roses, still sitting on the desk in their plastic wrap from the florist, a little wilted now. I had purposefully "forgotten" to bring in a vase. His eyes flicked from the bouquet to me. "I waited for you at the gym for an hour."

"I hope you still got your workout in." I said with the brightest fake smile I could muster.

"Come on, Mar."

"Could we talk later? I'm at work."

He left, and I immediately wished he hadn't. I went back to my typing.

That night I sat staring at my ringing banana phone. Somehow I knew it was Anthony. I finally picked up.

"I missed you yesterday," he said in a husky voice.

I steeled my heart against it.

"Get used to me being close to you. I accepted a job as a paramedic at your hospital." He hesitated. "I'll be at the gym by five tomorrow, Mar."

"Thanks for the heads-up." I hung up, half-satisfied and half-disgusted with myself. I hated these games.

I needed to take it easy. On *Days of Our Lives*, the women played it cool, kept a man guessing, played the cards close to their chests. I knew I had a good poker face because nobody could ever tell when I was lying. Still, I had the feeling I wouldn't be able to help but give myself away if I did that with Anthony.

The next day when I got to the gym at 4:55, I wondered if Anthony might deal it back to me and stand me up. I waited by the front desk, my heart beating faster and faster as the clock hands ticked closer to 5. I stopped breathing from approximately 5 to 5:02, until Anthony jogged up to the door. Breathing then resumed as usual.

"I'm not going away, Mar. So you might as well let me explain what happened."

"I know what happened. You broke up with me on New Year's

Eve."

"That's not the whole story—"

I turned away and headed for the stationary bike. What was I doing here with him? Sure, it had been my gym before he'd come home, but why had I caved and arrive when I knew he'd be here?

Anthony got on the treadmill. At the second row of machines, I pumped away at the handlebars, not caring about the sweat dripping down my face as if I'd been at it for five hours instead of five minutes. He jogged on the machine in front of me, his thick back muscles working under his thin shirt. The rhythm of his stride, the half glances back at me in the row behind, the way he kept wiping the sweat from his face—it all made me go weak at the knees. Watching him move, I couldn't help but wonder how he made it look so easy. His body seemed to be designed for it.

Snap out of it! I took a determined sip from my water bottle and kept going.

I didn't want to fantasize about him. I was afraid to let my mind go there. Afraid to forget what he'd done ...

I picked up my speed. Throughout our whole relationship, all the way back in high school, I'd wanted to get into shape for him. And now here I was, working out more, losing weight, thinner than ever. But not to get him back.

In those five months without contact, I'd tried to make myself happy. I ate better. I worked out. I spent time with my friends and, of course, lots of time with my family. Especially with Nonna. We'd passed countless hours sipping tea while she told me stories in her suite over the garage.

I'd dropped from a size fourteen to a size ten. I had to go out and buy new clothes. People noticed the change. Lots of guys asked me out, but I was trying to spend more time with Nonna.

Still, I felt more beautiful, more radiant, and more desirable than ever before.

Sweating on the bike, I realized I was giving Anthony the Disney princess version of myself, just as I expected him to be my Prince Charming. It was time to stop.

After our workouts and showers, we stopped at the local grocery. While he parked in a dark corner of the parking lot, I went in for a quart of spumoni and a pack of plastic spoons. Settling into the passenger side, I spread napkins on my lap and locked the doors. Nobody was leaving this car while the breakup still stood between us and there was ice cream left.

"I want to know what happened. Why did you say you were my boyfriend at the train station and then break up with me? And who's the other woman?" Might as well get everything out in the open, before the spumoni could melt.

He let out a groan as if he'd seen this coming.

"I started seeing her a few months before I came home. I didn't like Germany, didn't enjoy my work, so I was in bad shape. One of the guys fixed me up with her, and I went along with it out of homesickness." Anthony watched me open the container and spoon out an enormous bite. "She always invited me to her parents' house, where she lived, and I went just to have a real home for a few hours a couple times a week. I know I shouldn't have used her that way, but pretty soon, she started thinking we were a real couple—and so did her parents. Then it got bigger and bigger until they expected us to get engaged. I couldn't let her mom and dad down."

"But you did let them down. And you let her down." I licked my spoon and pointed it at him. "And me."

He pulled a spoon from the box and stuck it into the pistachio stripe of spumoni. "Believe me, I know. But as soon as I got home on leave, everything reminded me of you. And when I went back to Germany, I didn't know what to do. The best part of my leave was being with you. But her parents had become like family to me, and I owed them a lot."

I pulled a drippy spoonful of spumoni from the carton and admitted that my heart was thawing along with my dessert. How could I fault him for not wanting to break this couple's daughter's heart?

And how could I fault any woman for falling for my Anthony?

I lifted the melting cherry goodness to my mouth, then slipped it into his instead.

~~~~~

Anthony called me at the switchboard the next day at work. "Can you stop by my place before the gym today?"

We hadn't even talked about going to the gym today. But he wanted to see me—again. His house was out of my way from the gym, but only a few minutes. "I'll come over." I kept my tone chilly.

It was a gloomy, rainy day. The weather seemed to match my feelings. Would this ever go anywhere, or was I being delusional, and was he feeding into it, playing along?

As soon as I pulled up next to his Honda Civic in the driveway, he showed up at the door. Had he been watching for my headlights?

We made eye contact through the rain-streaked windshield. I jerked my head, gesturing for him to come over. If he wanted me back in his life, he was going to have to work for my forgiveness, my affection, and my heart—the heart I had tried to close to him every day for the past five months.

Without an umbrella, he stepped out into the drizzle. He opened my door and helped me from the car. His touch was light, sweet, supportive, as if I were something precious, something delicate.

We stood facing one another in complete silence, the drizzle leaving water droplets in our hair. What was happening here? Did he just want a ride to the gym? Were we not going inside? I maintained my space, my cool, and waited for him to do or say something. I thought he would invite me in, but he just stood there.

The intensity in his eyes heated the cold shoulder between us. I had been eager to follow my better judgment—my heart distanced and guarded. But the longer he held my gaze, the less sure I felt of this security system I had built around my heart. His eyes on my eyes. I remembered all those times I'd wanted him to lean in and kiss me under the bleachers, gazing at each other, just like this. The suspense was getting to me. The heat and the tension palpably rose.

As I began to lose feeling in the lower part of my body, I imagined it would only be seconds before the passion electrocuted my upper half—my heart.

He leaned closer. "You can tell me anything. I'm here for you now."

His invitation to safety seemed genuine. I fought against my naivety, which wanted to believe him. I was mad at him. I hated him. Before more words could escape either of our mouths, he moved in closer yet.

His hesitation excited me. One, two, three, four … By the fifth count, his knuckles touched the back of my hands. He seemed to contemplate kissing me. I couldn't promise not to slap him if he did. I also couldn't promise I didn't want him to try.

After what felt like a ten-minute tease, he finally grasped my hand, his movements tight and aggressive. He whispered soft in my ear and I instinctively tightened my end of our locked hands. "I promise I will never hurt you again."

He pulled me close by the small of my back. His eyes guided my body in his direction.

I was losing my control.

His fingertips swept my hairline at the base of my neck. My

head and my body were in complete war. How could I believe him? I distanced my heart with every ounce of strength I could find, but it didn't work. Trying desperately to keep hold of any poise and eloquence I had left, I relentlessly battled my temptation. What I knew to be an entire war zone between us had now closed to become more of a crack in concrete. My right hand gripped his left side at the belt loop of his jeans. My other grasped the chest of his V-neck and tugged him closer. His lips were so close to my neck, I could feel them, slightly pressing and slightly parted. He tugged with his teeth on the lobe of my ear just enough to make me jump.

He kissed slowly down my neck until his eyes opened in my direction. As he came up from my shoulder, I tightened my grip on his belt loop before releasing it to free my hand and acknowledge the rain. I ran my fingers through his short, wet hair and clenched what I could of it behind his ear. My hand steady along the side of his face, I leaned in to receive his kiss. I wrapped my right arm around the back of his neck and kissed him with more passion now than I had ever known.

Like the rain, the gentle pressure of his lips against mine began soft and passive. I could feel the pinch of my bite on his bottom lip. As his grip tightened below my waist and again around the back of my neck, he pulled me closer.

He kissed me harder. I gave in.

"I have to go," I blurted out.

"Call you later," he kissed me again on the mouth. I turned away and put my shaking fingers to my lips, hot and tingling.

By the time I made it back into my car, I was full-on sobbing.

I may not have worked out physically, but my heart sure had taken a run on the treadmill with a faster speed and higher incline than if I were on it myself. But I could get used to it.

I was sweating, out of breath, anxious, excited, and partially ashamed. What just happened? That was the last time I'd put myself in control of my own imaginary castle. Were the guards at lunch? Were the dogs out chasing the mailman? Who let the bridge down over the moat?

~~~~~

We started going to the gym every day after work for about a month. We'd work out and then spend equal time making out in my blue Camaro in front of his house. I think we both liked our routine. Sometimes we'd change it up and go out to dinner or a movie, but always a town or two over so no one would see us together. One of these days, we had to have a talk about that. But for now, we liked to explore new areas, new restaurants, although it was definitely a little exhausting, driving around so much.

Anthony called me at work on a Tuesday. "Want a ride?"

"I need to pick up my gym bag from the garage. Give me an extra fifteen minutes, and I'll meet you there." I'd been in such a rush for work this morning that I'd forgotten to throw my bag in the car. On the drive to the hospital, I'd called my dad and asked him to bring the bag with him to the garage.

"Can we go and pick up your clothes together? We can take your car."

I briefly imagined Anthony and my father staring each other down in the garage parking lot, like an old western. Each had a hand on his gun in the holster, just waiting for the right moment. I blinked. "I'll just meet you at the gym."

"Why? What's the big deal?"

"What don't you understand?" My heartbeat rose to my throat as my stomach flipped. "Once he meets you and understands what we're doing ..."

"Why? Because you're his little girl?"

He wasn't getting it. I was going to have to spell it out. "Because you're not Italian. Because you're black."

"Come on. It's the nineties," he finally said, his voice skeptical and high. "People aren't like that anymore."

"My parents are."

"I'll make them love me. Don't worry." Full of confidence, as usual.

When we approached the turn to my father's car garage, I briefly thought about throwing myself out of the car. But it wouldn't help. My father would recognize my car, and Anthony was in it.

Of course, my dad was in the garage when we pulled up. He stood up straight from the old Fiat he was inspecting, shielded his eyes with his hand, and then waved. He clearly hadn't seen Anthony at the wheel.

When we got out, my father strode over. Was he angry? How angry? I squinted to see his expression, but he looked fine, unbothered. After introductions, he stepped forward to shake Anthony's hand. I hid my horror as I watched their hands meet in a firm grasp.

"We were just on our way to the gym. Is my bag inside?"

"Behind the front desk."

"Thanks, Dad," I said as sweetly as I could. I gestured to Anthony to follow me into the office. I wasn't about to leave him out there alone to fend for himself. When we came back out, Dad had already returned to his work in the garage. I shouted goodbye, and we drove away, this time with me at the wheel.

"That went pretty well," Anthony said.

"I guess it did!" I still felt dazed. Part of me thought I might be dreaming. Was this real life? It felt as if we had already established the whole boyfriend-girlfriend thing and were just stopping by, no big deal. Had I made a way bigger deal out of this than it was? Had I merely imagined that my father would have such a big problem with me dating Anthony?

Nancy might have said differently. I guess I should have paid more attention to my father when he talked. Or had I heard only what I wanted to hear? A classic case of selective hearing … stereotypically a "man" thing, but I guess I'm a special kind of woman. Either way, I knew deep down that this wouldn't go unnoticed or ignored.

I tried to put it out of my mind during my workout. I watched Anthony, still in disbelief that he had wanted to meet my dad at all. He was serious. More serious than he'd ever been about me.

When I dropped him off at his house, he kissed me goodbye and said, "Call you later."

I'd put in a private line for my banana phone, and he had the number. We'd been in the habit of not only seeing each other every day but talking on the phone most nights, too.

Things had begun to work out for us, and it felt right.

The sun had just set and the last of its light stained the sky rosy pink, then faded into a deep, starry blue. My music blasted from the radio, and I sang along to it at the top of my lungs as I passed headlights on the road. Still, a flutter of nervousness built in my stomach. There was no way I'd avoid some kind of backlash. In our driveway, I put the car in park and took a deep breath. My good feelings faded as soon as I cut the engine and the music.

I stepped into my house. Although the temperature was in the seventies outside, my home was dark, frigid, empty. It was like December in June in there. Everyone should've been home by now. Usually, when I came home, I'd find my mom and Nonna preparing dinner or engaged in some kind of family activity in the living room. They all had to have heard the front door slam, but not one of my family members called out to me or even acknowledged my existence. Was anyone home? The house was never this quiet, especially with little Teresa running around.

I spotted the flickering light of a TV in the living room and hesitantly walked in.

I casually sat on the edge of the leather couch while my family watched their movie. No one spoke a word. I think if I were a ghost, they would have been more in tune with my presence in the room.

After nobody said anything for a few more minutes, I went into the kitchen, made myself a grilled cheese, and climbed the stairs to my room. I brushed off their iciness, telling myself I didn't care. I was in love. And nothing they could do or say, or not do or say, could get in the way.

The following morning, when I went downstairs for a quick breakfast, I stopped short. My father sat at the kitchen table, waiting for me. This wouldn't have been out of the ordinary on a Sunday, but this was 7 a.m. on a Tuesday.

Something was about to manifest itself.

Brace yourself. You're in the eye of the storm. There's no turning back.

"Have a seat," he said in his thick, broken English

I couldn't decide which chair of the five to sit in. I had to choose wisely. Man, if only this table was three feet wider and ten feet longer …

"Yes, Dad?" I said in what I hoped was a sweet, non-confrontational voice.

"The young man at the garage yesterday, the one who was driving your car—is he your boyfriend?"

Wow, nothing like making small talk.

"Yes." I answered so fast and firmly, it surprised me. Why hadn't I taken a moment to decide if I should lie or tell the truth? Before my brain could fully process what was happening, my heart and mouth teamed up to take the lead.

"I am so tired of sneaking around every time I want to see Anthony. It's exhausting to drive an hour to different restaurants and cinemas and constantly cover my tracks. I don't want to do that anymore. I just want to be open about it. It's not fair to him, me, or you," I said with a firm yet respectful attitude, probably offering more information than I should have. A moment of silence lingered between us. My heart pounded. My brain reeled, still trying to catch up and follow along.

"I understand." My father steepled his hands on the table, his disappointment seeping into his tone.

I started to feel better about my decision to have Anthony come with me to pick up my clothes. I got bolder, in my own head, anyway. Dad couldn't tell me what to do. Not anymore. If I was going to be in a serious relationship with the man I would probably marry, they needed to know about it. They needed to get with the program. Like Anthony said, it was the 90s, for crying out loud.

For a millisecond, I thought I was making progress. Maybe he could see beyond the color of Anthony's beautiful brown skin and had instead honed in on his heart and realized what a polite, caring, compassionate person he was. The day of our first kiss, with the bicyclist and the accident, flashed across my mind.

The next few moments of silence seemed endless. The clock ticked on the wall. Even the birds outside seemed to have stopped chirping. It was way too quiet.

He drew in a long, deep breath through his nose and exhaled ever so slowly through his mouth. The judge was about to rule. The verdict was in. Would he sentence me to life in this prison? Or would I get the death penalty?

"You know how we feel. It's up to you."

Up to me? An overwhelming, eerie sense of relief flooded my heart and then my eyes. I wiped away the tear before Dad could see it.

"It's him or your family," he said. "The decision is yours."

And then, in an instant, everything shattered. The judge had dropped the gavel and announced his ruling.

My heart fell to the floor. I felt cold. Numb.

I thought he'd said he understood. I thought for sure there would be a different outcome. My tears almost shifted from happy to sad, but then they abruptly dried up.

Adrenaline pumped through my body, and before I knew it, there my heart and mouth went again, running ahead of my brain before I could fully think anything through. He had made his choice. Now I had to make mine. It was my turn to strike. The gavel was in my hand.

I shot from my chair as if my seat were on fire. My legs burned. My heartbeat pounded in my ears.

"I choose Anthony. How do you like that? I bet that's not the answer you thought you were going to hear." I kept my expression and voice as neutral as possible, letting the words hang between us for a moment. "I will be out of your house by the end of the day."

I delivered the words as if it wasn't a problem. Easy-peasy, moving out was no big deal. *It doesn't bother me. Kick me out, see if I care. I have my love. I don't need you anymore.*

I didn't know where I'd go, but given this ultimatum …

It was an easy choice.

My father sat there, visibly allowing the words to sink in … going over each one in his mind. I watched him closely, expecting anger but seeing instead something else, something I couldn't quite identify. His elbow rested on the table, and his knuckles seemed to hold up his head. The glazed, blank stare on his face turned increasingly ominous. Slowly, he pushed his chair from the table and steadily stood up. Then he turned and walked out the door.

Bye Old House, Bye Old Life

The five-story ramp garage, where I parked, was unusually packed that day. I drove in what seemed like endless circles. How had I gotten here? My life had changed more in the past twenty-four hours than it had in the past twenty-one years.

"You're twenty minutes late," Garrett, my new supervisor, said as I rushed into the switchboard office. "You're never late. What's going on?"

"I'm going to try to tell you without breaking down," I said, my voice trembling, "but I can't promise."

"Try me. I've never seen you cry." He smirked, gesturing for me to follow him to his office.

This ought to be good. Did he think I was joking? I had just gotten kicked out of my house, and he wanted to joke about it? Men! Ugh.

As I recapped the morning's events, Garrett listened intently. "Your situation is worse than I thought. Take a personal day tomorrow if you need to. I'll help you any way I can."

It was nice to hear. But the day was long from over and the problem far from solved. I still had to tell Anthony. And find a new place to live.

The entire morning was eerily quiet. But in the afternoon, the switchboard lit up like the tree at Rockefeller Center. And not with emergency calls coming in. It was unnerving to hear my coworkers say, "Yes, she's here. No, she's fine—she's on another call." News sure did travel fast in my community.

Every time the phone rang, it seemed to be another concerned friend or family member trying to persuade me to change my mind, go home, and beg for forgiveness. I fielded quite a few and stayed strong—or stubborn, holding fast to my decision.

Until my father's friend, Vittorio called.

"First, I want to tell-a you that I no want to be involved, I no want to call you. But I no like-a the way you dad looked today. We've been friends since we landed together in this country. He's like a brother to me, and I tell-a you, he no looks so good today. He was walking on the highway, I ask-a him if he want a ride, but he said no. I felt so bad leaving him there. I called you mother as soon as I get home, but she no there either. I remembered when I see you and-a you boyfriend over there at the bus stop, you tell-a me you work at Santa Maria, so I call you. Anyway, I talk-a too long. You do me a favor, Mary Lou. You call your daddy and you tell him to call me. I worry about him, okay, okay? Goodbye."

He hung up the phone without letting me get one word in.

Stunned, I hung up too, lower than low. Lower than rock bottom. Nothing like Catholic guilt to make you doubt the most important choices of your life. So that's where my dad went when he left the house. He must've walked to work. On the highway?

I took a break in the nearest bathroom, sad gray tiles, brown stall doors, and contemplated my image in the mirror. Dad had given me a choice, but it didn't feel like it. "Him or us." No compromise offered. He hadn't even waited to get to know Anthony better. He didn't care. Hot tears pooled in my eyes.

I had waited for Anthony basically my whole life. My dad didn't know that, of course, but I couldn't let him take away my opportunity for love and the life I'd always dreamed of, just because Anthony wasn't his idea of the right man for me. I just couldn't. I would never forgive myself if I didn't give my shot with Anthony everything I had. Without meaning to, my dad had just pushed me deeper into my relationship and further from him.

I thought of my father's grim expression that morning, just before he left. I pictured him walking on the shoulder of the highway, hanging his head, waving Vittorio away. Why would he do that? It made me so sad. I knew, without a doubt, I had hurt him. I'd never wanted to do that. I just wanted to be in love and have my family's support. Were both so much to ask for? I splashed cool water on my face, took deep breaths, and went back out.

That day at work, between avoiding calls from Italian family and friends and answering actual work-related calls, I talked to Kristen, one of my co-workers and a dear friend, to ask if I could stay with her. I wasn't sure I wanted to go straight over to Anthony's. I still hadn't told him about the blowout, the ultimatum, my choice. Part of me felt nervous to tell him and wondered if he would steer me away.

You shouldn't have said that, I imagined him saying. *You belong with your crazy Italian family, Mary Lou. And if they won't have me, so be it. I'll just call my German girlfriend again.*

Please, no!

Getting into my car, I felt as if I had no pulse. I drove back to my house, possibly for the last time ever, to pack my things and say goodbye to my family.

The red brick colonial on the corner lot that had housed so many dinner guests and family get-togethers over the past six years was suddenly vacant. It was dusk and the lights were off. I cautiously exited my car and wondered if I had to give back my eighteenth-birthday present. I surveyed my surroundings like a seasoned Secret Service agent before I entered the house. It was intensely cold inside. Not so much the temperature, but the atmosphere felt inhospitable. I hadn't seen or heard anyone yet.

Carrying as many empty boxes from the garage as I could, I stumbled into the empty kitchen and proceeded up the stairs to my bedroom. Well, to what had been my bedroom, until this morning.

My former "sanctuary" was the room on the left at the top of the stairs. It was my sole obligation to keep it neat and organized. I took great pride in doing that. My bubblegum-pink room housed my most prized possessions. My Nonna's nightstand, a collection of cassette tapes, and perfumes, each in a beautiful unique bottle. Everything in my room had its own intended space.

I proudly displayed over four hundred cassette tapes, from soulful Luther Vandross to rapper Vanilla Ice. I had precisely the right array of music at my fingertips to get me through any mood on any given day. This held true for my perfume collection as well. The daily perfume of choice would depend on the attitude of the day. My usual pick was Anais-Anais, a light and refreshing flowery scent in an exquisitely frosted bottle.

I needed a more powerful aroma. The little bottle with the etched flowers wouldn't cut it. I needed something that would help me set the world on fire.

It was time to bring out the big guns. Holding a bottle in each hand, I puzzled over Obsession or Eternity, both poignant, strong, and intoxicating. After unsuccessful deliberation, I sprayed myself with both. I sat there, soaking in the powerful scent, reeling.

The sound of heavy footsteps stomping up the stairs snapped me out of my perfume trance. "Nancy, is that you?"

The door banged open. Nancy flew in, wearing a fierce scowl, her hair a mess. "How dare you, how dare you?" she yelled louder and louder.

"Are you angry because I am leaving or because I upset Dad?" I kept my voice calm.

"Both." Fuming in the entrance of my room, she whipped her head around until her eyes landed on the nearest, delicate thing—my tray of perfumes sitting on the bureau by the door.

She lunged for it.

"Don't!" I raced toward her.

She picked up the oval-shaped, mirrored perfume tray and hurled it with all her might across the room. The terrible sound of all that glass crashing into my perfectly painted pink walls was earth-shattering. The pieces of my perfume bottle collection tinkled to the ground, a sound too delicate for the brutal act. The pungent smell of sweet flowers meshing with citrus and spice hung like a dense, offensive cloud of smoke in my room.

My eyes were already swollen from crying, and now they burned and blurred from the dense perfume stench wafting over me. I cried harder.

I bent over, trying to salvage any fragments left on my hardwood floor. My tears made it hard to focus on the tiny shards of colored glass.

Nancy kept yelling at me in Italian. I was bringing shame to the family, to all Italians. How could I disobey Daddy like that? How could I be so rude and disrespectful? What kind of daughter was I?

I gave up collecting the shattered fragments of glass and sat limply on the floor.

Through all this commotion, I heard more footsteps pounding

up the stairs. With the perfume cloud starting to dissipate, my Aunt Evelina burst into the room. An adult, great. Here to interfere on my behalf, she's my mother's older sister and Nancy's godmother. I lifted my arm and extended my hand toward her for help.

Instead, the sting of her stern right hand smacked my face hard enough to knock me right over.

"If your selfishness kills my sister or my favorite niece, it will rest on your conscience. You are selfish. You are immature—a disgrace. How could you do this to me? To your family?"

My face stung as if a swarm of bees had attacked it. I could see the fragments of glass better, now that my face was parallel to the floor.

Aunt Evelina kept yelling at me, and I tried to tune it out, nose to nose with the floor.

And then I heard her voice.

"Basta! La shela sta!"

"Nonna," I cried. "Nonna, mia Nonna."

My eyes stayed trained on the wet, glass-covered floor as she argued with Nancy and Aunt Evelina until she badgered them out of the room and closed the door. Finally, there was quiet.

Nonna knelt beside me, casting me in her shadow under the overhead light. Her hand came to rest on my back.

"I heard what happened," she said softly in Italian. "I'm so sorry, Mary Lou."

She wrapped her arms around me and kissed the back of my head. She left the room and quickly returned with a dust pan and broom. In silence, we cleaned up the mess Nancy had made. I had nothing to say.

"This must be hard for you," she said.

I sat on my bed like a deflated balloon, trying to recover some strength before I set to work packing my life into brown cardboard boxes.

"Do you love him?"

I turned to meet her eye. "I always have."

"I know." She fell quiet for a moment. We sat holding hands on the bed, her palm papery and dry against mine.

Then she said, *"Ascolta al tuo cuore." Listen to your heart.* "I'm glad you stood up to your papa. It takes great strength, great bravery, to listen to your heart. You make me proud to be your Nonna."

Together Nonna and I put my clothes, my tapes, my posters, my shoes into box after box, and lugged my not-so-precious belongings down the stairs. Was any of it worth taking? If I had to leave with only one thing, it would be my favorite framed picture of me and my little sister, Teresa. I also made sure to grab the little angel statue my dad had given me. Holding her in my hands, taking in her serene face, I hoped somehow everything would blow over, that my dad would change his mind. I took with me this one little, happy piece of my dad. It pained me to leave the incredible antique nightstand with the "Q" and beautiful vine carvings. But I had to be realistic. There was no way I was dragging that thing anywhere again.

On my way out, I could hear my little sister talking to my mom in the next room.

"But Mommy," Teresa said in her sweet little voice. "Have you met him? How do you know you don't like him?"

The voice of a child also happened to be the voice of reason.

I heard the doorknob rattle. "Remember, your father told us to stay in my room. He told us to leave Mary Lou alone."

Maybe it was better this way.

Arms full, I stumbled out the front door, down the driveway. Dusk was settling over the neighborhood. The streetlights were coming on, people's houses lit with warm yellow light from the inside, shining out through the windows.

I glanced back at Nonna, standing in the doorway. She nodded, her smile encouraging me to be brave.

I firmly gripped the stuffed box and haphazardly shoved my boxes into the backseat of my car, slammed the door, and locked myself into safety. I let out a deep sigh. All I wanted to do was to get to Kristen's house.

I started the car and was about to throw it into reverse when I saw my godfather, Uncle Dominic, march across the lawn. He always seemed to have on a uniform: white tank top, too-short blue shorts, and knee-high tube socks with Birkenstocks.

Finally, someone else who cared. Someone on my side. Someone who loved me.

When he got to the car, he tapped hard on the window. A cold feeling started in my stomach. I rolled down the window.

He lifted his shirt, pointed to the gun in his waistband. "Listen carefully. If you bring shame to me or my family, I will shoot you, and then I will shoot Anthony."

For the first time in my life, I was terrified.

Shaken and heartbroken, I sank back into the hot leather seat of my car.

"Whatever you do, don't have kids."

I drove away, the lights of my house shrinking behind me. *'Bye, house. 'Bye, old life.* There was nowhere to go from here but forward.

When I got to Kristen's, I sat numbly in the dark for a minute. I reached back and pulled out the picture of me and Teresa.

After about fifteen minutes, I knocked on Kristen's door, looking like a complete wreck, I'm sure. When she answered, her face was the most welcome sight I'd seen all day.

Her cute rescue dog, Marty, greeted me at the door and

wagged his tail as if he'd been waiting his whole life for me. The little fox terrier jumped up and down and followed at my heels as I entered Kristen's house.

I stooped down to rub his ears. He stared up at me with a dopey look and tried to lick my face. Maybe he could smell the tears. Marty's unconditional love was uplifting and gave me an uncanny sense of hope.

"I have some homemade pasta and meatballs," Kristen said as she headed toward the kitchen. "I'll be right out."

"Take your time," I yelled back. "I'm not hungry these days."

"Then I'll get you a drink."

"No, I'm not thirsty."

"At least have a cup of coffee or a glass of ginger ale with me." She popped her head around the door to the kitchen and looked at me with big, pleading eyes.

"I'd love a glass of ginger ale."

After she disappeared into the kitchen again, I muttered, "Not really," under my breath.

She returned with the soda in a glass instead of the can. I held it up to my nose and sniffed lightly. Ah, the sparkling sensation of the bubbles ticking my nose brought a smile to my face.

"Why are you smiling?"

"I was thinking of the night I made my mom laugh so hard, the soda she was drinking shot out of her nose." I put the glass to my lips.

"Stop!"

I somehow managed to hold onto the glass. "What's wrong with you?"

"Please don't drink it ..."

Had she gone insane? "What's going on? I didn't want anything to drink, but you forced me to have soda, which I never drink. Now you're telling me not to?

The way she ducked her head confused me even more.

"There isn't poison in here, is there?" I wasn't sure if I was joking or not.

"No … not poison." Kristen kept her gaze on the floor. "It's holy water."

Holy water?

"Please don't be mad at me. I promised your mother—"

"My mother?" I gasped. "Of all the crazy—"

"Please believe me. It wasn't my idea. Your mom gave me this bottle and said I should sneak it in your drink if you came over." She turned around, reached into her lazy Susan, and pulled out a small, white, six-inch bottle with a little saint embossed on the front.

Yep, it was my mom's. "It's Our Lady Of Lourdes, straight from a grotto in France. Now coming to a kitchen near you."

"Are you mad at me?"

"At least you didn't sprinkle it on me while I was sleeping."

"That was the other option your mom gave me. I understand where your family is coming from, and I understand your side too. Marty and I are stuck in the middle. But you can stay on the couch as long as you need to." She embraced me in a long, tight hug.

Later that evening, I called Anthony and arranged to meet him for breakfast tomorrow.

At six-thirty the next morning, I told him the whole story over bagels and yogurt.

He pulled me into a tight hug. "I can't believe it."

"It's not you. It's them," I said.

He released me, blew out a big sigh, and ran one hand over his trim, curly hair. "Let's check the classifieds for an apartment for you. It's not fair to drag Kristen and her husband into our war with your dad."

Anthony was right. Despite her kind offer to welcome me, my presence as Kristen's roommate was probably inconvenient at best. However, with her policeman-husband in the house at night, I felt safe there. Part of me expected some of the more zealous members of our Italian community to hunt me down and threaten me until I broke up with Anthony and returned home.

Word must have traveled that I was staying there, because that night, her phone started ringing off the hook with calls from my friends and my family's friends. During dinner, Tanya Mancini called me. "I heard about what happened."

"Who hasn't?" I almost laughed.

"I think you're making a mistake. Don't you miss your family? Don't you miss home?"

Of course I did. I missed everyone, even my crazy father. But I had to stand by what I had said and done. To move back home now would be giving in way too easily.

"I have a message from your parents," she said. That got my attention. "From your dad. They want you to come home. He said you can date Anthony, but …"

Oh, here comes the "but."

"Your dad said Anthony can never come inside the house. He has to pick you up at the end of the driveway."

"What you and my dad don't get is that I love him. I'm not going to make him wait for me at the end of the driveway like a chauffeur."

"Hey, I'm just the messenger."

"You can relay this message to my dad: keep dreaming." I hung up the phone. The nerve my parents had. I would say I couldn't believe it, but the truth is, I could.

When Nancy called me later, I couldn't hide my shock. After all she'd put me through, she should apologize, but I didn't expect her to. Like everyone in my family, Nancy could hold a grudge forever.

We held our conversation entirely in Italian.

"Some nerve you have to call," I said.

"I'm sorry I broke your things."

"They weren't just *things*. I collected those my whole life."

"You can start a new collection now."

"What do you want?"

There was a long silence on the phone. I could hear Nancy breathing into the receiver. "We miss you. We want you to come home."

"Who does? That's not how it seemed last night."

"Look, Mar, you caught us all off guard. None of us expected you to up and move out. We didn't even know you were dating him."

"Yeah, and I kept it that way for as long as I could on purpose, because I knew something like this would happen when everyone found out."

"I did tell you so," Nancy snipped. "Remember when you introduced us? I told you."

"Not helping."

"Dad wants to make this right. Mom too."

"I don't think so." I switched the phone to the other ear. "Not as long as I'm with Anthony."

I paced in Kristen's kitchen. Marty watched me from his dog bed in the corner, his tail thumping hopefully on the floor every now and then.

"You won't even consider it?"

"I am considering it." I paused, pretending to consider, but I'd already made my decision. "I'm not moving back home. I can't go back now. I'm with Anthony, and I love him."

Nancy sighed another frustrated sigh. "Okay, I tried. Please think about what you're doing to the family."

For three days, I looked for an affordable apartment, to no avail. With no other viable options in sight, Anthony insisted I move in with him and his mom. Not into his room, of course. He helped me move my five boxes into his renovated basement—a temporary move until I found a place of my own.

His basement was clean, and his mother didn't mind that we rearranged the furniture. Anthony pulled out the mattress in the couch and helped me make the bed. We sat on it, kissing and holding each other for a few minutes until bedtime. Then he kissed me on the forehead and flicked off the overhead light, leaving me in the warm glow of the lamp on the end table. I listened to him climb the stairs. The door at the top clicked shut.

I took in my new surroundings: plain white walls, steel support beams holding up the ceiling. My five cardboard boxes gave the room a dingy, tacky feel. The beige carpet felt foreign and weird under my feet, instead of the hardwood floors back home. I mean, at my parent's house. It wasn't my home anymore.

I slid between the sheets and switched off the lamp. I thought about Anthony lying in bed in his room somewhere above me.

During my first night as a freeloader, a charity case, or a kindly adopted tenant, if you will, I couldn't sleep. It wasn't because I missed my pink bedroom back home. It wasn't because I missed limited privacy or rushing to get ready for the day in the shared bathroom. And it certainly wasn't because I missed being scolded, Italian style, by my father. I was the Amish runaway shunned by my village-sized family. I might as well have been wearing a scarlet letter. In any case, I desperately missed my little sister. Would I ever see her again? Only my love for Anthony outweighed my longing for my younger sister's company. She was more like my baby than my sister. But even my truest fear of losing her didn't constitute grounds for even entertaining the idea of packing up and moving back home.

I was Juliet. And in tune with every cliché, I wouldn't have dreamed of building my future without fighting for my Romeo. I never anticipated that the fight would entail campaign speeches, protests, and possible poisoning by holy water. But I was willing—and forced—to assemble my strongest forces to prove our fate as a couple to my family.

There was, of course, the slight hiccup that Anthony and I had been together only two months, not counting our six-year flirtation and courtship. We hadn't even said, "I love you" yet. And now I had moved into his house. Everything felt fast, but if it meant we'd get married sooner, I was okay with it. That night, I sent him mental messages urging him to propose, and also visions of our future living room furniture.

Fantasizing about our marriage calmed my mind enough to fall into a light, restless sleep for a few hours.

When I woke up, feeling ever so slightly refreshed, I looked around the basement. Not in re-evaluation of my decision, but more in optimism of making the best of it. I was delighted with my new living arrangement. *Steel and cardboard it is!*

The basement didn't have a closet. But Anthony's uncle, who owned a dry cleaners, gave me a steel rack to hang my clothes on. It looked splendid by the cut-open cardboard boxes I lived out of. However, on our way home from the gym the next afternoon, we looked at a more appropriate corrugated cardboard-box nightstand with flowers glued onto its three small drawers. Since I had been cut off financially, "clearance" was my new favorite word.

"I'll take it!"

Cardboard-brown and steel-silver go with just about anything. I told myself it was lovely. Besides, this war would be over soon, right? Either Anthony and I would get married and move into our own apartment, or my family would come around. How could they not? I knew how much they loved me, despite my position as the "problem child". But hello, Anthony's amazing. I had to believe they would eventually come to see what I saw. Part of me thought to pray the rosary that had somehow gotten mixed up in my boxes in my hasty move-out. But I believed more in the power of my thoughts, the power of my intentions.

Every night, I tried to direct my thoughts to my family, telling them I was sorry I'd left, but that I had to do it for Anthony and me. Begging their acceptance, hoping someday soon one of them would call.

I spent the next few days browsing apartment listings in the newspaper and moping over the loss of my family. I kept replaying the look of utter darkness on my dad's face the morning he walked out the door. The more I thought about it, the more I recognized that look as pain. Hurt. Disappointment.

I must've worn the exact same expression whenever I thought about what I had caused. My family, the whole community, was up in arms about me and Anthony. Or was it about my exodus? The fact that I just up and left? I couldn't tell, since the two were so intertwined.

I spent most nights moping, cuddling up to him while he stroked my hair.

"Will I ever get them back? Will I ever see my little sister again?"

"Yes," Anthony said.

I didn't believe him, but he kept saying it.

"Just you wait, Mar. By Thanksgiving, we'll all sit around the table together, laughing about this." He kissed the top of my head.

His faith confused and amused me. Still, I appreciated it, even if I couldn't believe it myself. I couldn't imagine, couldn't possibly see how all this would mend quickly, if ever.

"They'll come around. You'll see."

One night I went up to his room and found him on his bed, reading the Bible. Anthony was more religious than I was. He always asked if I wanted to go to church with him and his mom on Sundays. I think I said yes once, out of guilt, but most of the time I let him have his space with the Lord.

Still, it surprised me to see him praying. By the gentle light of the lamp on his nightstand, I watched his lips moving, just as Nancy did when she used to read in our bedroom. He was reading the Bible. When he came to the end of the verse he looked up and saw me. He jumped as if he'd seen a ghost.

"Didn't mean to scare ya." I walked into the room. "Whatcha doing?"

"Just reading the Bible. Praying for you. And your family. For all of us." He closed the Bible and set it on his bedside table. We sat down on the mattress and leaned in to each other. He wrapped an arm around my shoulders and squeezed.

Seriously, how did I get so lucky?

My love for Anthony propelled me down this path away from my parents, the family I held so dear. At the same time, I knew they were the ones who needed to change--not me.

Sure, I could have been more easygoing about my dad's ultimatum, but just like him, I could be hot-headed and stubborn. Proud, too. When he said, "him or us," I could've chosen him in a more gentle way, but instead I slammed down my gavel, and made a big show. I might have a slight penchant for drama.

Part of me also thought my dad was wrong not to give Anthony a chance, and my dramatic exit was my way of teaching him a lesson, showing that they couldn't control me anymore. They couldn't control what I did, and they couldn't control who I fell in love with any more than I could. Trust me, if I had been able to choose to fall out of love with Anthony, I probably would have, the second I got that phone call on New Year's Eve. I tried to put him out of my mind, but my heart had settled.

Anthony was a great guy. Nancy had seen it when we hung out all those years ago in high school. If my parents could give him a chance, they would love him. My dad had seemed to like him that day at the garage. The only reason he opposed our relationship was because I'm white and Italian, and he is black … and Protestant. Thoughts like these circled in my mind endlessly that whole summer.

While I stayed in his mom's basement, Anthony continued to help me look for an apartment, but they were too expensive for me alone, even in some of the seedier parts of town. I had some money saved up from working the switchboard, but a lot of it was already gone, since I helped Anthony's mom with expenses and groceries. If we didn't find something soon, I'd have to look for a higher-paying job or start working extra weekends.

"I don't like the idea of you living in a little apartment by yourself. You came from a huge Italian family. Won't you get lonely?" he said over one of our daily breakfast newspaper apartment hunts.

"I'll get used to it." But I knew I wouldn't. I wasn't cut out to live alone. I wanted him to offer to move in together. But something held him back.

"I don't want to live with anyone until we're married." He hesitated, and then changed the subject.

Will You Marry Me

Either my telepathy or Anthony's prayers worked.

The following Monday, my father called me at the hospital switchboard. When I heard his voice across the line, I froze. I couldn't believe it.

"Dad? Is that you?"

He asked if Anthony and I would agree to a meeting with him and my mother.

It sounded formal, but I'd take what I could get. Maybe there was a way to keep my man and my family, after all.

By the time I hung up, I had lost most of my enthusiasm. I started to worry. What if this was a trap? I fought my concerns actively. I continued to remind myself to stand by my decision, that I was right, and they were wrong. How hard could it be to convince them that Anthony was a gentleman and more than worthy of me and my family?

When I shared the news with Anthony, he was ecstatic, punching the air with his fists. "I knew they'd come around."

Tuesday afternoon, we drove to my dad's garage. I had high hopes that we would reach an agreement. A plea bargain, a peace treaty—*C'mon, anything.*

We walked through the garage reception area, down the main hall to my dad's office. The door was open, but it looked dark and ominous inside. It felt something like walking toward a guillotine.

I imagined my dad sitting in the shade of the blinds, hands steepled on his desk, reminding me of *The Godfather.* As we approached, I muttered to Anthony, "I'm gonna make him an offer he can't refuse."

Mom and Dad were in there waiting for us. My father, looking like Marlon Brando in his later years, sat at his big steel desk that stretched along the back wall. My mother had taken one of the metal chairs that the garage customers always sat in while waiting for their vehicles to be repaired.

My father stood. I checked his belt for weapons. Did he have a bat hidden under his desk? What was going to happen here? Why was he standing? I hated that I instinctively doubted his intentions.

My father extended his hand to Anthony.

Anthony stepped right up to meet him.

"I am Tony, Mary Lou's father," Dad said heavily. At least we started on a civil note. He pointed to my mother and introduced her as well.

"Nice to officially meet you, sir." Anthony's years in the Air Force were paying off. I almost wished I'd asked him to wear his uniform. It might've impressed them more.

We sat in the two loud, squeaky pleather chairs my father had in his office for clients and friends.

"Anthony," my father began. "Do you consider yourself a religious man? Because Mary Lou, our family, we are very religious."

"I was raised Baptist."

"You're Protestant?" My mom asked, more like gasped.

"No, no, no." My father shook his head. "This is the first reason you two will not work." He slapped his hands palms down on the desk.

The first? Oh, brother.

"We are Catholic. Italians are Catholic. Catholics and Protestants do not mix."

"They don't!" Mom chimed in.

I shot her a glare. "Not helping, Mom."

"Is-a like apples and oranges," my dad said. "They are similar but still very different. Too different."

Who was I, the orange or the apple?

This was a double whammy. Not only is he not Italian, but he's not Catholic either. Would they ever approve?

"Catholics and Protestants are far more alike than they are different, given all the religions in the world," Anthony said. "And if it's a problem, I'll convert."

Good counter.

My parents looked at each other again, but I couldn't read them. My father shrugged and moved on. "How long have your parents been married?"

"They're divorced."

At the mention of the D-word, my parents stiffened.

"Another difference," my father said. "A big difference. Italians do not divorce. We do not believe in it. Marriage and love are for life."

"I couldn't agree with you more," Anthony said.

There was no way they could come out of this meeting not liking him at least a little. I was falling more and more in love with him with every word. Still, my parents only looked more perturbed than before.

"You're from two different worlds. It will never work out," Dad said. "We don't approve."

After my dad finished his pitch, my mom took over.

"Anthony, she's extremely fickle, and she gets bored easily. This is a phase. A phase that's going to last three months. Four at the most."

My jaw literally dropped.

Then it was my father's turn again. We sat there respectfully and listened as my father told us we could be friends. He outlined the conditions we had to meet before they would "re-invite" me into the family. Anthony was not to come inside the house. He was not welcome in our home, and if we wanted to go out, he would have to pick me up at the end of the driveway, just as Tanya had relayed in her message. Our meetings couldn't be regular. And our relationship definitely couldn't be public.

It took all my might to keep a straight face while he demanded these babyish terms. Did he not realize we currently lived together? Someone would have told them by now. Did Dad think I would take these huge steps backward from my independence, just to live in their house again? It was so absurd to me that I started to tune it out and just waited for this meeting to be over.

When my father finally fell silent and nobody responded, Anthony stood and extended his hand, still the perfect gentleman. He thanked my parents for all their advice.

I bit my tongue and asked them to keep in touch. I gave them Anthony's mom's number. I didn't hug either of them goodbye.

Anthony and I walked out of their office, hand in hand, to the car. I knew they were watching from the tinted window of my father's office. Anthony opened the passenger side door for me, and I slid in.

I leaned in for a kiss from my Anthony before we drove away.

"Well, that went well," he said sarcastically.

"Have I told you how amazing you are?"

He shrugged. "Yeah, yeah. I bet they'll come around."

Humble, as always.

With his left hand on the wheel, right hand on my thigh, I never felt more sure of what I was doing. I had the man of my dreams, somehow, and he wanted me too, despite my parents' pathetic attempts to scare him off. Anthony and I were similar in a lot of ways. Neither of us would take "no" for an answer once we'd set our hearts on something. I was glad we had our hearts set on the same sight.

~~~~~

Anthony was particularly bright and chipper the next morning, as usual, practically skipping down the stairs from his room. "Good morning, beautiful."

"Good morning!" I beamed.

His mom was already at work, so it was just us two, making breakfast together. I smiled. Somehow, this was my life.

I brought over the eggs and sausage, and we sat down.

We ate in cheerful silence before beginning the morning ritual of apartment hunting in the local paper.

"I still don't think you should live by yourself," he said.

"I wish you would move out of your mom's and into a new place with me."

"The only way I'd want to move in together is if we got married." He paused, casting his gaze at me over the kitchen table.

Had he just said the M-word again? After yesterday? My parents must not have scared him off at all.

"Maybe we should get engaged. And once we're married, we can move into a place all our own and do this every day, without worrying about where my mom is or what she's up to." He winked.

Suddenly the house went silent. I ceased to breathe. My vision darkened at the edges into a tunnel, and all I could see was Anthony's face, waiting expectantly. I couldn't feel my hands or my feet. I took another sip of coffee to steady myself and to make sure this wasn't a dream. "Are you sure?"

He smiled a smug smile. He knew what a huge bomb he had just dropped on my life. Not a destructive bomb. More like a bath bomb, full of fizzing color and spinning with excitement.

"Was that ... a proposal?" Was this real? Was I dreaming?

Anthony reached across the table for my hand. Got down on one knee in the kitchen, looking up into my eyes. "Mary Lou, will you marry me?"

I said yes, of course, and the sixteen-year-old girl in me came back to life and did jumping jacks with pompoms as if she was on the cheerleading team.

This was literally my dream come true.

The man of my dreams, the only one I had ever wanted, had just asked me to marry him.

In some ways, it was inevitable. As I'd said that day when I brought him to meet my father at the garage, we had surpassed the point of no return.

Right away I thought about picking out the china for our future house. The china I'd been dreaming about for six years. And the home décor, the wedding registry ...

From the moment I said "yes," I began imagining the wedding—something I had done literally one thousand times already, but never with such clarity and purpose. It had always been distant, mystical, so far away, out of reach. And now it was just beyond my fingertips, dropping into my hands.

I envisioned the multi-tiered cake edged with frosted green vines and pink flowers, the little bride and groom standing hand in hand on top. My dress had to be princess quality, complete with beautiful beading, a wide, gauzy hoopskirt and a train decorated with yellow roses. The wedding menu would have Italian food, and maybe my mom would help cook.

Anthony wanted to get married as soon as possible, so we could move in together. He was kind of old-fashioned in that way. If my parents had been involved in the conversation, they would have approved. But they were not involved. They could not and did not approve.

Filled with mixed emotions, the most mixed I'd ever felt, Anthony and I drove into town to pick out a ring. Nothing too nice, because he didn't have much money either. But it was beautiful, and I wore my engagement ring proudly—my new favorite piece of jewelry. We were about to embark on life's biggest adventure together, and there was no man on earth I would rather do it with.

More than anything else, it confirmed that our love was worth the protest.

I went to the bridal shop by myself to pick out a dress to wear for the ceremony. I thought to call someone, maybe, but I had no one I wanted to share the news with. Although I couldn't wait to marry him, the day somehow wasn't quite stacking up to all I'd imagined it would be. Ignoring the disappointment weighing in my heart, I kept the news of this long-awaited day to myself. I had always imagined it as a huge, traditional Italian family wedding, with tons of food and dancing and loud singing and red wine from the basement. Nancy was supposed to be my maid of honor, Teresa the flower girl, and my dad was supposed to walk me down the aisle.

So, it wouldn't be the traditional wedding I'd always imagined. At least I got a wedding. And it technically was the wedding of my dreams, no matter what. The man I was marrying counted most.

A I sorted through the bridal gowns, walls of taffeta and lace, mermaid shape, sequins … something finally caught my eye. The clearance rack.

My hands landed on a perfect gown, sandwiched between cream and ivory. Strawberry frosting pink, the softest shade, it was a princess dress, like something Cinderella would've worn to the ball if she'd worn pink. Overlaid with sheer, delicate lace, it had elegant puffed sleeves. I tried it on and never wanted to take it off. I couldn't wait to wear it for Anthony on our wedding day. He'd love it. We'd talked about keeping the wedding as traditional as possible, but at this point it was going to be about as traditional as wearing orange on Christmas. If my dad wasn't going to walk me down the aisle, I didn't need to wear white.

It was unconventional. It was pink. It was perfect.

~~~~~

It was brutally hot in Anthony's basement that summer. I was used to dipping into the in-ground pool on High Meadow Drive when the temperatures got up to the high seventies. Now here we were, in the mid-eighties, nowhere near my family's pool or air-conditioned house.

Anthony decided he needed a job that could support both of us, so he set his eyes on medicine. He spent most of that summer studying in the library, so planning the wedding fell to me.

A few months ago, a friend had invited me to Manchester, Vermont, to attend a Precious Moments fair, a convention for lovers of the girly little porcelain figurines. They weren't my thing, but getting out of Connecticut, no matter the occasion, had sounded like a good idea at the time. When I accepted, I'd still been living at my parents' house. This was before my whole world flipped over like one of those upside-down amusement park rides. I felt ready to get off the ride now.

I pitched an idea to Anthony. "Destination wedding in Vermont. Let's elope in the countryside. It will be so romantic."

To my surprise, he went for it.

So it was settled. We were eloping to Vermont.

I set to work calling the Manchester Chamber of Commerce to find out what to expect and to arrange a Justice of the Peace to conduct our ceremony.

The night before we left, I was in Anthony's mother's kitchen, baking blueberry muffins, making sandwiches, and packing snacks. I headed upstairs to ask if he wanted anything special for the ride, but when I got to his door, I stopped short. It was ajar, and he looked deep in thought.

About the wedding?

Was I pushing him to do something he didn't want to do? If only I could hear what he was thinking …

I was afraid to ask, so I tiptoed back downstairs. *Please don't back out now.*

There were no signs suggesting he would. I snapped myself out of it and instead focused my attention on making sure everything was ready.

The following morning, we packed up his little red Honda Civic. He seemed nervous but in a bright mood. We passionately sang Luther Vandross love songs to each other and held hands for the entire three-hour car ride.

I had never stayed in a bed and breakfast, but after speaking with the owner over the phone, I was convinced it would be beautiful and romantic—more than suitable. I booked us two nights at The Inn at Ormsby Hill, a historic bed and breakfast in the heart of Manchester, Vermont.

The owners of the Inn, Don and Nancy, gave us a greeting as warm and inviting as the blueberry scones they'd set out for afternoon tea. Don looked like a quintessential inn owner, with his autumnal plaid shirt, suspenders, and light-wash jeans, despite the heat. Nancy looked as if she could have come off a maple syrup ad. Grandmotherly glasses, round apple cheeks, and a little apron with a pocket like a kangaroo pouch holding her current small knitting project. Every time I heard her name, I couldn't help but think of my sister, pang of guilt spoiling the moment.

The Lincoln room was the first room at the top of the stairs to the right. When we opened the door, we found a canopied, four-poster queen bed and a fireplace that set the perfect atmosphere for a romantic honeymoon. We unpacked our luggage and headed back downstairs where Don and Nancy were ready to "help us elope."

Don gave Anthony directions to the appropriate office so we could apply for our marriage license. Nancy and I called a local flower shop and ordered my bouquet.

Just prior to coming to Vermont, we had arranged to meet with the Justice of the Peace the Chamber of Commerce had recommended. He suggested that we hold the ceremony in an informal yet incredibly beautiful garden near the inn.

In keeping with the tradition that it is bad luck to see the bride before the wedding, the Justice of the Peace arranged to pick up Anthony at three o'clock on Saturday afternoon. That gave me one hour to get ready for my own wedding.

Yep, I thought as I watched Anthony and the Justice drive off in a beat-up, rusty old pickup. No horse-drawn chariot for me. This Cinderella had to drive herself in a red Honda Civic hatchback to marry her Prince Charming. Sure, this wasn't exactly how I dreamed my wedding day would be. But if you want something done right, do it yourself. If I didn't do things myself, for myself, I might never have known Anthony in the first place.

I took deep breaths and took my time. I would need only a few minutes to get ready, so I decided not to rush.

I slipped on my pink wedding dress and did my best to zip it up. I'd have to ask Nancy to help with the last two inches. I tied my hair back delicately and put on my makeup–soft white lids with a dusting of silver sparkles, a powdering of blush and a dab of lipstick. I stepped into my white two-inch heels and took a look at myself in the full-length mirror, reflecting the warm, cozy four-poster bed and fireplace in the background. I headed downstairs.

"Nancy, could you zip me up?" I asked as she looked up from her work at the desk.

"Yes, and your flowers just came." She zipped the last inch. She seemed as excited as I was for my big day. "I put them in the fridge on the top shelf so they wouldn't wilt in the heat. And you look incredible."

I thanked her and dashed to the kitchen to see them.

As I opened the door to the fridge, I instantly smelled the intoxicating blend of hydrangeas and roses. The different shades of pink and white were perfect, just like my day.

Driving myself to the ceremony, I sang our favorite love song, "The Power of Love" by Luther Vandross. I noticed an old, rusty, broken-down truck on the right side of the road. One of the two men leaned against the truck, perhaps sulking over his bad luck. The other was under the hood, hunched over and scratching his head. I was so distracted by my excitement that it took about ten full seconds to register that the man under that hood was supposed to read me my vows, and the man leaning against the truck was supposed to say, "I do."

Should I go back? Wasn't it bad luck for the groom to see the bride before the wedding? But it was worse luck if the groom wasn't there at all. Before I could decide whether to turn around or not, I'd reached road to the botanical garden. The gardens lay on the other side of a wall of hedges, out of sight.

As patiently as possible, I waited in the car for the groom to arrive. I played "The Power of Love" a second and third time, for good luck.

Before long, a truck lumbered up behind me. Anthony and our Justice of the Peace had arrived. I exhaled in relief. Only twenty minutes late. Not bad.

The rust-bucket wheezed to a stop next to my car.

"What happened? Did you pop a tire? Run out of gas?"

He got out and straightened his suit, dusted off the shoulders, tension in his eyes. "The truck stalled out, right on the highway. Maybe someone is trying to tell me something."

His anxiety-laden laugh sounded more like a sob. But his laughter came to an abrupt, calm halt when I got out of the car.

I stood in front of my soon-to-be husband, watching him watch me. His expression shifted from nervousness to clear astonishment.

He reached across the space between us and took my hand, drew me a step toward him. "You look so beautiful, Mary Lou," he said in his truest tone.

I pinned his white rose boutonniere onto his lapel before Gary, the Justice of the Peace, ushered us into the garden through a break in the hedge. We strolled hand in hand down the elegantly laid stone paths through the landscaped garden, past fountains and statues and all kinds of beautiful, exotic flowers and plants.

"I think you two are gonna love this spot. It's a local favorite for proposals and special events," he said over his shoulder. Anthony and I raised our brows. Whatever works.

As we strolled through the gardens, the heat of the day intensified. After a ten-minute walk through the maze, the path led toward a cedar bridge with pretty carved rails arching over a small pond. There were lilies and lily pads, and ducks paddled around below us in the water. It was perfect.

Anthony and I took our places on the bridge. Face to face, just us.

"We are gathered here today," the Justice of the Peace began, "to join Anthony and Mary Lou in holy matrimony …"

It was so hot, I had trouble focusing. My mind wandered to my family. What were they doing today? I imagined Nancy and Nonna sitting at the table, playing cards, my mom doing dishes. Nobody knew where I was or what I was doing.

"Is that all right with you, Mary Lou?"

"What?"

I blinked. Had I missed the "I do" part?

"Anthony has prepared something special for the ceremony."

"Of course! Yes!"

He had a small, almost embarrassed smile on his face. "I came up with this little tune last night, for this moment, for us. It's nothing too special, but I thought you might like it."

A song?

Anthony rolled his shoulders back and held my hand while he inhaled a big breath. He sang, "When a man takes a wife, he has found a partner for life." He sang in a bluesy, major, soulful melody. I loved it.

We recited our vows and said, "I do." Within ten short minutes, the same amount of time it had taken to walk through the garden maze to our altar, we were pronounced husband and wife.

"You may kiss the bride," Gary said with all the joy in the world, as if it was his first wedding ceremony.

Anthony and I shared a kiss—short, sweet, and just the right amount of lip.

Gary applauded us as we shared an embrace.

"Gets me every time." When we looked up, Gary wiped a tear from his eye. "I took the liberty of letting Ye Olde Tavern know you'd be coming in tonight. It's a nice restaurant and a tourist favorite."

When he gave us simple directions to the restaurant, he mentioned Cemetery Road. But this was a wedding, not a funeral. He set off to try to start his truck again. We gave him a head start and walked and talked around the garden a little longer. I hoped we wouldn't get lost and miss our dinner.

"Ye Olde Tavern on Cemetery road? He's not trying to undermine us, is he?" My mind was a jumble of nervous queries.

Anthony just laughed. "Why are Italians so superstitious? It'll be fun, I promise."

We drove into town, and I wished we'd thought to get some cans or streamers to attach to the back of the car, or some window paint to write "Just Married!" But then we'd just have to take it off before we went home.

The Justice's instructions held up. We found our way to Cemetery Road, a pretty, cheerful street, despite its name, and soon came upon Ye Olde Tavern. When we entered the restaurant, the hostess looked at her watch and loudly announced the time. "Four forty-eight. Great, you made it." She reached under the hostess stand, presumably to grab some menus.

With a raised eyebrow, I looked at my husband. "Made what? We didn't have reservations, did we?"

We were totally overdressed. Everyone else wore casual clothes, jeans, polo shirts, sneakers—and here we were, dressed for a black-tie event. We were also the youngest customers by thirty years. As the hostess escorted us to a small, round table, I couldn't help but notice the wide, uneven wooden floors, the slanted doorways, and the distinct smell of old wood. The restaurant was filled with patrons, but it was eerily quiet.

"This place should be called Ye Olde Haunted Tavern," I muttered to Anthony.

A few minutes later, another woman in a company t-shirt showed up. She wore a painted-on cheerful expression and looked to be in her mid-40s. As she pulled out her order pad, she too noted the time out loud.

Why were these people so obsessed with the time?

"You're cutting it pretty close, but you just made it for our early-bird special."

Anthony and I didn't try to hide our surprise. At least we'd get a deal.

Now I understood why the whole tavern was filled with elderly people... and most likely elderly ghosts, too. I flashed back to our date on the riverboat cruise, surrounded by senior citizens. Here we were, surrounded by the elderly once more. I decided they were signs that we'd grow old together.

Gazing around the room, I noticed an elderly couple sitting at the table across from us. They hunched over their plates in silence, intently eating their lunch-dinner. The only time they looked up was to take a sip of water.

"Will you look at that?" I said, jerking my head and rolling my eyes in their direction. "They haven't said two words to each other the whole time we've been sitting here."

Anthony squeezed my hand. "Promise we'll never be like that."

"That will never be us"

"Promise me, Mary Lou, that you will always tell me everything ... that we will always communicate."

"There's a perfect example of what we'll look like in fifty years." I glanced at an elderly couple holding hands, slowly making their way toward the door.

"I never doubted our future," he said.

Anthony grabbed my hand as we left, almost as if he was making a statement to the patrons still in the restaurant. The elderly couple shuffled toward their car too, parked next to us. I imagined they would get to it just as we were pulling into our driveway in Connecticut. Nonetheless, they appeared just as much in love as Anthony and I were, despite their sixty-year head start on us. Or perhaps because of it. It was so sweet and moving, I felt I had to speak to them. "May I ask how many years you've been married?"

The elderly gentleman lifted his gaze from the ground, peered into my face as if he could barely see me. "Fifty-four years. Four children, seven grandchildren, and two great-grandchildren." His hand remained tightly wrapped around his wife's. She still looked at the ground, her white hair falling around her face, and she took no apparent interest in the conversation.

"We were just admiring how, after all those years, you still hold her hand."

"Honey, if I don't, she will most certainly fall."

Anthony and I said the quickest goodbye ever. We got in the car and drove away before they made it to their doors.

We laughed about that until we reached the inn, and we kept laughing about it the whole ride back to Connecticut the next day. Our wedding weekend hadn't been exactly what I imagined, but it sure was full of laughs.

It has to Start with You

I knew it would be a weird day when I showed up at work on Monday with not only an engagement ring but a wedding band too. This transformation, which had occurred in a few short weeks, was not the Cinderella fairy tale I'd always dreamed of, but it was something I felt proud of, and something I felt was necessary. Anthony wanted to join our lives. He wanted us to live together, he wanted to marry me, and those were two things I had dreamed about ever since I was a little girl. Getting married and having a family were my life goals, the same way someone else might dream of becoming CEO of their own company. Well, my dreams had just come true. Not exactly in the way I'd imagined, but my wishes were still being granted. Beggars can't be choosers, as my father might have said, if he'd had a little more sympathy with my situation.

I took my first switchboard call before I'd had a chance to put away my purse. "Mary Lou, issa your father."

"Dad?" My heart dropped. I knew this was the time to tell him. I couldn't not tell him.

"Your mother and I, we were thinking, it might-a be nice to have you over for dinner this Friday. You and Anthony."

His struggle was evident in his words. I nearly cried with gratitude. Maybe this whole ordeal was about to end.

"Wow, Dad. Thank you …" I almost couldn't believe it, given how our last conversation at the garage went.

"Dinner is at seven. And between now and then, please," he said heavily, "try not to do anything stupid."

This was it. My moment.

My mouth hung open but no words came out. Finally, I managed to push something through.

"Dad," I began, and from my tone, my hesitation, I think he immediately knew. "I have to tell you. We went up to Vermont this weekend, and, well, we got married."

Silence on the line.

"Is it true?"

I could feel the pain in his voice. Why, why couldn't he be happy for me? "We were married on Saturday by a Justice of the Peace."

"Why did you do that?" he asked, his voice thick. With anger or tears, I wasn't quite sure.

"Anthony is a gentleman, a man of integrity. He didn't want to live together if we weren't married, and he didn't want me to live alone, so we felt marriage was our best option. Our only option. What's done is done. You can either accept it and have your daughter back, or you can reject it and lose me forever."

I paused to let him respond but heard only silence. "I don't know what else to say, except that you should have enough faith to know you raised me right. You and Mom did a good job."

Saying those words almost brought me to tears. Because they were true. My parents were amazing teachers, and they obviously raised me and my siblings right. It just hurt so much that they couldn't see through their own prejudice to understand I was marrying the right man for me, who would love and take care of me, just as they would want my husband to do.

Silence stretched on the line. *Please say something, please.*

Finally I heard a click. The dial tone.

Nothing.

In bed that night, I sobbed uncontrollably, clutching my picture of my little sister, while Anthony tried unsuccessfully to convince me this would blow over and my family would indeed start missing me soon.

"They'll come to their senses. I promise you we'll have Thanksgiving dinner with them this year," he insisted.

"I know for sure that Mr. and Mrs. Knight will not be invited over for dinner. If we are, you'd better wear a bulletproof vest, because Zio Dominic always has Thanksgiving at his house." Hollowly I recalled his threat at my car window. I couldn't imagine my dad still wanting us to come for dinner that Friday night. Not after I broke the news to him on the phone.

"Mark my words. We'll be there. You bring about what you think about. The only thing you should worry your pretty little self about is whether you're going to bring cheesecake or your éclairs to Thanksgiving." He looked me straight in the eye. "Time heals. In a week, your dad will feel differently. Goodnight, my love."

"Goodnight." I felt a little better, more in love with my Anthony than ever.

The next morning at the switchboard, I got another family call. This time it was from Nancy.

"We want you to come over for dinner."

"What?"

"You're still invited."

I took a second to process this.

"This sounds like a trap. Are you going to try to kill us before word gets out?"

No laugh from Nancy, which chilled my bones. "No killing. Please, just come. Let us get to know him."

Call me crazy, but I just couldn't believe they would want us to come over, after I'd broken the news to my dad like that. If I knew my family, they were hurt and insulted by what I'd done. Not just because I left the house, but also because I'd gotten married and invited no one. They wouldn't have supported me, and they wouldn't have wanted to come. Still, I knew I was hurting them by doing it the way I did. It had hurt me, too.

Thursday evening, my dad called the switchboard again. "Issa your father," he said, as if I wouldn't recognize his voice. My heart pounded double-time.

"Dad, hi." I tried to keep the tremble out of my voice. What did he want?

"I would like to formally invite-a you to our house tomorrow night for family dinner. Please, bring Anthony."

Now, since he'd called, I knew Nancy's invite had been true too. Here we went again on this rollercoaster: "It's all good." "No, it's not all good." "It's all good!" And then, "No. It's not all good at all."

I didn't know which part of my heart to believe. But I heard my dad asking me, genuinely, honestly, to come over for dinner.

"I'll think about it and call you back."

When we got home that night, Anthony and I discussed it.

He jumped right on board.

"Call him back and tell him we're coming." He was more excited to go than I was.

"I'm not sure what we'll be walking into, but if we bring brass knuckles and pepper spray, we should be all set."

So I called my dad back and told him we'd be there at seven sharp.

I made sure Anthony and I looked nice, but casual. It wouldn't be a fancy affair, because dinners at home happened every day. It was just another dinner, and I didn't want to overdo it.

Still, getting ready after work Friday night, my hands shook so badly, I dropped my earring as I tried to put it in.

"Shoot!" I bent down to grab it and smacked my head on the nightstand. I stood up quick and rammed the back of my head into Anthony's face. It was a wonder I didn't break his nose.

"Easy there, Miss Bull in the China Shop." He pinched and squeezed his nose, working it. "It's going to be fine."

I rubbed my sore scalp. "Easy for you to say. You don't know them."

We drove the twenty minutes to my parents' house. The main reason I said yes to this dinner was to see Teresa. I missed her almost more than I could bear.

Pulling onto High Meadow Drive felt surreal. I recalled the last time I was there, that terrible day when Nancy broke my precious collection of perfume bottles. I wondered if the floor in my room was stained and if it still smelled like a bunch of different perfumes had exploded in there.

In the driveway, I looked around, in case Uncle Dominic would storm from his house next door, gun in hand. Seeing no one, I took a deep, calming breath and opened the car door.

We stood on the front porch and rang the doorbell. It was so weird, waiting to be let into my own house. Rather, my old house.

Nancy answered the door.

Her gaze shot from my finger and the ring to my face. Then she pulled me into the tightest, longest hug I'd ever received from her. "I missed you."

"I missed you too," I said, and realized it was true. A little.

She released me, and then offered Anthony a hug as well.

That night was one for the books. It continued on the high note it had started on. Everyone was so wonderful and welcoming to Anthony and me that it shocked me. I couldn't believe how warmly my father treated Anthony. He took him aside after dinner and poured him some of his favorite homemade wine. They spoke intimately, just the two of them by the fireplace. Even though I felt nervous leaving him alone with Dad, maybe the shift had come, just as Anthony had predicted.

Nonna and I shared the longest, most giggly hug ever.

And Teresa—oh, my baby sister. She couldn't wait to show me all her new toys. While I played with her, I let the rest of my family have at it with Anthony. Nonna and I set up hopscotch on the back patio so I could play with Teresa. That was all the therapy I needed after the stress of the past few months.

We ended up staying not just for dinner, but for dessert, decaf coffee, and wine too. Toward the end of the night, Dad asked for a minute of my time.

I could tell he'd had a few. I hadn't consumed a single sip. I'd wanted to keep my senses alert and my guard up, just in case something like this happened.

We strolled out to the patio, to the little bench at the edge of the pool. We sat with comfortable space between us. For a moment, we watched our family moving around inside. It was like watching dolls in a doll house, or like watching a movie.

"He is very nice, Anthony," my dad finally said.

I turned to look at him as he looked straight ahead, into the center of the pool. "Thank you, Dad."

He turned to meet my eye for an instant before looking back at the water.

"He is nice man, smart, polite, accomplished. I like him." He said it like a concession. "He reminds me of myself as a young man."

I smiled.

"Is different, obviously. But I like him. And I like him for you."

I reached over and laid my hand on top of his. He squeezed back.

"Thank you, Dad."

"But the wedding," he went on. Of course there would be a "but." "How can we explain this to our friends and family? What will the community think?" He scratched his head. "Is so different than what they expect from us. How will they ever accept it?"

"How can you expect anyone else to accept it if you don't? Changing what our community expects starts with you. Don't you see that? If you accept him, if you go out and tell everyone at the garage how much you approve of Anthony and approve of us together, they will listen. If you accept us, the rest of the community will follow. I'm sure of it."

For a moment, I wondered where all that had come from. It sounded like something Anthony would have said. I felt proud of myself, and powerful. I was sure no one had ever proposed this idea to him before. And in my heart, I knew what I was saying was true.

I watched the thoughts settle inside my father's head. For a moment he didn't say anything, just gazed at the light reflecting the undulating patterns across the bottom of the pool.

"Is good to have you home, Mary Lou."

"Love you, Dad."

"I love you too, Mary Lou," he said after a beat, singing my name in his musical accent.

Olives and Walnuts

Three years later

Olives and walnuts. The faint, rich smell of olive oil and the buttery nuttiness of walnuts floated to my nose.

The room was small and dark with just one window letting in a square of gentle dawn light. The floorboards creaked under my feet as I crept toward the open door, resting my hand on the splintering door frame so I could lean out into the fresh Tuscan air. I breathed in the crispness of early morning and felt as if I could detect the fresh, green scent of every individual blade of grass on the hill. I looked around the empty rolling pastures outside the house in search of a little chimney of smoke or a baker carrying a basket. Nothing and no one was here but me.

There was that smell again. Where did it come from? I turned around and looked back at the empty room. I could almost see a thin

Italian woman, her long, dark hair hanging down her back in a heavy braid, standing where the stove would have been, cooking and roasting a humble meal.

I turned back to face the dazzling light of the rolling green countryside. At the top of the hill, I saw a huge, beautiful walnut tree, its trunk so thick, it looked as if it had been there since the dawn of time, growing wider and wider. Its branches stretched up and away, touching the clouds. The lower limbs sank toward the ground like a southern live oak. The rising sun shone behind it and between its leaves. Something told me to go to it, so I climbed the hill, eyes on the tree. As I drew closer, I saw someone standing under it.

Who would be out here by this tree at sunrise? I kept going. With the sun in my eyes, I still could not tell who the mysterious figure was, but as I got closer, both a great love and great sadness welled up inside me, a yearning, like a warm, heavy stone in my stomach.

I love you. I will always love you. Think of me here, like this, I heard someone say in beautiful Italian. I was almost at the top of the hill, almost in the dappled shade of the big branches. The tree grew even larger as I got closer, and the branches seemed to expand wider and wider. It was all I could see.

Standing beside it, his back to me, a boy of fifteen or sixteen leaned against the trunk. His hand pressed against his chest, his head bowed. As if he heard my footstep, he turned to me. *Mary Lou?*

"Mary Lou. Mary Lou, honey, it's time to get up." Anthony's voice swam in my ear.

My eyes sprang open, as if I was waking up from a nightmare. All at once, my dream was replaced by my life, the Italian boy by my beautiful husband.

"There she is," the love of my life said. He kissed me. His lips were always so soft. He stroked my sweaty forehead and then pulled back his hand. "Bad dream?"

I sat up in bed, the dream still rolling around in my thoughts. The sheets felt warm and damp on my skin. I kicked them off. "Not bad. Just weird, confusing." I realized I was drenched in sweat. My shirt was soaked. What kind of crazy dream had that been?

Then I realized it was a dream about the story Nonna had told me all those years ago.

"If you want to shower, you'd better go now." Anthony gave a big stretch and some shoulder rolls. "The clock's a-ticking!"

That early-morning bounce in his step drove me crazy, but I loved him for it.

From bed I watched him slip on a white t-shirt, the fabric glowing against his smooth brown skin. Next thing I knew, the white was covered by mint green scrubs. He managed to look good in any color. He was just as handsome to me as the day I first laid eyes on him in Sacred Heart High's foyer. *This is actually my life.*

He caught me staring and wiggled his eyebrows at me. "Chop-chop, miss." He pulled at the drawstrings of his pants and headed to the bathroom.

I closed my eyes and could still see that tree, the sunlight, that boy. The image stayed with me through my quick shower, rolling around in my head and chest as I scrubbed the shampoo into my scalp. The sweat may have rinsed off, but I could still feel the dream.

The dream took a firm hold on me and refused to let go but I had to keep to our daily routine and schedule. I tried to wake up Anthony, Jr., Michael, and Marcanthony and then started getting their breakfast ready. But the boys were having a difficult time waking up, so I went into their room again to help them get out of bed and dressed—oh, shoot. The toast was burning. All the while, I was reliving the vivid dream that I just couldn't shake. So, I made more toast, fried up some eggs and bacon. Afterward, it was a mad rush to get everyone out the door in time for me to go to work.

All morning, as I answered the phones, I thought of that dream. I thought back to all of the afternoons Nonna and I had spent together, stringing buttons into bracelets and necklaces, sipping tea and munching on Social Tea Crackers while she told me stories. I especially remembered her stories about forbidden love in Italy. They had helped me through some of the toughest times in my life. Not that everything had turned out all sparkles and roses after my family accepted Anthony, but it was good, pretty much the life I had hoped for. I had few complaints, because I had the two things that mattered most—love and family.

Nonna's tale of forbidden love streamed vividly through my mind—romance with the boy who lived on the property next door, beyond the walnut tree. It always reminded me of Romeo and Juliet—timeless, beautiful. I don't know how I knew, but my dream was about my Nonna.

Late that afternoon, just before Anthony was supposed to come home, my phone rang. Mom.

Her voice was heavy. "Mary Lou, it's Nonna. You should come to the hospital as soon as you can. It's her heart."

My heart sank. That same feeling of yearning from the dream I had this morning welled in my chest.

Pushing Michael and Marcanthony in the stroller while holding Anthony, Jr.'s hand, I entered Nonna's room.

She lay there, eyes closed, hands at her sides, tubes running into her arms, machines beeping all around her. Light spilled into the room through a big window, casting a golden hue at the foot of

Nonna's hospital bed.

My mom was there, holding her hand. Nonna's white hair was pushed back from her wrinkled face.

"Your grandmother's awake—just resting." Mom took the boys.

I sat down and held my grandmother's hand. "Nonna," I whispered.

She opened her eyes, very slowly. Nonna was so beautiful to me. She had always looked like an angel, today more than ever. It seemed to cost her a lot of energy just to look at me.

"*Maria Luisa*," she said in a rasping, quiet Italian. Her legs stirred slightly under the light blue hospital blanket.

Her eyes drifted closed. Every time they did, I feared they would never open again.

"I'm glad you're here. I want to tell you something." She drew a deep breath.

Would her words sap too much of her strength? I leaned close, so she could whisper if she had to.

"Alessandro." Her voice shook as she spoke the name.

"Alessandro?"

"The boy. I have to tell you the truth."

I felt as if I was back in her room on the third floor, on her couch with a sugary cup of tea in my hands, listening to her read from the diary.

"Let love be the force that drives you," she said. "Find it, fight for it, cherish it. Don't ever turn your back on love, because there is no promise it will come back to you."

"I fought hard for Anthony, with your encouragement," I reminded her.

"You followed your heart. Your decisions were your own. But

I didn't." She raised one shaky hand to her forehead, as if thinking hurt. She hesitated so long, I started to fear she'd made herself worse by telling me these things. Just as I was about to ask her not to tell me more, she drew a deep breath, seeming to grow weaker with the effort. "My parents decided for me. Alessandro, my Alessandro. Our hearts were bonded, but not our destiny."

Wait—what? Alessandro …?

"Reading my old writings and reliving that time brought it all back, including my love for him. I wish he were here."

I couldn't believe this. All those hours spent reading the diary, talking about Nonna's "mom"... "Why didn't you tell me it was you?"

"It would have brought shame to my family." She closed her eyes.

My heart filled with sadness for her as I watched each precious breath, each movement of her eyes or hand. She'd made her choices for others, out of selflessness. Because of this, her life had not been her own. A whole life without her true love.

"Don't feel sorry for me," she said as if she could read my mind. "My life is over, but yours is starting."

But what about my grandfather?

"I loved your Nonno," she said, clearly anticipating my question. "When my parents forbade me to marry Alessandro, a part of me died, never to be revived again. I didn't tell your grandfather. It would have broken his heart. I learned to live with it, thinking it would get easier, but it never did."

Silence filled the space between us. My head was numb. The mousy squeak of rubber soles on tiles outside our room brought me back to the moment. I blinked. "Where are the love notes?"

"You know. Think."

And all of a sudden, I knew.

Nonna's breathing slowed, shallowed. With trembling fingers, she pressed a wooden pendant, hanging from a length of twine, into my hand. "A gift from Alessandro. He wanted my parents to have it—and the nightstand—after I left."

I could only guess what my grandparents must have felt when they saw Alessandro with it. Regret? Shame? Her name was on the nightstand, after all.

"*Ascolta al tuo cuore.*" She closed her eyes.

Always listen to your heart.

Remember, everything in life is trade-off.

I laid Nonna's hand on the bed, repeating the Italian words to myself. Then I slipped on the twine necklace, the weight of the pendant sitting next to my heart.

That night, I let myself into Nonna's room and took in the familiar, dusty smell of her things. Her clothes still hung in the closet. Her bed was made. Dishes were stacked to dry in the dish rack.

I sat on the sofa where we'd shared so many secrets. After a time, I headed for my old bedroom.

The weight of the secret she'd passed on to me filled my heart with heaviness. Sitting on the floor of my bedroom, I ran my hand over the "Q" carved into the nightstand's door.

I took off the necklace and examined the wooden leaf. It resembled a heart. I thought of the boy who'd made it—and the lovingly carved nightstand. Pressing my hand to the smooth wood, I recalled the way it had sung to me when I'd first seen it in the shadows of Nonna's old house in Colle. Singing with a love unfulfilled, yearning. I imagined Alessandro, lugging the nightstand to Nonna's house, carrying it over the walnut-dotted hills and meadows between their houses, and finally, out of breath, setting it down at their door.

I never knew Nonna's parents. I can't imagine their faces. But seeing an innocent boy up close, whom they'd despised from afar, they had to have realized he was a nice boy, not so different after all, presenting them with a final gift. A peace offering.

It must have killed them. It had almost killed me.

Gazing at the nightstand, I noticed that a leaf was missing, only an indentation left, just under the knob to the cabinet door.

I held the pendant up to the spot. It fit perfectly. I pressed it in, waiting for it to click into place, when I heard a sound from inside. I opened the door.

I had popped loose a secret panel on the back of the nightstand door. A little hand-carved wooden bird sat atop a pile of papers.

Delicately, I lifted out their love notes and spread them on the floor before me.

One by one, word by word, I read them.

I read them all.

Every last love note between my Nonna and her Alessandro.

Your smile is more beautiful than the sun.
I don't deserve your love.
Every single day, I love you more.
Kiss me tonight under the walnut tree.
A thousand smiles and I love yours the most.
Our innocence is as beautiful as our love.
Your parents won and we lost.
The first time we kissed, I knew the reason I was put
on this earth.

They were the same age I was when I fell in love with Anthony. Fifteen.

I read the notes and then re-read them until the light of day had left the room. Carefully I stowed them into the nightstand, where they would remain our secret.

Ascolta al tuo cuore.

I felt the love of their letters in my heart, and I recognized my own heart in them.

Finito

About the Author

Mary Lou lives in Martha's Vineyard with her husband Anthony and 3 sons, Anthony, Michael and Marcanthony. Before she started writing comedic romance, she experimented with different occupations: travel agent, real estate agent, Health Care Access manager, but her favorite job is being a wife and mother to 3 amazing and successful sons! When she isn't working or writing, you can find her sea glass hunting on the beach.

If you want to know when Mary Lou 's next book will come out, please visit her website at http://www.theheartknowsnocolor.com , where you can sign up to receive an email when she has her next release. Or visit her on Facebook, Instagram or Twitter: theheartknowsnocolor

Writer and Editor Jenna Bernstein is at the start of a dynamic career generating and curating digital and print content. After graduating from the University of Virginia with a BA in English, Jenna is the co-author of Dear Jack: A Love Letter to My Son, and she worked on Trial By Fire, the autobiography of attorney Mike Burg. Jenna's writing has appeared in Arts & Ideas Magazine, Her Campus, and Resonance.

Made in the USA
Middletown, DE
01 February 2020